ENFANt TeRRIBLe

PART II:

HEADLINER

Gwydhar Gebien 06-01-22

BY GWYDHAR GEBIEN

ISBN: 978-0-578-38589-1 (Paperback)

Library of Congress Control Number: TXu 2-305-097

Front cover image by Emily Bratton.
    Cover photography by Sandy Morelli and Sebastian Ervi.
    Graphic elements by Banging Joints and Vecteezy.

Book design by Emily Bratton.
    The text of this book is set in Noto Serif by Google. Additional typefaces by Impallari Type, Misprinted Type, Tension Type, and Vic Fieger.

Printed by Ingram Spark, Inc. in the United States of America
First printing edition 2021.

www.gwydhar.com

www.enfantterriblenovel.com

* * * *

For my Best Belovèd, Danellyn

CONTENTS

WARNING

Second verse, same as the first, a little bit louder, a little bit worse...

So, you made it through Book I.

"That wasn't so bad," you're probably saying to yourself. "All those dire warnings for nothing. I didn't get triggered or anything. I never once had to retreat to a safe space."

Well, congratulations. It's all downhill from here. You don't *have* to turn back—it's a free country. You can do what you want. Go ahead and stare at the sun while you're at it: it will probably cause less damage to your retinas than the escalating indecency ahead.

Still here? God help you.

Kindly gird your loins for the following content: alcoholism, animal sacrifice, mental illness, attempted kidnapping, drug use, abusive relationships, politically incorrect stereotypes, and a litany of explicit language including, but not limited to *twatwaffle* and *dickpaste*.

Consider yourself warned.

ENFANT TERRIBLE:
HEADLINER

PROLOGUE: MUNGO

Clap. Clap.

Mungo Gordon was constitutionally incapable of entering a room without clapping his hands to map the acoustics.

Clap. Clap.

He stood at the entrance of Emmit's Pub with his head cocked at an angle as he listened to the space. He took another step, clapped again. Listened. Glancing around the room at the placement of the speakers as if he was looking for snipers, he reached into his pocket and shoved a pair of earplugs into his ears. Then, and only then, did he scan the shifting weeknight crowd to find me.

"Mungo!" I had to shout over the noise. I stood up from the bar to wave him over.

It annoyed me how much I blended in here: as if blue hair and facial piercings and full sleeve tattoos were the new normal. Or, at least, the new *ironic* normal for 2012 in the same way thick plastic glasses and suspenders were now the new *ironic* form of hip. I'd spent the last fifteen of my thirty years on Earth trying to punk my way out of the norm: I'd dropped out of high school, formed a metal band, run away to Los Angeles, and I'd run so hard and for so long that I'd circled the bases only to find myself back at home, face down in the dirt, while life's umpire waved his hands over my back and declared me *OUT*. Now, here I was at the hipster crossroads of Chicago trying to get my feet back under me.

Mungo spotted me and his strangely ageless, elfin face split into a slow half-grin. He wasn't old but his hair was almost completely white and his cheeks were etched with scars: a Glasgow smile from his youth when he'd been 'chibbed in t'Kelvingrove'. Whatever that meant.

He plunged into the crowd and appeared at my side a moment later.

"Damen, m'boy!" he greeted me. "Y'alreight? Heade'y'bin?"

I struggled to figure out how to respond. My ears weren't calibrated to his dense Scottish accent. Mungo sighed and rolled his eyes.

"How've You Been?" he enunciated.

"Oh, you know."

Mungo nodded. He did know. He followed news of the music industry the way other people followed sports teams and knew all about our fall from grace. My band, OBNXS, had hit the skids in June, and in a span of about two weeks, we were dropped by our label, kicked off our own tour, and abandoned by our manager, who had also absconded with all our money. Shortly afterward, our long-time agent cut us loose over slightly less-than-professional differences, leaving us broke and stranded in Chicago. And then, as if I needed any more reasons to hate my life, I'd turned thirty.

But Mungo had other things on his mind. He sank into the stool across from me muttering an ongoing train of thought in a gently conversational tone. "F'ayever ghet m'hands onem 'ets des*membered* GoatRodea fer'at advert'n telly I'mma ket 'em lengthweize,"

I caught 'GoatRodeo' which was the name of our only hit single, and 'dismembered', which was helpfully punctuated by a slashing gesture and a whistle through his teeth, and I could guess why he was upset. We'd licensed the rights to 'GoatRodeo' to an ad agency to keep body and soul together, and it now underscored a commercial for tires.

Firestone all-weather radials, my useless mind supplied.

"I take it you've seen the Firestone ad," I said aloud.

Mungo's expression was unimpressed. "Whet'd that song ever do t'you?"

"We needed the money. You know how it goes."

He gave a long-suffering sigh as if I had personally wronged him but didn't contradict me. It wasn't the fact that we'd sold out that bothered him—it was the fact that the quality of his engineering had been compromised to meet broadcast standards. I'd never met anybody more terrifyingly particular about sound quality. I'd seen him get into fistfights over compression depth.

He shook his head and turned his attention to the business at hand: "Areight then, so whet's this all aboot?"

"We're going back into the studio," I said.

Mungo looked surprised. "Ay? Yeh foond a new label?"

I shook my head. "Not a label—an investor. Says we can hire whoever we want. He's just interested in the money." In a normal recording environment, the producer would be in charge of running the show but our current bene-factor was a well-connected side of beef named Judge who spent his nights managing a strip club and his days doing who-knew-what for who-knew-who.

Mungo settled back and squinted at me. "Et's a good way to go skint. Dinna he know how t'music industry works?"

"I get the feeling he doesn't give a fuck." I felt certain Judge knew what he was getting into, and I got the impression he wasn't looking to turn a profit. There was money to be made in taking a loss. All I knew for sure was he had an affinity for cash business and was not someone of whom I was inclined to ask a lot of questions.

Mungo sucked in air through his teeth. "Ohh, laddie, y'promised I'd be yehr first call 'f you ever turnt bufty. Who've yeh gotten inta bed weth?"

"I'm not really in a position to be picky right now," I said. "You in or not?"

It would mean a lot to have Mungo in our corner. He was our go-to recording engineer, and if we were to have any hope of dragging our asses out of obscurity, the band was going to have to come up with mind-blowing, boner-in-ducing, panty-dropping original material.

No pressure.

Mungo rubbed his face, running his fingers up the lines of his scars and then down his jaw as he mulled it over.

"'F Ah'm producing yer album yer recordin' in a proper studio," he said. "And ah'm not waiving my fee. Producin' *and* engineerin' *and* mix."

"Give me your quote," I told him. "Best and final. I'm not wasting time getting other bids. I already know I want you."

"At's m'boy!" Mungo grinned and caught the back of my neck in a steely grip to plant an unexpected kiss on my lips. "Knew you'd come 'round one of these days."

Between the scars and his grizzled hair, he looked like a badass but Mungo was as gay as Sunday morning, and made a point of taking a pass at me every chance he got. But that wasn't what I wanted from him now so I caught him in a headlock and gave him a noogie.

"Alright, that's enough you fucking fairy," I told him. "Let's make some fucking music."

1

COR-TORTERED

*"S*ome father you are!"*

A woman's voice hit me like a gut punch, jerking me into wakefulness with my heart in my throat. I opened my eyes to find myself propped up on a heap of pillows in an unfamiliar bed in a room I didn't immediately recognize.

Where the fuck was I?

I glanced around to get my bearings while I struggled to catch my breath and realized that the more urgent question was:

Why the fuck was I naked?

I reached for a blanket to cover myself only to discover that my left wrist was handcuffed to one of the bedposts. From this, I could infer that something had either gone very wrong or very right the night before, but it still didn't answer either of my other two questions. Jerking my arm against the restraint I made an effort to sit up but the minute I moved, something tightened around my throat. With my free hand, I touched my neck to find a wide band of leather digging into my skin. My fingers recognized it as

COR~TORTERED   17

a belt. My belt. I fumbled with the buckle and wrenched it off my neck to take a deep, gasping breath of morning air.

"You're a bastard, you know that?!" the woman's voice spoke again and I realized it was coming from the other room. *"Why you gotta be like that?"* The woman fell silent as if waiting for an answer but before I could respond she spoke again: "You said you were gonna drop her off—you know I don't have a car—"

A phone call.

I breathed a sigh of relief to know I was not the bastard in question. Turning my attention to the room around me, I searched for clues about my whereabouts. Blades of morning sunlight slashed across tangled sheets on a bed in a room made up of warm colors and soft heaps. A little shelf of mementos ran the width of the room over the bed: a rhinestone tiara, a framed photo of a baby girl, a dried corsage of carnations, and a string of rosary beads. A Lladró figurine of the Virgin Mary.

Recognition dawned: *Melody's place.*

I'd been seeing Melody for a few weeks now but I still wasn't used to waking up in her bed. For as often as we hooked up, she was still pretty adamant that we were Nothing Serious and I wasn't in any hurry to contradict her.

Melody was a stripper. I was a musician. Our relationship was as inevitable as it was doomed. On the night that we met, I'd given her my badge for Lollapalooza in exchange for a lap dance. It had not been my finest moment. Alcohol may have been involved. The guys still teased me about it every chance they got. But in the end, it had been worth it because she came to the show to see me perform on stage;

and she came again afterward when I performed for her in private. More than once.

The rest, as they say, was history.

Now, I went to see her at the club every chance I got, and came home with her any time that she let me. It wasn't often. Melody had a five-year-old daughter and only let me stay the night when the girl-child was at her dad's for the weekend. Considering that I was handcuffed to the bed with my belt around my neck, it felt safe to assume that this was the case right now and that we'd spent the night getting as kinky as we damn well pleased. I wondered if any of it had left a mark.

A key lay on the bureau beside the bed within arm's reach. I picked it up and undid the handcuff to let my numb arm flop onto the bed. Blood seeped back into my fingers in a thousand pins and needles as I pulled off the covers and reached for my jeans. I made my way into the kitchen following the sound of Melody's voice still carrying on an annoyed, one-sided conversation underscored by a muttered litany of curses in Spanish. The back door stood open and I could see a hazy sliver of the Chicago skyline framed by a pair of steel brackets that were screwed directly onto the doorframe. A slab of two-by-four stood in the corner nearby—a massive homemade bolt against intruders.

Melody sat on the back steps with a rhinestone-encrusted cell phone pressed to her ear and a cigarette stuck between her lips. She was small and brown and smoking hot; dark hair, dark eyes, and curves in all the places that mattered. Her legs were bare but the cool, autumn air didn't seem to bother her; all her attention focused on the conversation taking place on the far end of the line. When I appeared in the doorway, she looked up with her eyes flashing but when she saw it was me she smiled and nudged my leg with her foot. She unloosed a final tirade of invectives—in Spanish, but requiring no translation—into the phone and then ended the call with a forceful prod of her thumb.

"I needa pick up Vico," she said as she took a final drag on her cigarette then stubbed it out in a painted flowerpot by her ankle "Can you give me a ride?"

This was new.

Melody maintained a strict separation between me and her daughter, Victoria. The fact she was asking me to come with her to pick her up struck me as significant.

"Sure, whatever you need," I said, failing to seize upon the obvious *yes, I CAN give you a ride, ifyouknowhatImean,* like I normally would have.

Melody stood and dusted off her butt. She was so tiny she only came up to my chest. "You hungry?" she asked. My eyes drifted to the twin points where Melody's nipples poked through the fabric of my t-shirt that she was wearing like a dress. A tantalizingly short dress.

"I could eat," I said. *IfyouknowhatImean.*

Melody hooked her fingers in the waistband of my pants and pulled me close.

"Good. What're you making?"

"Whatever you want," I said.

"I want eggs," she said. "I want meat."

"I'll give you meat." I put my arms around her waist and lifted her off the ground. Melody wrapped her legs around my hips and laughed.

"Meat in my mouth," she clarified.

"I'll give you meat in your mouth."

Melody bit her lip and smiled as I carried her back inside the apartment, kicking the door shut behind me.

Breakfast could wait.

✶   ✶   ✶   ✶

We stopped at a McDonald's for breakfast sandwiches for the two of us and a Happy Meal for the Girl Child before wending out way northward to a shady street where massive, designer townhouses stood shoulder to shoulder in a long row. Only about half of the units looked like they were occupied. It was clear that the neighborhood had been gentrified to within an inch of its life and then left for dead in the wake of the recession. The entire block stood as a hollow-eyed monument to affluence and conformity.

"Stop here." Melody pointed to a unit with a yellow Corvette parked in the driveway. I pulled the GTO to the curb and she climbed out.

"Mama!"

The front door of the townhouse banged open and a young girl burst out like a firecracker, running to meet Melody as she made her way up the sidewalk. Melody caught the Girl Child up and twirled her around, kissing the top of her head with a rare smile. It was easy to see the resemblance: the Girl Child was small and brown with dark hair and dark eyes. She spotted me through the still-open door of the GTO and her face split into a wide smile that was jagged with baby teeth.

"Mama—it's Damen!" she exclaimed, waving vigorously.

I waved back, surprised that she remembered me at all, much less by name. I'd only met her once before, by accident, when I'd dropped in on my sister while she'd been babysitting.

"That's right, baby." Melody kissed the top of the Girl Child's head and murmured something into her hair.

"Hey, kiddo. Come have some breakfast." I held up the Happy Meal where she could see it, and the Girl Child bounced on her toes in delight.

"Can I, Mama?"

"Uh-huh," Melody's eyes flickered towards the front steps of the townhouse where a bouquet of flowers rested on a plastic car seat, and her expression darkened. "Go wait in the car," she said, nudging the Girl Child in my direction. The Girl Child didn't need to be told twice. She bounded toward the car and landed in the passenger seat with a clang of springs, dropping her overnight bag into the footwell.

I handed her the Happy Meal and reached over her to close the passenger door, shutting the morning chill. Through the window, I watched as Melody marched up the front steps of the townhouse angrily. She picked up the flowers off the car seat and then banged on the door with her fist.

Beside me, the Girl Child opened the Happy Meal box to look inside. She sighed, disappointed with what she found.

"Can I have a French fry?" she asked.

"Eat your own."

"I don't have any." She showed me the contents of the box: McGriddle cakes. McApple slices. McYogurt. "Mama says they're junk food."

"I hate to tell you this but she's right." I put a fry in my mouth. "Delicious, delicious junk food."

Girl Child pouted. "Pleeeeeeeeeease?" she wheedled. "Share? Sharing is caring?"

I held up a fry in front of her—long and golden, and considered it. "Uhhhmmm...No," I popped it in my mouth and grinned at her.

"*Pretty* please?" She clasped her hands together in front of her—the picture of abject pity. Over her shoulder, I could see Melody arguing with a dim figure hidden behind the reflection of a storm door. Girl Child's father, I presumed. I'd never seen him before.

"What's your dad like?" I asked her.

Girl Child followed my gaze and sensed an opportunity. "I'll tell you if you give me a fry."

"Deal." I held one out to her but jerked it away when she reached for it. "Ah-ah, answers first."

"*One* answer," she said. "Cuz it's one French fry."

"You haggling with me?"

Girl Child's eyes twitched—it was clear she wasn't sure what 'haggling' meant but she wasn't about to admit it. "Yes," she said firmly.

"Good," I said. "Here's one for driving a hard bargain."

Girl Child pounced and shoved the fry in her mouth before I could change my mind. She grinned victoriously.

"What's your dad do?" I asked.

"I dunno. Some office job." She held out her hand for another fry.

"That's not an answer, Girl Child."

"Yes, it is."

"C'mon, you can do better."

"I don't know about jobs. I'm five."

"You want a fry or not?"

"Why do you want to know?" she demanded.

"You really are your Mama's kid," I muttered. The conversation on the porch was escalating and I could see Melody's back knotting up with tension.

"Mama hates him," Girl Child said, following my gaze. "I don't know why. He's nice. He gives her money and I get presents."

I handed her a fry. "Keep talking. You see him a lot?"

"No, but Mama says I got to see him more now 'cuz of cor-tortered."

"Cor-tortered?"

"Cor-tortred vista-tayshun,"

Court-ordered visitation. I handed her another fry. Melody's argument seemed to be reaching its climax. She reached down to pick up the car seat and turned on her heel to head toward the car.

"C'mon, baby—don't be like that—" The shadowy figure emerged from behind the door and resolved itself into a skinny white kid: lily-white. He was in his mid-twenties and dressed like a Yale legacy. Everything about him screamed white privilege.

"Don't fucking tell me what to do," Melody shouted back to him, shaking him off as he tried to grab her hand. "Don't *touch* me."

"Quick," I told Girl Child. "Hop in the back." I picked up her bag and tossed it in the back as she scrambled between the seats. I handed the rest of my fries back to her then opened my door and stood up.

"There a problem?"

Lily White stopped short in the middle of his front yard as he saw me. He sized me up but didn't move any closer.

"No. No problem," Melody said, still bristling with anger. Her eyes met mine as she marched toward the car, and it suddenly became clear why she'd invited me along: I was being put on show: *don't mess with me, I've got a new boy-friend and he can kick your ass.* I wasn't much of a fighter but Lily White didn't know that. I doubted he had the guts to fight me anyway. He looked like the kind of guy who didn't do his own dirty work.

"Who the hell is he?" Lily White demanded.

"None of your goddamn business," Melody yanked open the passenger side door and shoved the seat forward force-fully to chuck the car seat in the back.

"I'm entitled to know who's hanging around my girls."

He was entitled alright.

"I'm not *your* anything," Melody spat.

"Victoria's my daughter too—don't I pay your support checks?"

"I don't want your fucking money," she said. "I never did. I only ever took it so they wouldn't take my baby away."

"You were practically homeless!"

"Hey, buddy," I cut in before it could turn into a shout-ing match on the front lawn. "She's got a right to privacy. Calm your tits."

"Stay out of this, jagoff."

"Yeah? Or what?" I challenged him. "You'll beat your sunken little chest and piss on her leg? She's not your fucking property." Over the top of the car, I saw the bar-est flicker of a smile cross Melody's face as she climbed into the passenger seat and slammed the door behind her, emphatically punctuating the argument with a full stop.

"Who the hell do you think you are?" Lily White wanted to know.

"Don't worry," I told him. "You'll find out."

Lily White looked like he wanted to protest but before he could speak the Girl Child tapped on the window for his attention.

"Bye, Dada! I love you!" she called through the glass, waving.

Lily White turned his attention to her and his face split into a grin for a single, genuine second. "Bye, Punkin—be good! Love you!" he called, unleashing a barrage of air kisses in her direction with both hands. He might have been a privileged, self-important, human dildo but he loved his daughter.

Lily White turned his attention back to Melody.

"Same time next month?" he asked.

"As if I got any choice," Melody snapped. Then, under her breath, added; *"Culero."*

Even I understood that.

2

BIG BROTHER /
LITTLE BROTHER

I DROPPED MELODY and the Girl Child off at their apartment, and then headed back to the house I shared with my bandmates on the West Side of Chicago. The five of us occupied a derelict brick bungalow in Humboldt Park that we referred to as the Cursèd Place. It may or may not have been cursed but it definitely was a dump. Everything about it, from the sagging roof to the crumbling foundation, reeked of decrepitude. It was infested with pests that included but were not limited to, myself, an ex-addict, a trans-woman, a redneck, a runaway, and a strutting all-black rooster named Mary May whom I'd been told, on good authority, was 'unclean'.

Home sweet home.

I let myself in the front gate but no sooner had I crossed the property line than Mary May charged out from under the porch and launched himself toward my head in a hurricane of feathers and spurs.

Kra-kra-kraaawwwwk!

"Shit!"

I dashed across the lawn to the safety of the front porch where my bassist, Kilroy, reclined indolently in a lawn chair behind the smoldering chimney of a bong. Smoke seeped out of his mouth and nose as he laughed at my expense.

"Man, he *hates* you," he said.

"Nobody asked you, Dope Show."

Fucking roosters.

Mary May was a blight upon mankind. I'd saved his ungrateful ass from becoming roadkill on my first day back in Chicago which supposedly meant he was mine now but Mary May belonged to no man and wasn't about to let anybody forget it. He considered the front yard to be His Domain and lorded over it like a goose-stepping fascist. Not even I, his savior, was exempt from his self-designated supremacy.

Mary May eyed me from the front walk to see if I had any further intention of trespassing on his kingdom. When it was clear that I didn't, he took a victory lap and began to preen his feathers. I breathed a sigh of relief.

"Hey, do you owe someone money?" Kilroy asked.

"No more than usual, why?"

"There's a luxury car with tinted windows staking out the house."

His eyes flickered towards a Mercedes parked up the street that was trying, and failing, to look inconspicuous. I could see the lumpy shapes of two broad-shouldered figures behind the tinted windows. Periodically, a hand would emerge through the crack to flick the ash off a cigarette and I would see a gleam of gold jewelry and an expensive watch.

"Judge's people, you think?" I asked.

"Maybe?" Kilroy said but he sounded doubtful.

"How long they been there?"

Kilroy shrugged his bony shoulders and twisted the long braid of his goatee around his finger. "I dunno, since yesterday? They showed up about the same time as Gorey."

I felt my heart jump.

"Gorey's back?" I asked. Stephen Gorej, whom everyone called "Gorey," had been my best friend since high school, but I hadn't seen or heard from him in weeks—ever since we'd performed at Lollapalooza.

"Yeah, he's upstairs." Kilroy gestured vaguely toward the house as he turned his attention to once again sparking up the bong.

I found Gorey in my bedroom. He was slumped face-down on the mattress wearing nothing but gold jewelry, an expensive watch, and a cologne I couldn't name. His hair was shorter but it still formed an unruly top-knot on the top of his head, and not even the dread elders of his old-world Hungarian family had been able to persuade him to take out his nose ring.

"Where the hell have you been?" I demanded.

Gorey raised his head and made an effort to push himself up on an elbow. He held up a hand, sheepishly, and pointed the glint of a gold wedding band: a new star in his constellation of jewelry.

"Done got married," he said.

This wasn't actually news; a month ago he'd announced he was leaving the band to go get married. At the time I'd taken it with extreme prejudice, and I still wasn't over it. I stuck my hands on my hips and demanded: "And you didn't invite me?"

"It was just the Family," he said. I could hear him capitalize the *F*, drawing a line between us as if we hadn't spent the past thirteen years like brothers; touring the world, spreading music and anarchy everywhere we went and leaving a trail of chaos and destruction in our wake. Back then I thought family was something we'd both left behind in Chicago, but the minute we came back into town Gorey's family closed ranks around him, and once again I was on the outside looking in.

Gorey's people were a traditional bunch. Their notion of filial obligation consisted of Get Married and Have Kids to the exclusion of all else. The only reason they'd been willing to turn a blind eye to the fact he'd spent the past thirteen years as the rhythm guitarist in a touring rock band was because of the money he sent home every chance he got. But when the money dried up, so did his freedom, and now he was married.

And naked.

In my room.

In my bed.

"Yeah, okay, well this is my room now. Get lost," I told him, kicking the side of the mattress near his head. Gorey didn't budge.

"Fuck you," he said, "it's my *house*." This was true. His family had arranged his marriage and he'd gotten the house and the wife from his in-laws as a package deal. Curse or no curse, wedding or no wedding, a free house was a free house.

"Uh-huh, shouldn't you be off consummating or something?"

Gorey groaned. "Don't remind me," he said. "My wife—Jesus, that's weird to say: *wife*, she's twenty-three. She was a virgin 'til the wedding—"

"Overshare."

"—anyway, she's not a virgin anymore, and all she wants to do is fuck! It's like she waited too long to break the seal an' now she's got something to prove."

"I fail to see how this is a problem."

"She's tryin' to fuck the life out of me! I'm exhausted! I'm sure as hell not twenty-three anymore. I just...I dunno, need to get some sleep. Drink some Gatorade. She's got all my electrolytes—she's milked so much baby batter out of me I'm starting to lose bone density—"

"*Over*share."

"And the *chafing*—"

"Lalalalalalalalala*bananapannacottapie!*" I stuck my fingers in my ears. "Don't care, bro. *You're* the one with all the big talk about leaving the band and starting a family and making it all mean something."

Gorey winced as I threw his words back at him. "C'mon, dude—don't be like that," he begged. "I miss you guys! And I missed Riot Fest? C'mon—I heard it was bomb, too. And what's this about a new album? I gotta still make a living somehow, right? And...I dunno...maybe it wouldn't be such a bad idea to, you know, be on the road sometimes?" I saw him shift the tiniest bit beneath the sheets.

A musician going on the road to avoid getting laid: that was an un-fucking first.

"You sure changed your mind about that quick— "

Gorey opened his mouth to respond but was interrupted by the unmistakable shriek of something breaching Mary May's perimeter. He scrambled to his knees to peer out the window flashing me with an unambiguous display of his wedding tackle. He hadn't been kidding about the chafing. I reeled back.

"*Fuck*, dude!"

Gorey ignored me. Staring out the window, he huffed an annoyed breath at what he saw.

"Oh. It's them."

Over his shoulder, I could see a pair of dark-haired, male bookends standing on the sidewalk looking up at the house. Gold jewelry. Expensive watches.

"Friends of yours?" I asked.

"Anja's brothers. Don't worry about it." He turned away from the window and once again made himself comfortable on my bed.

"Your in-laws are staking out the house like a couple of mob goons and I'm not supposed to worry about it?"

"Yeah, it's nothing. Family business." Gorey batted away the question with a gesture. "Don't worry. They won't come in. Cursed, remember?"

"How long're they gonna stay there?"

"I dunno, probably till I come out. Self-important assholes. They think they're better 'n me cuz they're more...I dunno how to explain it—pure? They're worried I'm gonna knock her up with a cursed baby. You know—harelip or webbed fingers or something."

It made about as much sense as anything in Gorey's life ever made sense.

The bigger brother saw me standing at the window and gestured for me to open it.

"Hey, *gadjo*," he called across the yard as I leaned out. "Tell Stephen to stop slumming and come home. His wife is waiting for him."

"Tell him yourself," I said. "Gate's open. C'mon in." I gestured sweepingly toward the front door, welcoming them to walk right in but neither brother stepped across the property line.

"You don't want us comin' in there," Big Brother said in the tones of a threat, but his eyes flickered toward the black rooster patrolling the front path apprehensively.

"What's the matter? Afraid of a little Mary May?" I taunted.

Big Brother clenched his jaw around the comment he wanted to make and instead said: "He's gonna have to come out sometime"

"Yeah? Well, 'til then, fuck the hell off." I gave them the finger with both hands and then slammed the window shut. Gorey grinned up at me from the mattress.

"That was awesome, bro."

"You're sure they're not gonna come charging in here, right?" I said. If I knew anything about Gorey's family, it was that I didn't want to be on their bad side.

"Nah, dude—they take their curses seriously. D'you know they thought Anja was cursed? She useta have these fits— she was kind of an embarrassment. That's why they didn't force her to get married sooner. The good families wouldn't have her and our family was too..." He realized I was staring at him blankly as he rattled on about his family's Byzantine politics and got to the point: "Anyway, she's not cursed. Spoiler alert—turns out it was epilepsy—she was having little seizures. They never took her to a doctor—Granddad got her on some meds and Bam! Cured. I mean, not *cured* cured but...you know...cured enough—"

His monologue was interrupted by the sound of a crash followed by a tinkling of shattering glass from downstairs.

"What the hell was that?"

The two of us froze: listening. From the living room, I heard my guitarist, Tombstone, swear and cough.

"Fire!" Someone shouted in a choked voice.

"Aw, shit."

"Fuck."

We turned to the heating vent in the floor to see white smoke curling into the room in a silent plume.

"Fuuuuuck!" Gorey swore again, beginning to cough. "Get out the window! Quick!"

The smoke thickened in the room, burning my skin and lungs. I fought the urge to gag as I fumbled to open the window, groping toward the cool, clear air outside. I scrambled out onto the roof and Gorey clambered out after me, red-faced and wheezing with the bedsheet wrapped around his waist.

Down below, the front door kicked open and Tombstone emerged. Smoke streamed out of his shaggy, ginger hair making it look like his head was on fire. He had a scarf pulled over his mouth and nose which made him look like a Redneck Avenger. He was half walking, half carrying our household minion, a runaway teenager who lived in the pantry and we all referred to as 'Goose', out onto the bleached grass of the front lawn, where they both collapsed retching. Kilroy stood a safe distance away, placidly filming the whole proceeding on his phone.

"Fucking smoke bomb, man—" Gorey wheezed. He spat on the roof beside his bare feet and wiped his streaming eyes on a corner of the sheet. "Straight outta the slumlord's fucking playbook. I shoulda seen it comin'."

Little Brother brandished a second smoke grenade at the house. The pin from the first one was still wrapped around his finger. "You think you can do our sister like that? Come here an' drag this...*mahrime* back on her?"

"Fuck you!" Gorey made a rude gesture. "You think you're so fucking superior. I'm just as good as you."

Little Brother grabbed the top of the fence like he was planning to pull himself over it but Big Brother collared him and dragged him back onto the sidewalk. Glancing toward the glowing eye of Kilroy's camera, he took measure of the situation and murmured something in his brother's ear. He switched to Hungarian and lobbed a statement across the lawn that hit Gorey in the gut. He sat on the roof.

"Oh come *on* guysss," he pleaded. "I'm not runnin' around on her—I need to just ...you know...rest up."

Little Brother snickered and said something to Big Brother with a slap of his hand against his chest. Big Brother laughed as well. Gorey managed to blush even harder.

"Yeah, yeah. Laugh it up," he muttered through gritted teeth.

A black Escalade pulled up in front of the house and stopped in the middle of the road, unrepentantly blocking traffic in both directions. Ignoring the chorus of irate car horns, the Escalade's driver got out and circled around the front of the vehicle to open the passenger side door. An old man emerged. He was stooped and thin with a long, gaunt face, sharp, black eyes, and a curved blade of a nose: Gorey's grandfather. I'd only met him once before but once was enough to know that I wasn't going to like what came next. The last time I'd seen him was the day Mary May had come into my life and things had largely gone downhill since then.

"*Rom Laszlo.*" The two brothers recognized him and straightened up quickly.

"Aw, fuck me," Gorey said and buried his face in his hands.

Rom Laszlo approached the house at a measured pace, leaning heavily on a cane with a gold handle. He stopped at the fence line to glare down into the yard where Mary May stood frozen in mid-strut, one talon curled in the air. Mary May regarded the old man for a long moment with his beak open, tasting the air, then he squawked loudly and fled back to the safety of the porch.

Shit.

The old man surveyed the house. He took in the windows oozing smoke, Gorey and me on the roof, Kilroy filming from the porch and the rest of the guys coughing and wheezing on the front lawn. The old man pointed to Kilroy with a wizened finger.

"You vwill stop rechording now." The old man rolled the sounds around in his mouth before spitting them out one by one.

Even a stoner like Kilroy was astute enough to recognize the voice of authority when he heard it.

"Sure, dude, okay. Here, look—" He put up his hands, showing the old man the display as he hit the stop button.

Then he put the phone in his pocket and backed away like he suddenly wanted a lot of space between himself and the old man.

Next, Rom Laszlo turned his attention to Anja's brothers. The two of them shrank to the size of children as he looked them over with a knife-like gaze. Little Brother swallowed hard. Realizing that he still had the second smoke grenade in his hand, he hastily tried to conceal it behind his back but it was too late.

Rom Laszlo frowned at the canister with extreme distaste and unleashed a lengthy torrent of caustic Hungarian. I didn't have to speak the language to know none of what he said was good. With a vehement flourish, he rolled up his sleeve and stuck out his stringy arm, pointing to the blue number tattooed on his skin, then pointed to the canister in Little Brother's hand. Little Brother threw it down on the sidewalk like it had bitten him. Big Brother looked like he wanted to vomit.

"Bah!" Rom Laszlo made a dismissive sweep of one arm then leaned against the chain-link fence and lit a cigar. He turned his attention to Gorey.

"You vwill come home now," he said.

"Rom-Rom, please..." Gorey cringed to make himself as small as possible.

"Tchess?"

Gorey nodded.

"Tchess?"

"Yes, Rom-Rom." Gorey gathered the bedsheet around his waist with all the dignity he could muster and climbed back in through the window.

"Your granddad's a piece of work," I said, climbing in after him. The smoke had cleared, mostly, leaving only a faint haze in the air and an acrid chemical smell that made my eyes and nose water.

"Yeah, well, he didn't survive Birkenau with sweetness and light," Gorey said. His eyes were streaming and a cough seemed to tickle his throat with every word. He pulled a set of clothes out of a plastic garment bag and began to get dressed. "And trying to gas us out of our own property didn't win Tweedledumb and Tweedledumber out there any points." He grinned but it was weak around the corners. He fumbled with the buttons on his shirt buttoning it crooked twice in a row before tearing it open again in frustration.

"Fuck," he swore.

I realized he was scared—not just scared but terrified. I'd never seen him scared before. Gorey was a berserker. He was the kind of guy who ran headlong toward trouble like it was a Black Friday doorbuster blowout. But he was scared now.

"Hey—heyyy." I got in front of him and began to button the shirt for him.

"What if I can't do it?" Gorey managed in a voice so weak I could barely hear it. "Get her pregnant, I mean. What if I'm the last one with the family name?"

I focused on the buttons. I wasn't really in any position to be giving advice. Unlike Gorey, I was barely on speaking terms with my own family. I couldn't even sit through a family dinner without causing a scene. No one expected me to be the one to carry on the Adomnan name—I didn't even use it myself. I was a Warner, like my mom, and even she thought I was a piece of work. The only person in the family who didn't think I was a total shithead was my grandmother, Dearie, but now she was dying of cancer. My heart clenched around the thought, and I forced my attention back onto Gorey's problems instead of my own.

"Dude, please, it's not rocket surgery," I told him, finishing with the buttons and giving his cheek a gentle slap. "Go home. Fuck your wife. Have her pee on a stick. Repeat until you get the result you want. What's the worst that can happen? You die trying? There are worse ways to go."

Gorey managed a weak smile but looked relieved. "Thanks, bro," he said, catching me around the chest in a frantic hug. "You're always there for me." He gave my back a perfunctory no-homo double slap and pulled away, clearing his throat self-consciously.

"Go," I told him. "The sooner you get 'er done the sooner we can get to work on our album."

Gorey nodded and straightened his back. "Okay, well... here goes nothing," he said. "See you on the flippity-flop." And he headed out the door without a backward glance.

3

WOOD. STRINGS. INSPIRATION

NOW THAT the band was back together, I turned my attention to the task of writing a new album. We were overdue for some new material, and without a record label breathing down our necks, we had nearly unlimited creative control over our work for the first time since our garage band days; we could play whatever we wanted without regard for *marketability* or *consumer demographics*. All we had to do was write it.

Easy.

The music hovered all around me, pressing in on me from all sides, so close I could feel it. I could *taste* it.

I hit a note.

Wrong!

I hit a chord.

Wrong!

I tried a progression.

Wrong! Wrong! Wrong!

The notes were worthless and stupid. The chords were worthless and stupid. I was worthless and stupid, playing the same worthless, stupid progression over and over again, hoping it would resolve into something meaningful. The definition of insanity.

I banged my face down on the keyboard in frustration.

"Ohmigod, give it a *rest*, already!" Behind her drum kit, Jojo had her hands pressed over her ears like she was in physical pain.

"What even *is* music, anyway?" I mumbled, my face still ringing out a tone cluster in the key of desperation.

"Whatever it is, it sure as hell isn't that."

"I can't work on a midi," I griped, raising my head and glaring at the electric keyboard as if my utter failure to produce even the most basic four-chord melody was somehow its fault. "I need wood. I need strings. I need inspiration."

"So, get a piano. Stop torturing the rest of us."

"I asked Judge for one. Still waiting."

"Well, wait fucking *quietly*," she snapped, rubbing her temples and muttering something irritable in Korean. She looked as hungover as I felt. Her makeup was smudged and her long, dark hair hung in an artless tangle around a face swollen and pale from too much late-night debauchery and not enough fresh air and sunlight. She was wearing a t-shirt that had been shredded into wearable macramé and sweatpants bedazzled with sequins across the ass. It was either the height of fashion or the depths of poor taste. I was in no position to judge: I'd been wearing the same jeans and t-shirt for three days straight.

It hadn't taken long for our bad habits to settle into a routine. We spent our daylight hours sequestered in our rehearsal space: a derelict warehouse on Chicago's northwest side called 'the Gray Area,' boozing and jamming and generally fucking around with music until we got too fucked up to work. After that, we would head out Melody's club, Club Lure, and fuck around with dancers and drugs until we were too fucked up to keep our hands to ourselves. After that, if Melody was working, I'd hang around to drive her home and the two of us would fuck around some more until the sun came up and the whole cycle started over again.

The vortex of fuckery never stopped.

"Hot stab!" Gorey shouted from the direction of a tangle of wires. The lights dimmed fractionally as he plugged yet another cable into yet another splitter into yet another outlet but they didn't go out. He held up his arms in victory. "Winning!" he crowed.

"What are you *doing?*" I asked. I was reasonably certain I didn't want to know the answer.

"Just a thing. Don't even worry about it," Gorey said, and began to rummage through a road case for some unknown widget, whistling cheerfully.

Of the five of us, he was the only one whose nerves were not currently made of glass.

I flopped onto the couch and pinched the bridge of my nose where a headache sat between the halves of my brain like a wall of static. The cushions were still warm with the imprint of Tombstone's ass. He had stepped out of the room to take a phone call from his ex-wife that he didn't want us to overhear, leaving his guitar, Rita, unattended. Rita was a '69 pink paisley Telecaster, a true thing of beauty. She reclined against the faded cushions like a centerfold. The sinuous curves of her body called to me wordlessly: glossy and pink, as tempting as forbidden fruit. Wood. Strings. Inspiration.

Kilroy caught me looking at her and shook his head. "Duuuuude, don't even think about it."

"About what?" I asked as if the direction of my thoughts wasn't abundantly clear. No one with an ounce of sense would dare touch her without Tombstone's express permission. He had won her in a Devil-Went-Down-To-Georgia style guitar duel against Keith Richards, and she was his most prized possession.

"C'mon, bro, you know better."

"Do I, though?" I pulled Rita onto my lap and ran my fingers along her neck, trying to find the sweet spot that would make her sing. Kilroy looked to Jojo for support.

"Put her back," Jojo said without looking up from the drumhead she was replacing. "Tombstone'll shit a brick if he sees you foolin' around with her."

"Tombstone's not here, though, is he? What he doesn't know won't hurt me," I said. I struck a chord with too much force and Rita howled in protest and gave off an ear-splitting shriek.

"Ohmigod, *stahp!*" Jojo hollered, clapped her hands over her ears again. "Are you *tryin'* to get another black eye? Cuz this is how you get a black eye, jackass."

She was right, of course. I knew this from experience. It had only been a week or two since Tombstone and I had come to blows backstage at Riot Fest and he had given me a well-deserved black eye. It was only now starting to fade. We were back on speaking terms—as much as Tombstone could be said to be on speaking terms with anybody since he never spoke at all if he could help it, thanks to a severe stutter.

"C'mon, dude, you know how Tombstone is about his guitars," Kilroy said, wringing the long fingers of his hand into a knot. "Seriously, put her back."

"It's *fine*," I assured him.

From his heap of electrical detritus, Gorey cackled gleefully at my apparent lack of self-preservation, then announced: "For real, though, someone's coming."

I paused in my strumming to listen. He was right; from the direction of the hallway, I could hear the distant shuffle of approaching footsteps. Kilroy heard it too and went pale.

Shit.

"*Putherbackputherbackputherback!*" Kilroy hissed.

I hastened to comply, doing my best to settle Rita back on the couch in the exact position that I'd found her, then heaved myself off the couch to resume my place at the keyboard. My feet tangled in the web of Gorey's cabling project and I staggered but didn't fall. I tried to shake myself free of the snarl but the more I struggled the more enmeshed I got. Jojo watched me with her hands on her hips and a smirk on her face.

"Little help?" I asked. The footsteps were closer now.

"Nah."

I gave up on trying to get free and dove towards the chair beside the keyboard, pulling the web of plugs and cables behind me like a dragnet. My ass landed on the seat and I focused on the keyboard, affecting a posture of nonchalance as the door to our workspace rolled aside with a colossal rumble.

"Oh good, you're here."

The voice that spoke didn't belong to Tombstone. I raised my head to see our benefactor, Judge, filling the doorway from wall to wall like a troll guarding the entrance to a goblin kingdom. I breathed a sigh of relief.

"Jesus fuck, give us a heart attack, why don't you?" I blurted out, comfortably certain that I spoke for all four of us. Judge stuck his meaty fists on his meaty hips and peered at me over the top of his reading glasses.

"You would've known I was coming if you'd answered your goddamn phone," he said.

I cast a guilty look at my phone which lay face down on a table nearby. "I was *trying* to work," I said.

"Uh-huh. I'll believe that when I see it," Judge cast a meaningful look at the growing collections of bottles and trash and discarded women's undergarments accumulating on every surface. I followed his gaze: Kilroy cuddled up with his bong on the couch, Jojo rattling around her drum kit like a bad-tempered pinball, and Gorey crouched in his nest of wiring like an oversized squirrel, trying to pull the yellow coating off a length of Romex with his teeth.

"All part of the process," I insisted.

"Not my business," Judge said, waving it away. "Just keep your phone in your pocket from now on and answer it when it rings."

I picked up my phone off the table and made a show of putting it in my pocket for his express benefit. "There," I said,

"We good?"

"Don't be a shithead, I'm the one payin' your bills." Judge's tone was pointed. "Time is money, Crustbucket, when are you gonna start writing some music?"

Guilt stabbed me between the shoulder blades and I grimaced.

"I'm *working* on it, okay?!" I said, struggling to rein in my insecurity. "It's not like I can crap out a hit like it's the morning after taco night."

"Uh-huh."

"You want things to go faster? Get me a piano."

"I'm working on it," Judge said. "It's not like I can crap out a piano like it's the morning after—"

"Smartass."

"Well, if you're not gonna put out any music, at least do some press," Judge reached into the breast pocket of his bowling shirt and handed me a scrap of paper with the name *Blythe Phoenix* written on it along with a phone number.

"Who's this?"

"An influencer. You wanna get your name back on the streets she's the one to get you there. Text her. Set up an interview."

I groaned inwardly at the thought. 'Press' inevitably involved fielding a gauntlet of witless interview questions from journalists who didn't know heavy metal from a hand grenade and didn't care about anything I had to say. But Judge wasn't going to give two shits about my feelings, so I kept them to myself.

"I gotta catch a smoke." Judge stuck a cigarette between

his lips and tossed his head towards the door. "Walk with me." He turned on his heel and strode out of the room without looking back to see if I was following him.

I kicked myself free from the cables around my ankle and trotted after him, catching up with him halfway down the dim expanse of the Gray Area's service hallway.

"What's up?" I asked.

"Melody tells me she introduced you to Vico," Judge said sounding like he was trying to sound casual. "You two getting serious?"

"Not unless Hell is freezing over," I said, trying not to let my bitterness show. I still didn't know how to define my relationship with Melody but she continued to make it excruciatingly clear that it was Nothing Serious.

"She's not some groupie you can fuck and forget about, y'hear?"

"Yeah, no diggety."

Judge pivoted suddenly and shoved me up against the wall with one meaty arm. My heart leaped into my throat and I swallowed around a tongue so dry I expected it to crumble in my mouth.

"The fuck, dude?!" I gasped.

"You better start takin' Melody serious if you know what's good for you," he growled. An exposed bulb overhead swayed, casting Judge's face in and out of deep, skull-shaped shadows. I held up my hands in what I hoped was a placating gesture.

"I'm not trying to be an asshole," I managed hoarsely. "I care about her, I just—she says she doesn't *want* anything serious."

"If she's introducing you to her kid, it's fucking serious," Judge said. He stuck a thick finger in my chest and used it to punctuate each word as he spoke. "Don't. Fuck. With. Her. You fuck with her you gonna be fucking with me, and if you fuck with me, I will top you so hard even the lifers down in Pontiac Max won't have any use for you when I'm done."

"Fuck, tell me how you really feel," I managed.

"Just so we're clear," he said.

"We're fuckin' clear."

"All good, then." Judge backed off as quickly as he'd pounced and gave my chest a slap. "Now, go write a fucking album. And call Phoenix."

Then he stumped off towards the exit leaving me breathless in his wake.

✴   ✴   ✴   ✴

"What'd Judge want?" Jojo asked when I made my way back into the rehearsal space. She caught sight of my expression and her eyes narrowed. I forced myself to smile.

"He wants to fuck me," I told her.

"Oh god, be serious."

"Says he wants to top me so hard—"

"Okay! Okay, I'm sorry I asked—" Jojo pressed her hands over her ears to shut out the images I was painting in her head.

I grinned again, for real this time, and exchanged a look with Gorey who grinned back.

"You'd make a cute couple."

"Shut the fuck up."

Gorey turned his attention back to his wiring and I turned mine back to the keyboard. I tapped my fingernails against the hard plastic keys, trying to pretend it wasn't because my hands were still shaking from the run-in with Judge. I'd always known, abstractly, that Judge was dangerous. From the moment we met, he'd struck me as someone with dark secrets, and if there was one thing I knew for sure, it was that I didn't want to become one of them. But this was the first time he'd ever threatened me. A thousand thoughts swirled in my head as I flailed for something to anchor me against my turbulent emotions.

Just write the fucking album. I told myself. *Sitting around waiting for inspiration is for amateurs, just do the work.*

I resolved to myself that I would keep my ass firmly planted in my seat until I got something written. I closed my eyes and took a deep breath but before I could play a note, the fuse box in the corner exploded in a shower of sparks and the room plunged into darkness. For a moment there was nothing but stunned silence and the smell of burning ozone.

"Nobody panic," Gorey called from the gloom. "Everything's under control." Then silence. Then the airy roar of a fire extinguisher discharging.

Kilroy flicked his lighter to reveal Gorey crop dusting the room with a coating of flame-retardant chemicals. Gorey grinned and gave us the thumbs up.

"S'all good! We're good. Everything's okay!" he announced.

I couldn't work like this. I got to my feet and picked up my jacket.

"I'm going out," I said to no one in particular. No one in particular watched me go.

4

RAFFI

THE ONLY place I could think of where I would have ready access to a piano was my grandmother's house: a grand four-story brick house on the Near North Side that everyone referred to as 'the Big House'. It stood as a monument to both the Adomnan family and the Adomnan family business: Metron, a development company dedicated to maintaining the balance of the universe by building up the city of Chicago faster than it could tear itself down. Under normal circumstances, I avoided it as assiduously as I avoided a wasps' nest and for much the same reasons. The last time I'd been there, I'd come away stung by the news that Dearie had been diagnosed with stage four cancer. The wound was still fresh.

I stood on the sidewalk and screwed my courage to the sticking place. Visiting the Big House meant dealing with my family, most of whom considered me a nuisance at best. Dearie was an exception but getting to Dearie usually meant dealing with my brother, Edward, who lived with her as an in-home caretaker. Stupid, perfect Edward—as beautiful and beloved as a bar of gold, and just as dense.

He'd been in a car accident as a kid and the resulting brain injury had left him so dyslexic he could barely read. Everybody loved him anyway, no matter how hard he failed at life. Neither of us had finished high school but I was the only one they called a 'dropout.' Neither of us had ever held down a regular job but I was the only one they called 'jobless.' He was a grown-ass man still living in his childhood bedroom at home but I was the only one they told to 'grow up.'

But Edward wasn't the only one at the Big House that I wanted to avoid—now my mom was living there too. Edward may have cast a long shadow but it was Mom who called down the blinding light of judgment on everyone and everything in her path. The frost of her disapproval could wither crops and heave asphalt. More powerful men than me had shriveled into twisted husks under her scrutiny. Her most recent act of devastation had involved calling a family dinner to announce that after twenty-eight years of marriage she was separating from her husband, Michael, so that she could 'consider her identity' whatever the hell that meant. Dearie had invited her to do this soul-searching at the Big House and Mom had moved in shortly afterward. She had taken it upon herself to get the house in order and the last time I'd visited had been in the process of cleansing the household with a thoroughness that bordered on mechanical debridement.

I hoped she wasn't home.

I climbed the front steps and knocked on the door but it wasn't Edward who answered and it wasn't Mom either. Instead, I found myself confronted by a stranger: an enormous Native American dude in an aloha shirt. He filled the doorway like a mountain range.

"Can I help you?"

"Who the hell are you?" I asked, startled.

"Who the hell are *you?*"

"Uh...Damen...?" It came out sounding like a lie—like I wasn't even sure of my own name.

The stranger squinted at me for an endless moment until suddenly recognition lit up his face. "Holy sh—" he grinned. "I *know* you!" He glanced over his shoulder and lowered his voice to a fervent undertone. "You're Damen Warner! Right? Tell me I'm right."

"I'm sorry, who are you exactly?"

"Raff—Raphael—Raffi. Raffi Lujan." He shook his head as if he were trying to shake off a dream. "I gotta be dreaming, right? If I am, don't tell me—I don't wanna wake up. But seriously, are you for real?"

"I think so?" I hazarded, still trying to gather my wits. The longer this went on, the less certain I was about the state of reality.

"No way."

"Way."

"No way!"

"*Way,*" I insisted.

"Wow! *The* Damen Warner! I love your music, man—big fan!" he gushed. "What are you doing here? Sorry, that sounded super aggro—I didn't mean it like '*what are you doing here,*' but, you know, why are you here? I guess, I mean, cosmically speaking, why are any of us 'here,' right? But I mean literally: why *here,* here, of all places?"

For someone who asked a lot of questions he sure as hell didn't leave a lot of air space for answers.

"This *is* still Dearie's house, right?" I asked. I cast a furtive look towards the brass number bolted to the brickwork as if there could be any chance in a thousand hells that I'd gotten it wrong.

"Dearie?" Raffi shook his head and looked blank.

"Sophia Adomnan?"

"Oh, yeah!" Raffi's face softened and he bobbed his head with a grin. "This is her place."

"Cool, so...can I come in? Or..." I gestured towards the interior of the house beyond his bulk but Raffi didn't budge.

"She expecting you?"

"Probably not."

"How is it you know her?"

"Uh...she's my fucking grandmother?" I snapped as annoyance got the better of me. *Who the hell did this guy think he was?*

"Hey, heyy! Sorry! I didn't realize you two were related." Raffi held up his hands in a placating gesture and at last stepped aside to let me in the house. "I'm her new assistant. I'm still gettin' my feet under me if y'know what I'm sayin'? She said she neededa sleep an' didn't wanna be disturbed so I shouldn't let anybody in. I mean, I know she's an important lady an' all but I gotta admit, I wasn't expecting to be opening the door to a literal rockstar—" Raffi closed the door behind me, once again spinning out an endless chain of semi-interlocking thoughts without ever coming to a full stop. "And, I mean, c'mon—you're a Warner an' she's an Adomnan? Right? Not exactly an obvious leap. You can see where I'm comin' from, right?"

"Uh-huh. Sure." I started towards the living room, lured by the piano's gleaming surface but Raffi blocked my way.

"Sorry, pal, she's sleeping right now. Don't want to wake her. You want a cup of coffee?" He gestured to the kitchen with a pursing of his lips. "We can talk 'til she wakes up. She'll be glad to see you." Raffi ambled towards the kitchen towing me along behind him like an erstwhile caboose to his ongoing train of thought. "I love your music, man, I first heard 'GoatRodeo' when I was in my last semester of school; the story of my life, man—always something fallin' apart, barely holdin' it together. I was working day and night—drivin' this crazy commute every day—and that stretch of road is *dark;* the only thing keepin' me awake was your album; played it over and over for *months."*

Once in the kitchen, he bustled around from cabinet to cabinet like he'd lived there his whole life. He tipped coffee grounds into a fresh filter and punched the 'on' switch on the coffeemaker to start it brewing before turning to face me.

"Sorry, I kinda run my mouth sometimes," he said with a sheepish grin. "I got the gift of the gab; thought I'd go into radio for a while—I worked at this radio station for a while—*KTAO! 101.9 Alternative!* But then the whole recession hit and...you know...had to pay the bills. Anyway, sometimes I forget myself when I'm in a conversation with people who can talk back, you know?" Raffi shook his head at his mortal failings and then a thought seemed to occur to him. "Sorry if I'm talkin' too much. I'll shut up now—let you get in a word edgewise, right? God, I even talk too much tellin' you I talk too much. Ha! But, I mean, c'mon, I'm makin' coffee for *the* Damen Warner! How often does a rockstar show up on the doorstep? It's a first for me, that's for sure! Sorry. Doing it again—Hey, when're you all gonna be putting out a new album?"

The coffeemaker beeped to signal it was finished brewing and Raffi poured out two mugs of coffee. He handed a mug to me and I poured in a generous helping of sugar straight from the container realizing belatedly that he had lapsed into eager silence because it was a question he wanted an answer to.

"Fucked if I know," I mumbled into the coffee mug but Raffi's attention flickered towards something over my shoulder and he straightened.

"You're up!" he said.

I turned to see Dearie standing in the doorway looking like she might've still been half asleep. Her feathery, silver hair stood on end on one side.

"I thought I heard voices," she yawned, brushing a hand across her eyes. Her gaze settled on me and she smiled. "Oh, it's you! Have you come to visit me? I'm sorry, I wasn't expecting company." She plucked at the folds of her over-sized sweater as if she felt guilty to be seen in something inappropriate. As if it weren't nicer than anything I owned.

"I came to use the piano," I said. "Sorry, I should've called first."

"Nonsense! You're always welcome. I see you've met my Raphael?" She pronounced his name like she was spinning the vowels into glass, and patted his hand as he guided her to the table. "Isn't he wonderful?"

"I dunno—he almost didn't let me in the door," I said. "You could've told me you were getting a new...assistant." The word wasn't right. I didn't know why but it was somehow sharp on my tongue. I caught myself knocking my piercing against my teeth around the shape of it. "Where's Edward, anyway? I thought he was your lackey."

"At the office, I suppose," Dearie said.

"The office?"

"Yes, you recall he has gotten a job with Metron, of course." She floated the reminder into the conversation as gently as a soap bubble but I still kicked myself inwardly for forgetting that Michael had gotten him a job. The family did own the company, after all.

"I thought he was a janitor?"

"I understand he was recently promoted," Dearie smiled. "We're all very proud of him."

"Christ on a bike." I shook my head. Imagining Edward in an office job hurt my brain. It was like imagining a snail on a razor blade. I couldn't think of a single person who was less suited to an office job. But that was Edward: failing upward as usual. As charmed as a cat.

"Let's get you a seat," Raffi said to Dearie solicitously. "You sleep alright, ma'am?"

"Still a bit loopy I'm afraid," Dearie said.

"That's normal."

I watched as he guided her to a chair and settled her into it, holding her by the wrist. Her wrist, I noticed, not her hand. He held it for a moment too long, uncharacteristically quiet as if listening for something.

It wasn't the kind of thing an assistant would do.

"You're a nurse," I blurted out.

Raffi looked up at me in surprise then looked to Dearie to answer before taking a notebook out of his breast pocket to make a note.

Dearie sighed. "Yes, that's right," she said. "I was rather hoping to keep it discreet."

"Why do you need a nurse?"

"Damen..." Dearie's expression was sympathetic. "You know why."

"But it's too soon! I thought you said you had months—"

"I did—I *do* but...it's time for me to get my affairs in order. Raphael is here to...help me prepare." Dearie said as if she'd hired him to do her taxes. "He'll be staying here at the house to help me manage my appointments, my paperwork, and...when the time comes...his specialty is palliative care."

Palliative. I'd heard the word before but I couldn't re-member what it meant. I couldn't think. The ringing in my ears was suddenly so loud I could feel it in my teeth.

"Hospice," Raffi supplied quietly when it was clear I was still trying to understand. He wasn't running his gab now. "I'm a hospice nurse."

"No. That can't be right!" A tempest of dread swirled in my guts, threatening to swallow me whole. "It's too *soon!*"

"Well, it's not going to happen tomorrow," Dearie assured me. She tried to catch my hand but I was pacing in earnest now. "Damen, please sit down—"

She looked to Raffi with a pleading expression. He caught me in a full-body hug that trapped my arms across my chest and threatened to crush my ribs if I struggled. He outweighed me by about two hundred pounds, and from the feel of it, most of it was muscle. It was like being hugged by a grizzly bear.

"I'm so sorry, Damen," Dearie murmured. "I know how much it hurts to hear that someone you love is dying. But I am." The corners of her mouth twitched upward but it somehow made her look sad. "I need to make the most of the time I have left."

Gradually, her words found their way through my reeling mind and my distress began to fade, leaving me as brittle and empty as an eggshell. I sagged against Raffi's arms as the new reality settled into my mind.

"Lemme go," I mumbled at last, "I'm fine."

Raffi held on a moment longer, waiting until he was absolutely sure I'd gotten a grip on myself, and then relaxed his clinch. I pushed him away, and rebounded from my own force, stumbling out of the kitchen into the living room where I collapsed on the couch. It creaked under my weight—an ancient walnut frame upholstered with fading tapestry. I stared at the blank face of the fireplace cover and ran my hands over the fabric as if I were trying to read the thread count through my fingertips.

Dearie settled lightly on the cushion beside me and laid a delicate hand on mine—her fingertips cold against my skin. I wrapped my fingers around them to warm them.

"Did I hear you say that you came to use the piano?" she asked. "Would you play for me for a while?" It was a gentle request but it might as well have been a command: no force on earth would have given me the strength to tell her 'no.' I nodded and got to my feet. The piano's glossy curves and blood-colored wood gleamed reassuringly in the dimness of the room. The sight of it quieted my mind. I ran my hands over the silky wood and took a deep breath, feeling calmness settle across my shoulders.

I slid onto the bench and pulled off my rings one by one before running a scale. The notes rang true; Dearie had gotten the piano tuned. My left hand landed in the shape of a chord and I launched into Dearie's favorite: *Moonlight Sonata.* The music rose inside me, pushing the agony of Dearie's approaching death to the far edges of my mind. The music evolved into Liszt. Then Chopin. Then Gershwin. I followed the thread of the music out of my murky thoughts, feeling it rising through my fingers and filling the room around me. As long as I kept playing the music kept me safe. It filled my mind like a ring of firelight that kept the hungry wolves of my emotions at bay. The feelings weren't gone, I could still sense them in the darkness; still hungry, still circling—but for now, I was safe.

When I ran out of classics, I turned to some of my music: aimless, shapeless fragments of songs I kept in the back of my mind and sometimes played as an exercise to keep myself in practice. I found my attention drifting back to the progression I'd been struggling with at the Gray Area. I tried to let go and let it rise to the surface. The first few notes rang true and my heart leaped but then my fingers fumbled the notes and the music once again tangled.

"Sorry," I mumbled. I tried to pick up where I'd left off but couldn't find the tune. I floundered for a moment, aware of Dearie's eyes on me, and then gave up. Switching gears, I started to play a polka. Dearie laughed in surprised delight, throwing her head back and I smiled in spite of myself, and we rolled out a barrel together for a while.

When I ran out of songs to play, I let the last note ring out and dropped my hands into my lap. I stared into the distance, waiting for the magic to collapse and reality to come crashing in. Instead, I felt Grandma Dearie's hands settle on my shoulders in a benediction.

My throat closed up and I turned to put my arms around her waist. For a while, all I could do was hold on. My cheek pressed against the soft cotton of her shirt as she rocked me gently, humming something I could only hear through the ear I held pressed to her chest.

"That was marvelous, Blue, thank you," she said, at last, kissing the top of my forehead. "You are such a sweet soul."

"I'm pretty sure you're the only one who thinks so," I said.

"Come now, you know that's not true." Dearie slid beside me on the bench and pressed a hand to my cheek until I turned to look at her. Her gaze was steady and serious. "I love you, Damen. You know that, right?"

I tried to look away but Dearie pulled my face back.

"Right?"

I nodded, feeling a knot form in my throat the size of a human skull. "You're the only one who does," I managed. It came out in a voiceless croak.

"No, I'm the only one you are willing to hear it from."

A bitter laugh escaped me. It sounded like a sob. I knew she was wrong—no one else even cared that I was alive, much less loved me.

"Damen, please listen to me," Dearie brushed the hair back from my forehead and forced me to look into her eyes.

"I wish I could make you see how deeply you are loved by everybody around you. You must let go of this belief that you are not worthy of it. *Please.*" Her fingers gripped my hands so tightly that my knuckles popped. "Will you at least try? For me?"

I pulled my hands away and dropped my gaze to my lap. "I don't think I can," I managed, my voice barely a whisper.

Dearie slid her arms around my elbow and leaned against me. "You must try, nevertheless."

There was no arguing with a 'nevertheless.'

5

ALL BENEFITS.
NO FRIENDS.

I T TOOK me a few days after my encounter with Dearie to get my head on straight again. I moped around the Cursèd Place in a depressive funk, too wrapped up in self-pity to write any music or to go looking for mischief with the rest of the guys. I was lying on my mattress in a listless half-doze when my phone buzzed. I wrenched my eyes open far enough to peer at the screen and saw a number I recognized.

Melody.

I sat up sharply, feeling the world swirl around me as the blood drained from my head. I was awake in an instant. Melody had never called me before. The boundaries of our relationship were explicit: if I wanted to see her, then I would go to her at the club. She dictated whether or not we hooked up, and when she was finished with me, she sent me home. No discussion. No outside contact. *Nothing serious.* I'd given her my number weeks ago but she'd never sent me so much as an emoji.

"Hey, where you been?" she asked without preamble.

"New phone, who dis?" I said, mustering every ounce of control I had to play it cool as my heart beat against the wall of my chest like it was trying to escape.

"Don't be a tool; it's me, Melody."

I smiled in spite of myself. The sound of her voice pierced the haze of my angst like a sunbeam cutting through cloud cover.

"Oh, hey."

"Don't 'oh, hey' me. You haven't been to the club in days. How come?"

"Too busy being an international man of mystery."

Melody gave a sigh in the shape of an eye-roll and let the question drop.

"Okay, well, I need you. Can you meet up?"

Need. The word sank into my brain like a hot knife cutting through butter. *Melody needed me.*

"Sure, where and when?"

"Soon as you can. I'll send you the address," she said, and then ended the call without saying goodbye.

✳   ✳   ✳   ✳

The address Melody gave me turned out to be an elementary school. Shrieking kids in all shapes and sizes swarmed across the wet pavement of a basketball court in a shapeless mob. I assumed the Girl Child was among them but I didn't see her in the crowd.

At the end of the block, a line of moms stood on the sidewalk outside the chain-link fence staring expectantly towards the kindergarten entrance. Melody was easy to spot among them. She stood out as the only splash of color on an otherwise gray street in her neon-bright high-heel boots and a coat trimmed with fur that looked like it might have come from a Muppet. She might as well have been wearing a sign that flashed "STRIPPER" in neon letters. The rest of the moms were all as drab and shapeless as pigeons, and they twittered among themselves as they cast contemptuous looks towards her back.

If any of this bothered Melody, she didn't let it show. Her attention was fixed on the school doors with such a laser-like intensity she probably hadn't even noticed. She had an overnight bag clutched to her chest and was holding onto it like she expected someone to try to steal it from her. The Girl Child's car seat rested at her feet.

I ambled up the sidewalk behind her, setting off a new surge of whispers and titters, and swooped around to kiss her on the cheek.

"Jesus Christ!" she gasped, flinching so violently I immediately felt bad.

"Sorry! Sorry."

"*Hijueputa!* Don't sneak up on me like that!" She smacked me in the stomach with the back of her hand hard enough to sting even through my coat.

"Hey! I said I was sorry!" I danced away to what I hoped was a safe distance and held up my hands: *not touching*.

Melody glowered at me and got a handle on herself.

"Sorry," she mumbled. "I've had a shit day."

She took out a pack of cigarettes and stuck one between her lips, struggling to light it one-handed. I took the lighter and cupped my hands around the flame to hold it steady for her.

"So, what's all this about, anyway?" I asked as she drew in a deep sip of smoke and rolled the tension off her shoulders.

"My *stupit* babysitter."

"Who, Evelyn?" I asked, confused. I knew my sister sometimes babysat for her but as far as I knew she and Melody were on good terms.

Melody shook her head and huffed an annoyed plume of smoke out her nose. "No, my weekday girl. Bitch got locked up tryin' to lift a Juicy bag—it wasn't even *real*—an' I got an afternoon shift but now I got no one to watch Vico. So, I hadda call her daddy an' now the bastard wants her for the whole weekend." She gestured peevishly towards the overnight bag and the car seat. I got the feeling she was more upset about having to call Lily White for help than about the plight of her babysitter. "An' on top of it all, now I gotta find a new goddamn babysitter."

"I could watch her," I offered but Melody just laughed.

"Ha, yeah right."

"Why not? It's not like I have a day job," I said, trying to pretend I didn't feel stung by the brush-off.

"We don't got that kind of relationship," she said. *All benefits, no friends.*

"Judge sure thinks we do," I said.

Melody frowned. "Judge? What's he got to do with anything?"

"He came around our rehearsal space asking if we were getting serious." I leaned against the chain-link fence and shoved my hands in my pockets, dreading the question I had to ask next. "What's your deal with him, anyway? You two got some kind of...thing going on?"

Melody snorted derisively. "Ew. No."

"Cuz he sure feels some kind of way about you. He about nailed my ass to the wall when he found out you introduced me to your kid."

"Oh, that." Melody dismissed the episode with a wave of her hand. "He's just protective is all."

"Yeah? Well, so is a handgun—that doesn't mean it won't kill me."

"He's not gonna kill you, don't be dramatic."

Before I could protest further, Lily White's Corvette rumbled to the curb behind us and he revved the engine to get Melody's attention. Melody acknowledged this by giving him the finger but didn't turn to look at him. He rolled down the passenger side window and leaned across the seat to shout at her, "Hey! Is Victoria ready to go?"

"Don't you yell at me out a car window," Melody snapped. "Get out an' talk to me like a goddamn human."

Lily White threw the Corvette into park and climbed out as if he were doing us all a favor. His eye fell on me and his expression darkened. "What's *he* doing here?" he demanded.

"That's none of your business," Melody told him.

"I'm not babysitting so you can sleep around—"

"Ohmigod, STOP!" Melody cut him off. "I'm goin' to *work,* asshole. He's giving me a ride."

"Yeah? Well, maybe you shouldn't schedule work if you don't have someone to watch Victoria," he said, still glaring at me, his expression stubborn and mean.

Before Melody could respond, the school bell rang and kindergarteners began spilling out of the building onto the playground. I saw the Girl Child push her way out the door wearing a yellow raincoat that was slightly too short in the sleeves. She scanned the fence line and beamed when she spotted us.

"Dada!" she cried, galloping towards us across the wet pavement. She crashed into the chain-link fence with an echoing rattle.

"Hey, Punkin!"

"Are you here cuz of cor-tordered?" she asked.

"Nope, I'm here just to see you, kiddo," Lily White told her. "Waddya say? Wanna spend the weekend with your Dada?"

"Yes!" the Girl Child said, giving a little hop of delight.

"Go on to the gate," Melody ordered, gesturing to where a playground supervisor was releasing children to their parents one by one. The Girl Child scampered off to get in line and Lily White once again turned his attention to Melody.

"I'm just saying, don't think you can make a habit of this," he said. "I'm not some child care service you can call up for free any time you feel like it."

Melody gave an irate growl. "You know what? Forget it. I don't gotta listen to this." She jabbed at him with a pointed finger. "*You* were the one that wanted more time with her but you don't wanna watch your daughter? Fine. I'll find someone else—"

She turned on her heel to storm away but Lily White got in front of her.

"Okay! Okay, fine. *Stop.* I said I'd watch her, so I'll watch her."

"Don't do me any favors or nothing," Melody snarled at him. Lily White held up his hands in surrender and said nothing. Still smoldering, Melody thrust the car seat toward him but Lily White didn't take it.

"I don't need it. I bought a new one—a good one." He gestured toward the passenger seat of the Corvette where a top-of-the-line car seat was already installed.

"What, my car seat not good enough for you now?" Melody demanded but before Lily White could respond the Girl Child pushed her way out the gate and tackled him around the middle.

"Hey kiddo!" he exclaimed, once again all smiles. He swept her up and braced her on one hip to address her at eye level. "You ready for some fun?"

"Yes!"

"You know what we're gonna do? We're gonna go downtown to the American Girl store, and I'm gonna let you pick something out—whatever you want. Something you can keep in your room at my place when you come to visit."

"Yes!" Girl Child squealed.

"No," Melody said.

"But Mamaaaaa."

"You wanna go spendin' that kind of money on her maybe buy her a real goddamn coat, not some *stupit* doll," Melody said.

"That's what your support payments are for: necessities," Lily White said. "She needs a coat; *you* buy her a coat. I can buy her whatever I want."

Jesus, he was a weasel.

Melody fumed but couldn't argue. She held out a hand to Girl Child imperiously.

"C'mon, Vico, let's go get you in your seat."

The Girl Child slid down Lily White's side and Melody dragged her towards the Corvette, every line of her body vibrating with rage. Lily White watched her go with a shake of his head.

"Women, amirite?" he said, once she was safely out of earshot. He turned to me with a smirk like he expected me to take his side.

"Sure, whatever," I said. I could feel him staring at me but I stuck my hands in my pockets and avoided his gaze.

"I know who you are," he continued. "You're Damen Warner."

"Yep, that's me."

Lily White pulled his lips back to show his teeth but it wasn't really a smile. "The first time I saw you I thought you looked like a piece of shit," he said. "I thought 'what's she see in this guy?' But now? I get it. Big musician. Can't really blame her—nothing like fame to get a girl to open her legs, right?"

"Yeah? You got a lot of experience with that?" I challenged him but I had to admit it was true: fame was the world's best social lubricant. I certainly wasn't laid on my charm, my money, my good looks, or my social grace.

Lily Weasel shrugged off the question.

"Listen, *rockstar*," he said, somehow managing to make 'rockstar' sound like an insult. "Don't think you're gonna... you know, get away with stuff cuz you're famous."

"Okay, cool. Good talk." I turned my back on him but Lily White shouldered his way in front of me.

"Hey! Don't walk away from me, I'm talking to you."

I tried to step around him but Lily White blocked my

way. It was just a matter of time before the temptation to punch him in the mouth got the better of me.

"Lemme guess," I said. "This is the part where you tell me she's your woman and that I better keep my distance if I know what's good for me?"

"Listen, we both know you could have any woman you want. Why get tangled up in some single-mother baby-mama drama?" he said, a veneer of nonchalance scraped too thin over the jagged edges of his desperation. "Just... move on. Find someone new."

"Why? You think if I'm out of the picture Melody's going to come back to you?" I said, realizing as I said it that I'd hit upon the truth. "It's over, bro. Let her go. Move on."

"Move on?!" he hissed. "She's the mother of *my* daughter. I have a right to be a part of her life."

"Dude, she *hates* you."

"She'll get over it."

"Why're you so hung up on her, anyway? Is it because she got away?" I caught a guilty flicker in Lily Weasel's eyes as my words landed close to the mark. "That's it, isn't it? A rich kid like you—used to getting everything you want? But not Melody. And it drives you crazy."

I could see it was true: Melody didn't give a flying rat's ass about Lily White's money. She didn't give a flying rat's ass about my fame either but Lily White didn't know that. He'd lived his whole life at the center of the universe. Everyone and everything had always orbited around his wants and needs, and he'd never had to waste one single privileged minute thinking about what anybody else did or did not want. Until now. Now, I was on the scene. Now,

Melody had a choice, and she wasn't choosing him.

"Melody's *mine*," he insisted, red-faced.

"Melody doesn't want you."

"Well, it doesn't matter. Victoria's *my* daughter. I got a right to be a part of her life. And I'm gonna fight for it. If you don't wanna step aside, then..."

"Then what?" I asked, waiting for a threat that I knew would never come.

Lily White glared at me until his silence answered the question. I patted him on the head.

"You're cute when you're mad," I said. "Have a juice box. Take a nap. We'll talk again when you grow the fuck up."

He snatched up Girl Child's overnight bag from off the pavement and slung it over his shoulder. "You're going to regret this," he growled. Then he turned on his heel and stalked back towards his car.

6

THE ODDKAT

JUDGE WAS true to his word. Within a few days, a piano appeared in the Gray Area accompanied by neither fanfare nor explanation. The only indication that it had come from Judge was a Post-It note stuck to the front with the directive: *Call Phoenix* written on it. The piano itself had seen better days. She was a battered, blonde upright with a scarred case, yellowing keys, and a statistically significant amount of sophomoric graffiti that made me think she had probably been acquired from the Chicago public school system during a recent round of budget cuts. Because fuck the arts.

I called her 'the Oddkat.' As in Strange Pussy. As in something you banged around with on the side—good for practice but not something you were ever going to get serious with. I felt certain that Mungo would tear himself in half before he let me use her to lay down a track but she was good for songwriting, and she stayed in tune. Mostly.

As long as the weather didn't get too hot.

Or too cold.

Or too humid.

Despite her many obvious faults, the Oddkat's arrival signaled that it was time to stop screwing around and do some work. Judge had made it clear that his role as our producer began and ended with the money, which left me in charge of producing the actual music. This should have been a dream come true—I'd always fantasized about having the chance to record whatever the hell I wanted without adult supervision—but so far, the only thing I'd managed to develop was a new and malignant form of procrastination.

Finally, I gave up and called Mungo.

Mungo was neither a producer nor a musician: he was an engineer all the way down to his component atoms but what he may have lacked in the way of creative vision he made up for in rigorous exactitude. His was a reality made up of waveforms and amplitudes. To Mungo, the entire universe and all its mysteries could be distilled down to a cosmic stream of vibrating energy, and his purpose in life was to capture it, refine it, and bend it to his will.

"Chreesht on a bloody cracker." He arrived in the doorway to the Gray Area and surveyed the room with his face carved into an expression of grim distaste. "Werkin' hard et hardly werkin', isit?" he asked but the question was largely rhetorical. Jojo was sprawled out on the floor with her head nestled on the pillow in her bass drum, sleeping off her hangover from the night before. Gorey's attention was absorbed by his accumulation of computer monitors and gaming consoles, playing an MMORPG on two screens while scrolling endlessly through an array of social media feeds on two others. Kilroy had taken a monster dose of edibles and was so high he was verging on uselessness. Most of his limited attention was focused on picking a hole in the threadbare upholstery of the couch where he sat. I couldn't tell if it was a new hole or if it had been there when we'd picked it up off the side of the road.

"Welcome to Bedlam," I said. "Enjoy your madness."

Mungo shook his head and pinched the bridge of his nose, then clapped his hands to listen to the space.

"Creesht..." he winced. He took a step into the room and clapped again. Shuddered. Stepped again. Clapped again. Shook his head. "Gei me th'boke," he said, pressing his fingertips to his lips as if the shape of the room's acoustics made him physically ill. He looked at me with pleading eyes.

"That bad, huh?"

"Ef ah wanted a skelpit lug ah'da callt mah gran," he said.

It was unclear whether any of this was English. What *was* clear was that there were certain acoustical standards from which he was not prepared to deviate even for the sake of rehearsal. He set to work re-arranging the space according to the laws of his personal auditory feng shui.

Mungo's biggest pain point was Jojo's drum kit. He insisted that it was out of alignment with the space and spent the next forty minutes clapping his way around the room to demonstrate some finer point of tone management that was so far over our heads it might as well have been in outer space. Something about nodes and ringing overtones.

Jojo was having none of it.

It had taken her weeks to fully decompress her kit and a solid third of the rehearsal space was now given over to her. She was not prepared to move it. Anywhere. For anyone. Especially not at the behest of a *bloviating sack of dick paste.*

Mungo thought this was rich coming from a *weapons-grade plum.*

Jojo didn't know what that meant—none of us did—but she wasn't about to take it lying down. She planted herself defiantly on her throne and proceeded to stomp out a one-two beat on the kick drum while Mungo appraised her intelligence, character, family history, personal hygiene, and career prospects in a harangue of irate Scots.

It probably didn't help matters that I took it upon myself to underscore their argument with an improvised piano accompaniment.

"Yeh'r tone's *flat,*" Mungo insisted, to a dramatic, ascending minor second interval, his face red with frustration.

One. Two. One. Two.

"Sorrray, I just don't heaaar it?" Jojo said, her inner Kardashian dialed up to full volume. I accentuated it with a descending tritone, somewhere around a diminished fifth.

"Yeh'r flatter 'n a witches tetty."

One. Two. One. Two.

"Just how flat aarre witch titties?"

Flat as a B-flat minor melodic arpeggio. I exchanged a sly grin with Tombstone who snickered but Mungo gave a roar of aggravation and punted an empty cardboard box to the far end of the room with a vehement kick.

"Ahm skunnert wit'cher glaikit jobbies!" he sputtered, inchoate with fury. He tangled both his hands in his hair like he was prepared to rip it out of his scalp.

"Omigod, guyssss, CHILL OUT..." Kilroy hollered blurrily, at last cutting through the bullshit to bring us back to reality. If Kilroy was getting annoyed then things were getting serious. Jojo let the beat clatter into reluctant silence and held up her hands in surrender.

"He started it."

"D'yeh want t' record yer album or not?"

"Enough! Stop!" Kilroy cut them off before they could regain any momentum. "We're all tryna do the same thing here, right?"

Jojo and Mungo glared at one another but subsided into silence. Kilroy waited until he was sure the tensions had cooled at least as far as room temperature and then turned his attention to me. "What do you think about maybe doin' a cover?" he asked, floating the idea out into the space between us, dangling from a question mark.

"A cover."

Kilroy shrugged, embarrassed. "Yeah, you know... something...catchy?"

"We're not a fucking cover band," I said at last.

"I know, dude but..."

I exchanged a look with Gorey who shrugged. "People like hearing songs they already know, right?" he offered.

He had a point. I looked to Tombstone who seemed to be considering it. He shrugged: *maybe.*

"What've yeh got in mind?" Mungo asked.

"I been thinking 'bout alla our bad luck n' stuff?" Kilroy fumbled in his pocket for his phone, dropped it onto the carpet, and struggled to pick it up again. "Made me think 'bout that Stevie Wonder song? 'Very Superstitious' or whatever it's called?"

"'Superstition'?" I supplied. "You wanna cover 'Superstition'?"

"Yeah, that's the one, you know, as a single. For shits n' giggles." Kilroy began to giggle at the very suggestion but pressed on: "An' we could make a...you know...music video? Like, you know, like...gorilla style."

Tombstone looked at him, perplexed, and made a motion as if beating his chest.

Gorilla style?

Kilroy seemed to realize this wasn't the right word and giggled harder. "Gorilla style..." he reiterated, hunching his skinny shoulders and puffing out his cheeks. I'd never seen anybody in the world who looked less like a gorilla in my life. He beat his fists on his chest but only managed to knock the wind out of himself, which made him laugh harder until he crumpled onto the floor.

Tombstone cued up a video on YouTube and hit 'play' with the stab of one finger. He angled his head angled towards the phone, listening intently to the song's distinctive guitar line before slinging Rita around to his front. He fiddled with her tone knobs for a moment, then fell into the groove of the melody as easily as child's play. He grinned. He liked it.

Jojo recognized the tune and picked out the beat on a high hat, gaining momentum as she went along. Gorey ditched his wall of electronics and ran to strap on his guitar, quickly improvising a series of harmonies that, objectively, sounded awful but somehow threaded together with the melody in a way I couldn't have anticipated. I felt the hairs on my arms stand on end. Even Mungo recognized an epiphany when he heard one. Nodes or no nodes, he hastily produced a Zoom recorder and set it to record, trying to bottle the lightning while he could.

I had to admit, it wasn't the worst idea to ever come out of Kilroy's burnt-out brain. Covers were an easy sell, and with GoatRodeo out of our rotation, we were going to need a new opening number. And a video could go viral. There were plenty of Columbia kids who'd be happy to shoot it for us. Guerilla style.

"I think you might be onto something," I said when the song ended. "You wanna ask Judge about the rights—"

But Kilroy didn't respond.

I looked down to find him sprawled out on the carpet by my feet: tied up, dried up and dead to the world.

"Hey, Kil—" I reached down and slapped his cheek, but he lolled his head to the side and let out a colossal trumpeting snore that almost certainly disrupted the room's nodes and ringing overtones. Not dead, just out cold.

Jojo rolled her eyes. "Situation normal: all fucked up."

Tombstone frowned. He kicked the sole of Kilroy's sneaker, then fell into a crouch beside him. Picking up one of Kilroy's bony arms, he peered at the inside of his elbow. Then he checked between his fingers and pulled off his shoes to check between his toes. It didn't take a mind reader to know what he was looking for. The fact that Kilroy was a recovering heroin addict was never very far from any of our minds. And while he did a lot of pot, it was pretty rare for him to be this fucked up in the middle of rehearsal.

Tombstone let Kilroy's bare foot drop to the carpet and looked up at the rest of us with a shrug: *nothing*.

"Check his dick," Gorey supplied, helpfully.

Tombstone gave him the finger, trying not to smile.

"Christ," Jojo groaned. "The last thing we need right now was for him to take a header off the wagon." She produced a package of Sharpies and selected one before holding it out to me. I took one and passed it to Tombstone. One by one we all settled around Kilroy's body like vultures, united in vandalism.

"You're not missing any pills, are you?" I asked.

"Not that I know of but I'll check. I haven't been keeping them in the house. You know, to be safe." She and Mungo seemed to have formed an unspoken truce and were now taking turns writing swear words on Kilroy's chest. Tombstone had peeled back Kilroy's oversized beanie and was sketching a combover on his shaved skull while Gorey completed the look with a handlebar mustache and a dense unibrow.

I had just begun work on an enormous winged boner emerging from Kilroy's beltline when my phone buzzed in my pocket. I answered it, tucking it under my ear without looking at the screen.

"I'm *working*, I swear," I said, expecting it to be Judge but it was a woman's voice that spoke.

"Oh, hi, Damen? Sorry. I didn't mean to interrupt."

I pulled the phone away from my face to look at the Caller ID which read 'EVIL SISTER': my sister, Evelyn.

"Oh, hey, no worries," I said, softening my tone. "What's up?"

"I need a favor."

Evelyn was asking *me* for a favor? She was the most sensible, capable, responsible person I knew. I couldn't imagine what I could do for her that she couldn't do better, faster, and more legally.

"Uh, sure," I said. "Tell me where the body is and I'll take care of it."

I hoped I was joking.

"Wouldn't you be surprised," Evelyn said, dryly. "But no, it's nothing like that. Can you swing by?"

"Sure, where you at?"

"Home," Evelyn said.

Evanston, my mind translated.

"I'll be right there," I said.

7

NIGHT TERROR

EVELYN HAD her coat on when I arrived.

"Thank God—" she murmured, ushering me into the house and closing the door behind me. "Something came up and I have to run out. I don't really know how long it'll take."

"Cool, where're we going?" I asked trying to guess what would induce her to rush out of the house in the dead of night. Her appearance offered no obvious clues. It seemed unlikely she was headed to the Botanic Gardens, where she worked during the day, or the Renaissance Faire, where she worked on weekends. At night she bartended at the club where Melody danced but she was hardly dressed for nightlife in pajama pants and a faded Northwestern sweatshirt. Her smooth, fair hair was pulled back in a ponytail and her face was clean of makeup. Her breath smelled like toothpaste.

"Not 'we,' *me,*" she clarified. "I need you to stay here. I'm in the middle of babysitting and I need someone to be here in case the kiddo wakes up. Could you hang out for an hour or two?"

"Hang on, you needed someone to babysit and you thought of *me?*" I asked. I could think of a lot of people who were probably a better choice. "What about your roommate? Or, hell, even Mom?" If I knew one thing for sure, it was that Evelyn wasn't stupid, if she'd chosen me, she'd done so for a reason.

"Gracie's on graveyard shift and I don't need Mom asking me a million questions about my business," Evelyn said, "And besides, it's Vico. Melody asked me to watch her for the night; she already knows you. I don't want her waking up to a stranger. Are you cool with that? I mean, it should be super easy, and there's food in the fridge—you're welcome to whatever you want."

"Sure, Evil, I got you," I said.

"Thanks, you're a lifesaver." Evelyn breathed an audible sigh of relief and began rattling around the room to gather her keys and phone and wallet from various surfaces. "Vico's in the den on the couch." She nodded toward a small study area off the kitchen where a lumpy form was stretched out on a secondhand sofa. A glowing lamp made out of salt suffused the room with a soft warm light. It was so painfully domestic it made me long for a pair of slippers and a pipe. "She's out cold but...you know, just in case."

"Cool. I got this," I assured her. "You wanna tell me where you're headed?"

"It's not really any of your business," Evelyn said. She shoved everything into her purse and gave a little hop to kiss me on the cheek. "Thanks, though. I'll owe you one."

And then she was gone.

*   *   *   *

Comedy Central was rerunning classic episodes of South Park, so I took up residence on the living room couch with a bag of potato chips and settled in to watch Cartman fart fire. I'd just about reached a satisfying level of comfortable stupor when an unholy shriek from the back room startled me upright.

I lurched to my feet in panic and ran to the den. The Girl Child was on top of the covers writhing in a fit. I ran to her side. Her cheeks were streaked with long, wet trails of tears and her mouth was a wide square of terror, showing all her baby teeth around a hollow, clenching throat.

"Lemme go! Lemme go! Lemme out of heeeeere!"

No one else was in the room. Nothing was even touching her—she'd already kicked all the blankets off the couch in her struggle.

"Vico, hey! It's okay! You're okay!" I shook her shoulders gently but she twisted and kicked, whimpering out a low, animal moan. In the dim light, I saw that her eyes were open but when I waved a hand over her face she didn't respond—still asleep.

Don't panic, it's just a night terror. I told myself, then laughed inwardly: *Just.*

Night terrors weren't just bad dreams; they were a kind of sleep-panic that happened deep down in the lizard brain that knew the world only as That Place Made of Imminent Death. I knew this from experience: I'd had night terrors as a kid. I'd wake up half the neighborhood with my screams and then have absolutely no memory of it in the morning.

"Lemme goooo!" The Girl Child's voice cracked into the

high, whistling scream only small children could manage, and my ears shrieked in harmony. I felt a sudden sympathy for Mom, sitting up with me screaming bloody murder night after night until the neighbors called the cops.

The cops.

Shit.

If she kept this up, someone was going to think I was killing her or worse. The cops would take one look at me and throw me in jail. Evelyn would get in trouble. Melody would be fucking furious. And then Judge would get involved and I'd spend the rest of my worthless life down in Pontiac Max taking proton torpedoes up the exhaust port.

I had to make her calm down.

Contrary to conventional wisdom, it wasn't dangerous to wake someone out of a night terror but it was difficult. I'd be waking her out of deep sleep and I wasn't sure my perforated face was going to be much comfort to her but physical pressure sometimes helped. I captured her flailing hands and pressed them to her chest, crossing her arms over her heart and wrapping her in a firm embrace.

"S' okay, Girl Child," I murmured in her ear, smoothing her hair back as best I could with my free hand. "S'okay. You're okay."

Girl Child drew in a monster breath in preparation for her next scream, and I pressed her head against my chest and crooned the lowest note I could hit, deep down in my guts, letting it sustain as long as I could. The Girl Child's howl never came: she held the breath in her chest letting it out bit by bit in little hitching whimpers but didn't cry out again.

"Lemme outta here," Girl Child sobbed, quieter now: no longer a scream. "I uwanna go...I want my Mamaaaa. I...wan...my...Mammaaa."

I took another breath and crooned another low note, holding her close, smoothing her hair. It was the only thing that ever got me to calm down as a kid. When the neighbors called the cops, my stepfather, Michael, was the cop that responded. Somehow, his crooning embrace was enough to smooth my anxious mind back into sleep. Mom used to joke that he'd stayed the night so many times she might as well marry him.

Back when Mom told jokes.

The Girl Child's breath was calmer now. I could still feel the frantic butterfly of her heart against my chest but she stopped struggling and slowly settled back into stillness. I rocked her some more until the fit seemed to be over, then gently laid her back on the sofa. Using the front of my shirt, I wiped away her tears and picked up the blanket off the floor. It was too thin; the autumn cold was seeping into the room through the window panes. I dumped it on the back of a chair and picked up Grandma Rose's heavy, knit afghan off the back of the couch and draped it over her instead, and then started out of the room.

"Mama?"

The Girl Child's voice reached me at the threshold sounding bleary and hoarse but awake. I tucked myself behind the doorframe where she wouldn't see me.

"She's at work, Girl Child," I told her.

"Where's Evie?"

"She had to go out," I told her. "It's me, Damen."

"Damen?" The Girl Child didn't sound alarmed. She sounded almost...pleased. I hazarded a peek around the doorframe and saw her roll over under the blankets to sit upright.

"You had a bad dream," I told her. "It's over now, you can go back to sleep."

"I'm not sleepy."

"Just close your eyes."

"I can't, there's monsters."

"Not while I'm around there's not."

"I *caaan't*."

I sighed. She was awake now. Getting her to go back to sleep was a battle I wasn't going to win without resorting to cough syrup, and I wasn't prepared to explain to a grand jury why I'd drugged my stripper girlfriend's five-year-old daughter.

"You like cartoons?" I said at last.

Together we made our way back to the living room and the Girl Child scrambled up on the couch beside me to snuggle under my arm like a puppy. I pulled a blanket over her and she settled in against my side to stare at the colors flickering on the screen as aliens wreaked havoc on a quiet mountain town.

"What's an 'ayno pro'?" she asked as Cartman signaled to the aliens using a satellite dish coming out of his ass.

There was a good chance I'd never be allowed to babysit again.

"Uhh, it's something people think aliens like to do."

"Oh," The Girl Child said and fell silent until one of the characters swore. She giggled. "He said a bad word!"

"Yeah, he did. Don't repeat that to your mom, okay?"

"Okay."

Cartman launched into a lengthy blue streak and I put my hands over her ears until it was over. "You know what? You probably shouldn't repeat *anything* you hear on this show, okay?"

"Okay." The Girl Child lapsed once again into silence and was quiet for so long I thought she might have fallen asleep until she asked: "What's a 'slut'?"

"What did I just say about repeating stuff from the show?!" I said as I mentally rewound the last fifteen minutes of dialogue, trying to remember if it had been among the litany of swears pouring out of the screen.

"I didn't hear it from the show," Girl Child protested.

"Then where did you hear it?" I asked.

The Girl Child looked cornered. "Nowhere?"

"C'mon, Girl Child, I know that's not true. Tell me where you heard it."

"Is it bad?" The Girl Child's voice was tiny. I realized she thought I was going to yell at her for asking me about it. I softened.

"Heyy—you're not in trouble for asking, okay? It's just not a nice word."

Girl Child nodded.

"Where'd you hear it?"

"At school."

"From a grown-up?"

Girl Child shook her head.

"From another kid?"

A nod.

"Another kindergartener?"

"Mno. One of the big kids. They were saying bad stuff about Mama."

"Bad stuff like 'slut'?"

She nodded. "And they laughed at me cuz I didn't know what it means."

"You're not supposed to know what it means," I told her. "It's a mean thing grown-ups say sometimes and you shouldn't be hearing it yet."

"But why would they say that about Mama?" she sniffled as tears welled up in her eyes. I felt my heart go out to her.

"They're just being little shits," I said then winced. "Don't repeat that, okay? They probably heard it from a grown-up." I remembered the barrage of jealous side-eye from the other moms outside the schoolyard and figured I knew who the real culprit was. "Do you know what your Mama does at her job?"

Girl Child nodded. "She's a dancer. I think she's pretty. I wanna be a dancer too."

"Maybe someday," I said. *Some parent I would make.* "Well, some people don't like that she's pretty and dances to make money and are going to say mean things about her."

The Girl Child scrubbed her face and nodded, still upset but trying to hide it.

"Listen, if they make fun of your Mama again, you knock them down. You tell them 'No one makes fun of my Mama.'"

"But that's *fighting.*"

"It's standing up for yourself," I said. "Sometimes that means knocking someone down."

"I'll get in trouble."

"They won't tell," I told her. "They won't anyone to know they got beat up by a girl. I mean, don't go around starting fights but if someone else starts one you can sure as hell finish it, okay?"

"Okay." The Girl Child smiled tentatively.

I put my arm over her again and she snuggled down under the blanket, snug as a bug in a rug. Within minutes she was asleep, snoring gently against my t-shirt. I could feel her little ribs rising and falling beneath my arm: peaceful and soft. I flipped off the television and eased out from under her, then stretched out on the floor beside the couch to keep the monsters away.

Just in case.

8

BITCHWHIP

EVELYN DIDN'T return for the rest of the night. I didn't know if I should be worried. I sent a handful of messages throughout the night but the later it got the less I expected a response. She still wasn't back by the time dawn broke and Melody knocked on the door.

"What the hell are *you* doing here?" she demanded as surprise and suspicion flickered across her face in rapid succession.

"Hey now, take it easy," I managed around a yawn. I stretched, feeling joints pop and crack, stiff from spending most of the night on the floor. "Evelyn had to step out so she asked me to stay with the Girl Child—didn't want her to wake up to someone she didn't know."

Melody narrowed her eyes. "Why, where'd she go?"

"You'll have to ask her," I said. "She told me it was none of my business."

"So, this wasn't your idea?"

"Why would it be my idea?"

"I told you, we don't have that kind of relationship."

"Yeah, you've made that pretty fucking clear." I felt a

surge of annoyance and bit down on it. What had I expected? A medal? I forced myself to take a deep breath and
watched it plume into the raw morning air like smoke. "It
was a favor for Evil," I assured her in my calmest possible tone. Melody chewed over her doubts, frowning, and
peered past me into the living room where the Girl Child
was asleep on the couch. "You wanna come in, already? It's
freezing out." I gestured her through the doorway grandly:
an engraved invitation.

Melody gave an annoyed sigh. "You know what? Fine.
Whatever. I don't got time for this." She pushed past me
into the front room and began to gather up the Girl Child's
belongings. I turned to follow her inside but a voice called
me back.

"Hey! Crustbucket!"

Out on the street, I could see Judge's beat-up Cadillac
idling by the curb. The window on the passenger side rolled
down and Judge's meaty hand gestured me over. I stepped
out of the house and immediately regretted it. The concrete was icy beneath my bare feet, and the damp wind
blowing in off the lake seeped through the thin fabric of
my t-shirt like the touch of clammy fingers. There hadn't
been a frost—not yet but it wasn't far off. I stooped to peer
in the window, feeling a welcome waft of heat blowing out
of the vent in the dashboard. The interior was cavern-like
even in the morning light. The air was hazy from Judge's
cigarette. Styx blared from the radio.

"You babysitting now, Crustbucket?" Judge asked through
a wall of teeth that was not quite a real smile.

"Favor to Evelyn," I said.

"Uh-huh."

"It wasn't my idea, scout's honor," I told him. "Just trying to not fuck things up."

Judge's eyes glittered with mistrust but he gave a curt nod. "You plannin' to drive her home?" I nodded and he reached a ham-like hand into the back seat and handed me a hunk of molded plastic through the window. "Here. You'll need this."

The car seat.

Whipped.

I reached out to take it, but Judge didn't let it go. "You call Phoenix yet?" he asked.

"Not yet."

"Do it." He tapped his wrist meaningfully. "Time's a-wastin'." Then he threw the car into gear and roared away, chewing over the cigarette crushed between his teeth like it owed him money.

I retreated to the warmth of the house where Melody was bundling Girl Child in her coat and the too-thin blanket from the den. She glanced up when she heard the door close.

"You gonna give us a ride, then?" she asked, nodding to the car seat in my hands.

"Figured so," I said. "You want breakfast? Evil won't mind."

"Can't. Gotta get Vico to school," Melody hoisted Girl Child onto her shoulder with a grunt of effort. Wrapped in blankets, she was nearly as big as Melody herself.

"Here. Gimme." I set down the car seat by the door and took Girl Child from her—fifty pounds of sleeping deadweight. It was no wonder Melody was so strong. The Girl Child stirred and wiped her face on my shoulder, but didn't wake up.

Melody made a circuit of the room picking up shoes and toys and shoving them into an overnight bag. She yanked on the zipper and swore when it pulled apart in her hands but slung it over her shoulder anyway and disappeared into the kitchen. I heard the sound of the refrigerator door, and she returned carrying a metal lunch box held together with band stickers.

"You ready?"

I nodded and shoved my feet into my boots without lacing them. Picking up my coat and the car seat in my free hand, I fumbled my way out the door, managing to bang the car seat on the door frame, the storm door, the porch railing, the mailbox, and myself in my ungainly exodus.

Melody pulled the door shut behind us and followed me to the GTO parked at the curb.

"Keys?" she asked.

"Jacket pocket," I held it up and she fished them out to unlock the passenger side door. Pushing the seat forward she tossed the overnight bag into the footwell and pitched the car seat in like an afterthought.

"You wanna plug that in?" I asked.

Melody gave me a look. "You really think you're going to get *her* into *that*, fast asleep, in a two-door car?" she asked in a tone that suggested I was being stupid. "Just put her on the bench, she'll sleep the whole way."

"That's illegal," I protested. *Since when did I care about what was legal?* That was a goddamn first.

"So, don't get pulled over."

Swallowing my aggravation, I tucked Girl Child onto the bench seat in the back and buckled a lap belt around her waist. It wasn't perfect but I figured it was better than nothing. Melody rolled her eyes.

"Hurry up, it's freezing."

I pushed the seat back into place and held the door open while she climbed in. Closing it behind her, I circled the car, stomping my feet to try to settle them into my boots, and tugged on the driver's side door handle.

Locked.

Melody had the keys. I knocked on the window with a knuckle and she looked up from her phone, annoyed.

"What?"

I tugged the door handle again. "You wanna go or what?"

She bared her teeth in a savage smile. "Did you lock yourself out?" she taunted. She held up the keys and jingled them at me. I felt a surge of anger and bit down on it: this was what I got for trying to help. I looked back at Evelyn's house, wondering if it was too late to go back inside but I was sure it was locked.

"You're the one who's got someplace to be," I said.

Melody scowled and reached across the driver's seat to tug on the lock peg.

"You're no fun," she said when I climbed in.

"You're a cunt," I muttered. I held out my hand for the keys but she held them out of my reach.

"You take that back," she said. Her voice was hushed and threatening.

"Or what? We'll sit here all day?"

"Judge can give me a ride," she hissed. "It's not too late. I could call him and he'd come."

I didn't doubt it but I wasn't ready to give in. We stared

at one another in a tense stalemate, both of us too proud to back down. I glared at her, still smarting with wounded pride. Too angry to apologize. Too angry to think of any other option.

Melody watched me, calculating my reaction. She reached across the gear shift and rested a hand on my leg, a hot spot against my thigh. High up. I felt my breath catch as arousal insinuated itself into the equation.

"Take it back," she murmured again, leaning in close.

I ground my teeth in frustration. All it had taken was one touch. One touch—and I couldn't think straight. My body was prepared to betray me and I was prepared to let it.

"You're a cunt and a bitch," I whispered.

"Take it back," Melody persisted. Her hand crept up to my crotch. I licked my lips and glanced at the Girl Child still out cold in the back seat, suddenly terrified she would wake up.

"Give me the keys."

"Take it back." Her fingers stroked me through the denim and her lips curled back in a cruel, ferocious smile as she felt my hardness responding to her touch. I grabbed her wrist and pushed her hand away, snatching at the keys with my other hand. She jerked them away, holding them by the far window, out of reach.

"You're hurting me," she said. I realized I was gripping her wrist with all my might. I let her go and swiped for the keys again, leaning across her as far as I could reach.

"Give me the goddamn keys!" I felt her breath on my ear, and then her teeth sank into my earlobe with a crunch. "Ow fuck!" I jumped back, touching the bite in disbelief.

"I'll scream," Melody said, smiling at me with bloody teeth. She held up her phone. Judge's number was already cued up—his chubby jowls split into a grin as his profile photo gave a double thumbs-up. "I'll say you offered me a ride and you grabbed me and the only way I could fight you off was to bite you." She pressed the call button with her thumb. Faintly, I heard the far end of the line begin to ring.

I felt an icy stab of fear—how had it come to this? One minute I'm giving her a ride home like a pussy-whipped bitch, and the next thing I know she's calling me a rapist. I sat back in the driver's seat fuming, trying to rein in my rage. Also, I had such a boner.

Judge's phone continued to ring.

"Fine," I said. "You win. I take it back."

A second ring. A third.

"Say it like you mean it."

A click on the far end of the line and then the tinny sound of Judge's voice: "Hello?"

"I take it back! Jesus, I take it back!" I said. My mouth tasted like copper.

"Melody, you there?"

Melody let me dangle at the end of her mercy for a moment longer then put the phone to her ear: "Sorry, hon," she said. "Butt dialed." She disconnected the call and dropped the keys into my hand, her eyes glittering with victory. I breathed a sigh of relief unaware I'd even been holding my breath.

Breaking her stare, I put the keys in the ignition, and fired up the engine trying to drown out the pounding of my pulse in my ears. The radio blared out the horse laughter of a morning DJ, braying out a segment on celebrity head-lines. Melody twisted it off.

"You're going to make it up to me," she said.

"Fine. Whatever." I eased the car onto the street, gripping the wheel to keep my hands from shaking. Melody took out a pocket mirror and inspected her teeth, scrubbing away any sign of the blood with the tip of a forefinger. I touched my ear self-consciously. It throbbed but didn't seem to be bleeding anymore. I could feel a crescent of tooth marks.

The streets were clear this early. I made it to the high-way and roared down to Melody's neighborhood, making good time. The streets around the school were crowded but I found a space across from the school where park-ing was only slightly illegal and came to a stop. Melody reached over the seat to give Girl Child a nudge.

"Wake up, baby," she murmured. "Time for school."

"Iunwannago..."

"Vico! School!" Melody climbed out of the car and pushed the seat forward to gather her bags. "C'mon, you're gonna be late!"

The Girl Child groaned and sat up; the hair stuck to the side of her face. She smoothed it back and squinted at me still lost halfway in sleep.

"Where's Uncle Judge?"

"At home probably."

"Are you gonna take me to school?"

"We're already here, kiddo," I said, nodding out the window at the procession of parents and kids ambling towards the entrance gate. On the playground, a knot of boys fought over a basketball. The Girl Child saw them and tensed. I remembered our conversation from the night before.

"Those the kids that've been picking on you?" I asked.

The Girl Child nodded, still regarding them sideways out of the corner of her eye. I reached back to unbuckle the seatbelt around her waist.

"Well, now's your chance to do something about it. Remember what we talked about last night? If they start making fun of you, knock them down."

"But they're bigger than me."

"So? I'm bigger than your mama and she kicks my butt up and down the block." I touched the raw spot on my ear again and felt a hard shell of dried blood.

"Yeah but she's *Mama*."

"And you're your mama's daughter," I told her. "I bet you're even stronger than she is. I bet you could knock me over right now."

"No, I can't."

"Sure you can. C'mon, let's practice." I climbed out of the driver's seat and circled around the car to hold the door open for her. The Girl Child dragged herself to her feet and stood on the sidewalk sullen with reluctance. I crouched on the sidewalk in front of her so that she could look at me eye to eye.

"Okay. Give me a good hard push right here." I patted my chest with both hands to show her where to shove. The Girl Child thrust out her hands and gave me a half-hearted push. I rocked backward but didn't fall. "C'mon, you can do better than that," I told her. "Hard, like you're pushing someone on a swing."

The Girl Child shoved again with more force.

"Again. Harder. Push with your feet."

Girl Child shoved harder.

"Again. Push!"

Girl Child ground her tiny teeth and let out a roar, charging at me with her head lowered. She collided with my body with her full weight, and I toppled over backward.

"Knockout! You win!" I exclaimed. I got to my feet and heaved her up over my head. I held one of her arms over her head in victory and put on my best Macho-Man Randy Savage voice. "We have ourselves a champion, OHHH, YEAHHH!"

The Girl Child shrieked with laughter and gave a victory roar.

"See? You can do it. Knock them down and say—"

"—don't talk about my Mama that way!" Girl Child crowed.

"Vico! You coming or what?" Melody stood beside the gate and gestured impatiently towards the schoolyard where the other kids were beginning to file into the building.

I set the Girl Child on the ground and I handed her the lunchbox. "You don't start fights but you sure as hell finish them, right?"

"Right!" The Girl Child grinned up at me.

"Attagirl. Knock 'em dead."

The Girl Child grinned up at me and wrapped her arms around my knees in a hug before bounding towards the gate with her lunch box rattling in one hand. Melody hustled her into the school yard as the bell rang and the security guard closed the gate shutting Melody out. The

Girl Child trotted across the asphalt basketball court towards the building.

"I love you, Vico!" Melody called after her.

Girl Child turned at the door and gave a wave and then disappeared inside the building. Melody waited until she was out of sight and then turned her attention to me.

"You got a good kid there," I said.

"Yeah, I know," she said. She moved in close until she was pressed against my chest. I wrapped my arms around her, enveloping her in my coat. I felt her unbuckle my belt.

"Hey now, ma'am, we don't have that kind of relationship," I murmured into the fragrant tangle of her hair. I felt her smile without seeing it.

"Don't we?" She tilted her head back to smirk up at me. "What good are you then?"

"I don't mean to brag but I did a pret-ty good job babysitting."

Beneath the folds of my coat, Melody undid my zipper and slid her hand down the front of my jeans. I felt my breath catch. "You think you deserve this for babysitting?"

"I think I deserve it because I'm awesome at it," I managed hoarsely. "Lots of practice."

"Uh-huh." Melody gave me a squeeze and extracted her hand from my pants. She shrugged off my arms and turned on her heel to stalk off down the block. The ache of her withdrawal took my breath away but I watched her go without following her. Five or six steps along the sidewalk she turned to look back.

"Well?" she said. "We doing this or not?" She smoked me with a look and tossed her head in the direction of her apartment. My heart leaped and I trotted after her before she could change her mind—as whipped as a bitch, and without one single regret.

9

HELLS BELLS

I CONTINUED TO bombard Evelyn with text messages throughout the morning until she responded with a succinct: *'Sorry, fell asleep. Home now.'* I could relax knowing that she hadn't been trafficked into white slavery, abducted by a cartel, killed in a mob hit, arrested, assaulted, dismembered, incapacitated, maimed, or mutilated but she offered no explanation for her disappearance and deftly ignored any follow-up questions I sent. I got the feeling she was hoping I would let the matter drop.

Foolish mortal.

After several days spent pelting her with questions that never got answered, I drove out to the Botanic Gardens to track her down at work. I found her in the Visitor's Center supervising a crowded market selling what appeared to be dried turds in all shapes and sizes. A host of ladies in red hats were shoving them into canvas NPR tote bags as fast as they could. A banner overhead proclaimed it to be *Bulb Fest!*

"So, where'd you disappear to the other night?" I asked, sidling up next to her in the crowd. She jumped in surprise at the sound of my voice.

"Jesus, Damen—don't sneak up on me like that," she said glancing around like she was afraid to be seen with me. It was a clear day and the schools were closed for Columbus Day, so the gardens were overrun with North Shore families inculcating their precocious spawn with cultural enrichment. I doubted anyone there would recognize me but I'd bought a hoodie from the gift shop to hide my hair anyway.

"You didn't answer my question," I persisted.

"Yes, cuz it's none of your beeswax," Evelyn said firmly, turning on her heel and heading towards the checkout counter.

"Look, asking me to cover for you while you run out of the house for a few hours in the middle of the night with no questions asked is one thing," I said, chasing her down, "But you disappeared the whole night without a word!"

"I'm a grown woman, I can handle myself." Evelyn stopped by a register long enough to flip through a stack of inventory sheets, drumming her fingers irritably against the clipboard.

"A grown woman who sneaks out in the middle of the night."

"Uh-huh. Thanks, *Dad.*" She ripped a page out of the stack and waved it toward a cashier before dropping it into a manila envelope and heading for the door.

I followed her outside, doing my best to hold back my surge of annoyance. "I was worried, okay? So, fucking sue me."

Evelyn softened slightly and turned to face me. "Listen, I'm sorry, okay? I'm not in trouble or danger or anything, it's just something private."

"You know what? Fine." I took a deep breath and felt calmer. "Just lemme know if you're going to be gone the whole night next time."

Evelyn nodded and gave me a cautious smile. "Was Vico okay?" she asked, directing our steps along a path beside the parking lots toward the administrative buildings beyond.

"The Girl Child was fine. She woke up after you left so I sat with her," I said, then added: "She's probably going to have some questions about anal probes."

Evelyn stared at me. "What on earth did you tell her?" she wanted to know.

"Don't blame me, blame 'South Park'."

"Damen!"

"Oh, please, it went right over her head. She just liked the fart noises."

"Melody's never gonna trust me with her again!"

"You mean *aside* from abandoning her kid with your mutant brother in the dead of the night?" I said. "I don't think 'South Park' is gonna be the headliner of that conversation."

We were walking through a stand of trees blazing with fall colors. Wind moved through the branches sending a rain of bright leaves onto the ground beneath our feet. I strayed off the path toward a cluster of gnarled apple trees that were heavy with fruit.

"Damen? What're you—" she protested as I pulled an apple off one of the trees and tossed it to her. "Don't pick that! You're not supposed to pick the fruit! It's garden policy."

"C'mon, Evil, live a little. What're you gonna do? Kick me out?"

"I'm supposed to, yeah."

Evelyn stuck her hands on her hips, waiting for me to come back to the path. I grinned at her and pulled down a second apple feeling like a little kid doing something naughty. "It's one apple, nobody's gonna miss it."

I sank my teeth into the apple's flesh and regretted it immediately. It was so spittingly sour my tongue began to wither. Evelyn watched in amusement until I gave up and spat it out on the ground.

"That tastes terrible," I said. I threw the remains of the fruit under the tree, raising a cloud of yellowjackets.

"Serves you right," Evelyn said. "That's a King David. It's for cooking. Also, it's not ripe yet."

"Okay, plant lady, you're smarter than me," I said. "But I can still do *this*," I picked her up and slung her over my shoulder to carry her down the path.

"Omigod, put me down! I'm working!" Evelyn smacked the back of my head with her envelope—which did nothing. A family with a pair of small children passed us going the other way wearing wide-eyed expressions of shock. The parents looked like they were torn between taking a picture and calling security.

"Everything's fine, folks," Evelyn assured them from over my shoulder. "Nothing to see here. The visitors' center is down the path on the right. Can't miss it."

She waited until they were out of sight then reached under my sweatshirt to grab the waistband of my underwear and gave it a warning tug. "Put me down or I'm gonna give you such a goddamn wedgie—"

She spoke my language.

"Okay, smarty-pants," I said, and I set her down. Evelyn smacked me with the envelope again but she was laughing now. I missed making her smile.

"So, where we going?" I asked, continuing to dog her steps along the path.

"*I'm* going to my office," she said. "Are you going to follow me all day?"

"I got nowhere to be."

"Great."

We made our way along a tree-lined drive to an administrative building and went inside. The main room was divided into a grid of cubicles, as shadowless and stark as an accounting firm. Offices lined the perimeter of the space making it clear that *windows* were for *closers.*

"Nice place you got here," I said with a distaste I hoped was audible.

"Home, sweet home," she replied navigating through the mouse maze of cubes to drop the envelope in a mail tray on someone's desk. "You really shouldn't be back here."

"C'mon, show me where you work. Give me the grand tour."

"This is it," Evelyn said gesturing sweepingly to the main room. "Very glamorous. C'mon, let's go." She grabbed my arm and tugged me towards the door, her eyes flickering anxiously towards a corner office where shadows moved behind a wall of frosted glass.

"What's with all the secrecy, Evil? It's a botanic garden, not the CIA."

"Yeah? Well, my boss wants to hire his nephew, so someone's gonna be getting fired soon. I don't want it to be me."

The door to the aforementioned corner office opened but before I could see who was inside, Evelyn grabbed me by the collar and yanked me around a corner.

"What's the hell—"

"Shhhh!"

"Don't 'shhhh' me!"

Evelyn gave me a hostile look and drew a finger across her throat with enough force I didn't doubt she'd resort to slitting my throat if I didn't shut my hole. We were in a bland hallway lined with doors. It dead-ended in a fire door that read "EMERGENCY EXIT ONLY, ALARM WILL SOUND" in large letters.

Trapped.

"*Shit!*" Evelyn swore, realizing her mistake. She pulled open one of the doors, apparently at random, and shoved me inside. Following close on my heels, she eased the door shut, cloaking us in darkness and hushed silence. A set of footsteps passed, and a sonorous male voice could be heard carrying on an unintelligible conversation of vowel sounds through the thick door. I suddenly realized how quiet the room was.

"Is this place soundproofed?" I flipped on a light switch before Evelyn could stop me, illuminating a smallish office space of industrial carpet and foam-covered walls. The majority of the room was occupied by a wooden console supporting a double row of wooden levers. It looked like a piano designed by someone who thought keys were for sissies.

"What the hell is this?" I asked, fascinated. Evelyn was still hovering worriedly by the door, cracking it open to peer down the hallway.

"It's the practice carillon," she said. "Don't touch it."

Too late.

I gave a lever an experimental push. It moved easily but no sound came out. I tried to guess where the notes were, stretching my fingers wide to guess at the cords. Evelyn saw me fucking with it and slammed the door shut.

"Get the hell away from there!" she said.

"Oh, come on—what's the worst that could happen?"

"Um. I could get *fired.*"

"You won't get fired." I searched around for an on switch and found it along the side and clicked it on to a faint electric hum. I struck the lever again and the sound of a bell tolled out over a pair of speakers overhead. I made myself comfortable on the bench and started to pick out a tune, finding the notes as I went. My foot reached for the sustain pedal automatically, but instead, a sonorous gong of one of the deep notes rang out. There was an array of pedals on the floor for the lowest notes. The bells took their time decaying—I struggled to reign in my enthusiasm to play slowly enough for a tune to hold together.

"Shit!" Evelyn went to the door and peered out the door again. "So help me, if you get me in trouble, I'm never speaking to you again."

"Don't be lame; live a little," I called over the pealing that was now filling the room from wall to wall. I could see why the space was soundproofed. "Why does the gardens have a 'practice' carillon, anyway?"

"Because we have a real one."

"A real what?"

"A real carillon—out by the lake."

"What, with bells and all?"

"Yes. With bells and all—*ohmigodstop!*" she begged as I danced my way up a scale, using only my feet.

"Whatever." I began to play "Hells Bells".

"They do concerts in the summer. People come from all over the world to play. This is so they can rehearse without ringing it over the whole gardens."

I flubbed a note.

"Like that?" I asked, continuing to play, flubbing another note, and then another until she realized I was doing it on purpose. She smiled in spite of herself and I grinned. Neither of us heard the door open until it was too late.

"*What* is going on in here? Evelyn? You know this room is *off-limits.*"

The voice sounded middle-aged and I didn't need to turn my head to know it belonged to Evelyn's boss. I continued playing but switched to something by Bizet and kept my back to the door, glad that the hoodie was covering my hair. Out of the corner of my eye, I saw Evelyn cringe, resigning herself to the trouble she was about to get into.

"Harold this is—"

"Oh, pleassse, don't be ridiculous, he knows who I am," I interrupted, adopting a slightly sibilant inflection that I imagined would belong to the kind of person who styled themselves a *carillonneur*. "I told her she could stay, Harold. I don't mind."

I'm supposed to be here.

It was the oldest Jedi mind trick in the book.

Don't you know who I AM?

"I, uh...Excuse...me?" Harold faltered. He didn't know me from Adam and I knew it. From his place in the doorway, all he could see was my back, and from the back, I could have been anyone. Without seeing my face or hair, he wouldn't have been able to pick me out of a crowd of two but I was almost certain he wouldn't be willing to admit it in front of someone he considered a subordinate.

"*So* sorry to show up unannounced. Terribly rude, I'm sure. But you *know* how it is when the muse is upon you. Inspiration is *such* a cruel mistress." Evelyn's eyes bulged in incredulity as I doubled down on the role. "This young lady was kind enough to show me to the room so I could rehearse, so I said she could stay."

I felt Harold's eyes on my back doing a hasty inventory of my appearance, checking off the details his mind considered relevant: tall, male, good posture, fussy attitude, Botanic Gardens souvenir sweatshirt, playing the carillon—*how many people knew how to play carillon?*

Surely, I belonged there. I sounded like I belonged there. I could practically hear the wheels turning as his mind re-wrote reality.

"Anywayyyy, *so* sorry to inconvenience you. Perhaps I should go—"

"No, no! No problem," he insisted as I made as if I were going to stand up. "Sorry to interrupt, please continue—" His voice took on a conciliatory tone and I settled back onto the bench. I chose a song by Holst and resumed playing, winking at Evelyn who was still white-faced with anxiety.

There was a faint hiss from the door as Harold began to retreat from the room.

"I do hope Miss Evelyn isn't in trouble on my account?" I called after him before he could leave.

"Oh, uh—no, of course not."

"She really has been *such* a help."

"Good! Good, glad to hear it."

"You're so lucky to have such *exemplary* people. It's *so* hard to find good staff." Evelyn's face went from white to red in the space of a heartbeat and her eyes shot daggers at me, begging me to quit while I was ahead.

"Of course, of course. Evelyn is one of our best."

"You must be offering something special to retain her—in *this* job market? Talent like that can go anywhere. I cannot *imagine* the nightmare it would be to try to replace her."

"Well, actually—"

I didn't let him finish the thought. I hit a wrong lever to make a sour note ring out.

"She's a keeper. That is all," I said, resuming the melody. "Now if you'll excuse me? I need to concentrate?"

Dismissed.

Whatever Harold may have wanted to say to or about Evelyn was suddenly relegated to second priority as he hastened to retreat. "Of course, of course—I'll leave you to it," he backed out of the room and allowed the door to fall closed behind him. The muffled sound of his footsteps receded into the distance and Evelyn deflated into a heap on the floor, pressing her forehead to the ground in relief.

"Only you, Damen," she mumbled into the carpet, shaking her head. "Only you."

10

B@D BEH@V!OR

"**W**HAT DO you think about bells?" I lobbed the question at Tombstone more to see what he would say than because I thought it was an actual good idea. The two of us were holed up in the Gray Area listening to a drizzle of autumn rain patter on the skylight overhead and trying, at last, to stitch together a new song without much success. He looked up from a notebook of song lyrics and squinted thoughtfully into space as he considered it, then shrugged:

Maybe.

Turning his attention back to the notebook, he pulled Rita onto his lap and began noodling around with a progression of chords. It was the same progression of chords that I'd been knocking my head against for weeks but now it was Tombstone's turn. He'd been fucking with it for the better part of an hour but had made no obvious progress.

I felt a dark satisfaction at the fact he couldn't get it to resolve either.

Kilroy's suggestion to cover 'Superstition' had given us a kiss to build a dream on but one cover song did not an album make. Our weeks of aimless jam sessions had yielded a motley collection of riffs, licks, harmonies, rhythms, and chord progressions, which Mungo had dutifully recorded and archived into a library of musical fragments—all labeled with an eldritch system of filenames that included such gems as 'Numpty.03,' 'StochasticCocksplat.w/reverb.05,' and 'SlutHarmonics.wet.13.' This last was a tooth grindingly atonal series of metallic shrieks so jarring that they made me want to curl into a ball with my hands over my ears and beg for the sweet mercy of death.

I planned to use them on the new album even if it killed me.

I snatched up the notebook from where it lay on the low table between us and glanced at the page.

Verse. Chorus. Verse. Chorus. Bridge. Chorus. Coda.

Tombstone was a hell of a writer. For someone who looked like Joe Dirt and who almost never spoke he sure as hell had a way with words. The lyrics were already nearly fully formed, laid out in tidy segments written in Tombstone's careful, schoolboy handwriting. All I had to do now was put them to music. That was our system: he wrote the words, I sang them. I wrote the music: he played it. A perfect storm of symbiotic co-dependence.

"It's good," I admitted, grudgingly.

I set the notebook on the piano and counted out the syllables, tapping them out on the Oddkat's battered frame with one of my rings to get a feel for them.

Don't overthink it, just fucking play.

"Okay, what d'you think of this?" I said, with no real plan in mind. I stretched my fingers out over the piano keys and let the tune bubble up to meet me. The tune that came was simple—painfully simple, like the sing-song notes of a schoolyard taunt but it didn't need to be complicated to be a hit: we just needed a few basic notes that would carry over a crowd.

Tombstone squinted into the middle distance as he listened and bobbed his head from side to side: he didn't hate it. He fiddled with a few tone knobs and then strummed a chord on Rita, sketching in a harmony.

I shook my head. "No, minor," I insisted. I modulated the chord for him on the piano.

Tombstone played it once or twice then wrinkled his nose and shook his head, modulated it in a different direction, and played it again. Stubbornly, I hit the minor chord on the Oddkat again. The two chords together formed a jarring tower of notes splintering with overtones and close harmonies.

It was terrible.

It was magnificent.

It was Slutharmonics.wet.13.

I felt the hairs on my scalp begin to stand on end and looked to Tombstone who grinned and shivered with delight.

"Holy shit."

I approached the chorus with a descending progression as Tombstone's instincts pulled him in the opposite direction. If anything summed up my relationship with Tombstone, this song was it: a tug-of-war of competing impulses inextricably bound together to the wicked end, both of us fighting to play the melody to the other's harmony.

But we were onto something. The music warped and warbled but there was something there. I pounded out the low end on the piano, imagining Gorey's guitar and Kilroy's bass fitted together in lockstep, sick with grit and distortion while Tombstone's guitar soared over the top like light trails.

We made it to the bridge and I let the piano drop out to see where Tombstone's instincts took him. He rolled into an improvised solo, bending notes and sliding until the melody soared into new and heady heights. He modulated through a key change and the high note split into a jarring tritone that was sudden and painful in its beauty.

"Holy shit..."

It was rare and beautiful. It was perfect. There was only one problem: I couldn't sing it. I tried the melody on for size but my voice cracked and fell short.

"Shit."

I tried again. Still couldn't hit it.

"I can't hit that note," I said. "I'm not Axl Rose—I'm gonna give myself a hernia trying to hit that night after night when we go on the road." My voice was low: my natural range was a baritone, and although I could sing most of the tenor range I could only push it so far before risking the kind of vocal strain that would end my career.

Tombstone shook his head and played the melody again: just the middle notes—all in my range, then played it again, hitting the high notes, and then, with a slight qualm of hesitation, he pointed to himself.

I snorted a laugh. "Ha! Okay, you're funny."

Tombstone's cheeks darkened until his face was the

same color as his hair and I felt bad. He was a good fucking singer, and his vocal range outstripped mine handily in both directions but his stutter had always held him back. Not to mention his crippling stage fright. The thought of him singing on stage was laughable, surely, but Tombstone wasn't laughing.

"Hang on, you're *serious?*" I asked, doubtfully.

Tombstone swallowed hard and nodded.

I tried to imagine it: Tombstone striding out to center stage to hit that high note night after night as the crowd went wild the way they went wild for his guitar solos. In my mind's eye, I could see him reveling in the cheers, arms, and guitar raised in victory.

"Alright—show me what you got."

Tombstone replayed the bridge this time singing along with his eyes screwed shut in a rictus of abject terror. But his voice rang true. The high note lifted out of him as easily as wind through a whistle. There was no sign of his stutter now.

"Shit, dude, what the hell do you even need me for?" I asked when he finished.

Tombstone opened his eyes and grinned shyly, then made a gesture over his face.

Pretty face.

"Fuck you, dude."

No, really—what will he need you for? A traitorous voice spoke up in the back of my mind, sending fingers of paranoia into the soft matter of my brain. *He writes the words. He plays the guitar. Now he wants to sing? What the hell will he need you for? It's a matter of time before he forces you out—replaces you...*

I forced the thought to the back of my mind. We were finally back on speaking terms and I didn't want to fuck it up over a high note. It wasn't a problem until it was a problem, and if it became a problem? Well, it wouldn't take much to psych him out.

Stage fright was a bitch.

I glanced at my watch and sighed.

"Fuck, I gotta go do an interview." I stood and stretched. Our diehard fans, The Legion, had caught wind of the news that we had a new album in the works and had been clawing themselves to pieces for details ever since. It was this fact, more than Judge's pointed reminders, which had forced me to sober up enough to text Phoenix to set up a meeting. I was already regretting it. Her responses read like strings of code:

'Nu fone who dis?'

'O hai u want 2 haz meet 10/13?'

'kk, c u l8r kthxbai'

If this was the future of journalism, we were all fucked.

Tombstone tossed his head sympathetically and made a gesture that roughly implied *good luck.*

"Thanks, I'm gonna need it," I said. "She's a Manic Pixie Dread Nightmare."

"By 'Manic-Pixie-Dread-Nightmare,' I assume you mean me." A new voice spoke up from the direction of the door. Tombstone and I turned in unison to see an androgynous hipster standing in the doorway surveying the Gray Area's comfortable squalor with the blasé expression of the chronically unimpressed. "You must be Damen. I'm Phoenix."

Phoenix had the pallid, undergrown look of someone who spent a lot of time in the blue light of a computer monitor. Her outfit consisted of an assortment of shapeless knits carefully curated to look like they'd been pulled at random from a laundry bag. Hobo chic. The knees of her skinny jeans were artfully ripped. The color scheme of her vintage-cartoon-character t-shirt matched the colorful laces on her brand-name indie sneakers.

"Nice place you got here," she said, striding into the room and flopping down on the couch beside Tombstone. "What band are you with, again?"

"Uh, *excuse* me?" I managed, wondering where the hell Judge had managed to dig up this Millennial nightmare. He'd insisted that she was the mouthpiece we wanted and he'd never been wrong before but there was a first time for everything and I was beginning to think this was it.

"You're excused," Phoenix said, snapping her gum. She produced a smartphone from a satchel and clicked a photo of me without asking, then sighed when she looked at the results as if everything she saw was a nuisance, and began typing away with her thumbs.

"What magazine are you with?" I asked, still trying to gather my wits.

"It's not a *magazine*," Phoenix scoffed, heaping scorn on the word 'magazine' like I'd asked her about a buggy whip. "It's a *blog*. I have three million followers."

"Bully for you." I gritted my teeth. I was way too sober for this. Everything about her rubbed me the wrong way and I could already feel myself beginning to tense into a tight, angry knot. Phoenix resolutely failed to notice. She turned the phone sideways and aimed the camera at me.

"Your band?" she asked again.

"O-B-X-N-S" I spelled it out for her. "Pronounced 'Obnoxious'."

"Why not spell it 'Obnoxious'?"

"We did."

Tikaticktickatickticka

Every tap of her thumbs chipped off another tiny piece of my nerves.

"*Okay,* why 'Obnoxious'?" She made air quotes with her free hand.

"Because 'Redneck-Tranny-Gypsy-Jew-Bastard' was already taken," I snapped, as her derision eroded my patience to the breaking point. Phoenix remained unphased.

"Can I quote you on that?"

"You're a piece of fucking work, you know that?" I said. "You come in here, you don't even know what band you're interviewing— we could've been Rebecca Fucking Black for all you would know.

"No, if you were Rebecca Black, I'd know who you were," she said with a savage smile. "She makes music people talk about."

"Oh, they talk about it alright."

"I didn't say they were saying nice things. No one cares if it's good as long as it drives traffic. Clickbait is internet gold."

I resisted the urge to make a fist. It took all my might. "Do you even know a single one of our songs?"

"I know the one on the commercial."

"You know what it's called?"

"Goat something. GoatNPonyShow?"

"GoatRodeo."

"Yeah, whatever." She shrugged. She stood off the couch, still filming with her phone, and approached until the camera was inches from my face. I gripped the edge of the piano bench to keep myself from slapping it out of her hand. "Nobody listens to *music* anymore, anyway. I mean seriously, who even cares about metalcore? That went out with the aughts."

I could see the display from her phone reflected in her glasses, turning her eyes into two miniature screens reflecting my face again and again in smaller and weaker and more distorted iterations until I was nothing at all. I felt a sudden, plunging sense of vertigo. The ringing in my ears drowned out all the sound in the room.

"Everything's online now," Phoenix continued. "The internet is the great equalizer. Any basic bitch with a ukulele can have a YouTube channel. Soon, there won't be any more labels, no more radio. Music'll become truly democratic. If it's *good*, it'll rise to the top—"

I stopped listening. Music didn't rise to the top of the internet for being good, it rose to the top of the internet for being popular, pandering, sarcastic, stupid, or all of the above. Internet popularity meant the likes of 'Gangnam Style' and 'Dumb Ways to Die'.

And Rebecca Black.

Getting-down-on-Friday Rebecca fucking Black.

"Shut the fuck up! Just shut up!!"

I leaped to my feet knocking the piano bench over, and wrenched the notebook off the music stand, hurling it across the room as hard as I could.

"Do you have any fucking idea what you're talking about?"
I screamed at her. I felt Tombstone's arms catch me in
a bear hug and pin my arms to my sides before I could
knock the phone out of her hand. I writhed and struggled
against him but he held on with an iron grip. I kicked out
both legs as hard as I could and planted my feet against
the upper part of the Oddkat's case. I pushed off with all
my might, trying to knock him backward but Tombstone
held his ground. The Oddkat rocked under the force and
then slowly, like a majestic, groaning cow, toppled over
backward until it hit the floor with a crash I could feel in
my bones.

The force of the concussion shocked me back to my senses. Tombstone dragged me down and pinned me to the
carpet with his arms locked around my chest so hard his
knuckles were turning white.

"Buh-buh-be k-k-kc-cool!" he managed, spitting down my
neck as he struggled to force the words out.

I stopped struggling and closed my eyes, trying to force
myself to get a grip. I took a deep breath and opened them
again. The Oddkat lay on her back with her two legs sticking out sideways like a dead horse. The lid was open. I could
still hear the strings resonating painfully over the sound
of my ragged breathing.

"I'm cool," I told him. "I'm cool. We're cool."

Tombstone reluctantly relinquished his grip and I shook
him off. I scrambled to my feet to walk an angry circuit
around the room, still trying to regain my control. When I no
longer felt like I was going to kill somebody, I looked up

at Phoenix. She was still filming, her expression as bland as tapioca.

"Keep going," she said, snapping her gum. "Don't let me harsh your buzz."

"Are you fucking kidding me?!" I surveyed the shambles of the rehearsal space and the poor, toppled carcass of the Oddkat on the floor between us. Tombstone shot me a warning look reminding me to keep myself together. "What the hell kind of journalist are you?"

Phoenix sighed and stabbed the screen with her thumb before letting her arm drop.

"I'm not a journalist, I'm a *content* creator," she said as if having to explain herself was a colossal nuisance. "I make trash. Clickbait trash. 'You-won't-believe-what-happens-next' Barnum and Bailey trash." She relinquished her stranglehold on apathy long enough to make eye contact. "I didn't name my channel '*B@d Beh@v!or*' to be ironic. You think I like being a blogger? I have a Master's degree in journalism from the University of Chicago and the student loans to prove it. I *ought* to be investigating bank fraud and pursuing a Pulitzer for the Fourth Estate but the only way any of the established news outlets are gonna take a chance on a twenty-four-year-old straight out of academia is by making them work as an intern for ten years. For free. Ain't nobody got time for that. Personally, I like to fucking eat. So, sue me. You wanna be a purist? Fine, starve to death for all I fucking care. Otherwise, get off your tiny little high-horse and join the viral revolution."

It was the first real thing she'd said.

Content Creator. *B@d Beh@v!or*. Viral revolution.

She wasn't here to talk about music, she was here to make us go viral, and one look at the poor toppled Oddkat told me she knew what she was doing. She had fucking played me like a goddamn fiddle. Judge was right: she was exactly the person we wanted.

We were in the presence of a master.

11

ROLLY

T HE VIDEO of my temper tantrum went viral overnight. Within hours of going live, it caught the ravening eye of social media, and by the time I emerged from Melody's club, Club Lure, the next morning, it was the topic of the day. I landed in the GTO's driver's seat in time to hear my voice blaring out of the radio:

"Do you have any [BLEEEEP] idea what you're talking about?" CRASH!

The morning show hosts whooped gleefully and replayed the soundbite before launching into a Greek chorus of ongoing commentary.

"Dude kicked over a piano!"

"We love OBNXS, man—"

"—yeah, we had them all in the studio last year—"

"They're good guys but holy crap is Damen Warner a hot mess these days—"

"The whole band's a wreck—they say they're working on a new album—"

"D'you see them at Riot Fest? Y'know, they had to cut the set short cuz they had a fistfight before going onstage?

"So, they get into a fistfight, then to go onstage? Can you imagine?"

"That's rockstar alright—dudes go hard. You look at the video, you can see Warner looks like he went a few rounds with Mike Tyson—"

"There's gotta be something goin' on—you know—behind the scenes—"

"Did you see the one from Lollapalooza?"

"Or the airport? Where he's naked in the security?"

"Hellooo."

There was a chorus of raucous laughter.

"Hey, call in and tell us: what's the maddest you've ever been? You ever been so mad you've kicked over a piano?"

"I've been mad enough to poop on a car—"

"Lisa's pooped on a car—who's gonna top that? Call in or text. We got tickets to the Brat Stap for the best story—"

I listened to them rehash the video for the entire drive home including two station breaks and one musical interlude, and when I reached the Cursèd Place I went straight to a computer to call up the *B@d Beh@v!or* homepage. *DAMEN WARNER LO$ES HI$ $H!T!!!!* screamed the headline in lurid yellow letters. Beneath it, the footage of the Oddkat's inglorious downfall played on a loop. Phoenix had a good eye for camera angles and had captured it all from a low, tilted angle, transforming the piano into a towering edifice against the Gray Area's industrial ceiling. Nearby, Tombstone and I wrestled like shapeless titans, backlit and grunting as I screamed at the camera and kicked wildly, toppling the piano again and again and again.

It was a five-second cinematic masterpiece.

The suddenness of my internet notoriety took me by surprise. Every time I went out in public now, I found myself followed by whispers and stares and the not-so-subtle eyes of cellphone cameras waiting to capture my next act of self-immolation for fun and profit, so I retreated to the Cursèd Place to lay low while I got used to my new reputation as a deranged basket case. The isolation proved to be nearly as bad as the attention, and it was only a day or two before I was climbing the walls.

"Save me," I begged Melody over the phone, after spending a week cooped up in the house, staring at the same four walls for hours on end.

"I got my own problems to worry about," she said. "Avi says if I don't give him a weekday then I'm fired, an' where else am I supposed to go? The fucking Admiral?" I got the feeling she was more annoyed at having to work on a weekday than she was worried about getting fired: she was one of the most popular dancers at the club and prided herself on being able to dictate what days she worked. "So, now I need someone to watch Vico during the day. I ast Evie but she's busy."

"Dang, that sucks," I said. "If *only* you knew someone with a lot of free time on their hands who was bored out of their fucking skull."

"Yeah, if only."

"You know, I'd offer to watch her but 'we don't got that kind of relationship.'"

"Yeah, well, that was then, this is now," Melody said. I could practically hear her grinding her teeth on the far end of the line as she said it and I couldn't help but smile.

"So, we *do* got that kind of relationship now?"

"God, you're such an asshole."

"Whatever, you love me. It's okay, you can admit it. This is a safe space."

"You gonna watch her or not?"

"I'll be right there."

✳ ✳ ✳ ✳

I arrived at the apartment to find Melody already shoving clothes and shoes into a bag for work. She suffered to let me kiss her cheek briefly and disappeared into the bedroom leaving me standing in the doorway.

"Oh, hey, good to see you too," I called after her. "You're welcome for this, by the way."

Melody did not respond. I sighed and looked to the Girl Child who was sitting on her bed looking gloomily at the dark television.

"What's the matter, Girl Child?" I asked, settling down beside her.

"She is *grounded*," Melody called from the other room. "And it's your fault."

"My fault?"

"What were you thinking? Telling her to fight with other kids?"

I looked at Girl Child. "That true?" I asked. She cringed away, afraid to look at me.

Melody came back into the room fastening on a pair of earrings as she spoke: "I got a call from the principal that she knocked down a fourth-grader and called him a 'fucking bitch' and threatened him with her lunchbox.

Which they took away."

I looked at the Girl Child in surprise. "You did all that?"

"You said he wouldn't tell," she mumbled.

Melody slapped the back of my head.

"Ow. Narc."

"What's a 'narc'?"

"Someone who tattles," I said.

"Don't you blame her for this!" Melody glared at me. "She's in *kindergarten.*"

"Are you kidding? I'm proud of her. She took down a fourth-grader for Chrissake. She's a stupendous badass—don't repeat that," I told the Girl Child. "And if this kid tattled to the principal, he deserves to be called a fucking bitch."

"Yeah. He's a narc," Girl Child said, emboldened to have a grownup on her side.

"You—" Melody started to scold her but I cut her off.

"Did you ask her who started the fight?" I asked.

"The principal said they didn't know."

"Yeah, but did you ask *her?*"

Melody pressed her lips together. She hadn't.

"We don't start fights—" I prompted Girl Child.

"—but we sure as hell finish them," she finished.

"How did the fight start, Girl Child?"

"He was saying bad things," Girl Child said. "He said Mama was a ho."

Melody's mouth dropped open but I held up a hand to keep her from interrupting.

"And you pushed him?" I asked.

"No, I said 'don't talk about my Mama that way.' An' he

made fun of me for calling her 'Mama' like a baby an' said his mom says Mama's a slut and a welfare ho and—" Girl Child was on a roll now. I put a hand over her mouth before she could gather any more speed.

Melody stood in the middle of the room, momentarily speechless as she absorbed this new revelation. I could see her anger begin to change direction.

"That fucking bitch," Melody swore. She stewed for a minute then said: "Thirty minutes of television. You're still grounded for losing your lunchbox. Go put away your backpack."

Girl Child hugged me around my middle and hopped down off the bed to trot into the other room. Melody reached for her phone but I caught her hand before she could dial.

"Don't," I said.

"That *fucking* bitch," she hissed again.

"Don't give her any more ammo," I said. "Calling her now will make it worse."

"I wanna fucking kill her."

"Me too," I said, "but there are better ways to do worse things to her."

I pulled her in close until I could wrap my arms around her waist. I rested my chin on her belly and looked up at her.

"Like what?"

I had to admit I didn't know. "Don't worry about it right now," I said. "You got work. Let me try to handle it. If it's still a problem by the time you get home, you can open up a can of whup-ass. I'll even help."

Melody stewed on it a moment longer and then nodded. She sank onto my lap and put her hands on the sides of my neck to kiss me, properly, on the lips.

"Fine," she said. "You got until I get home. Make this go away."

And then she left.

The kid's name turned out to be Rolly. I found his home address in the elementary school directory and bundled Girl Child into a coat.

"Where are we going?" she wanted to know.

"We're gonna go see Rolly."

"But whyyy," she whined.

"So he won't pick on you again."

"How are we gonna do that?"

"You're gonna apologize," I said.

Girl Child started to cry. "But he was the one being mean to *me!*"

"Hey!" I got down to her level and looked her in the eye. "You wanna make sure he never makes fun of you again or not, Girl Child?"

Girl Child nodded reluctantly.

"Do you trust me?" I asked her.

She nodded again.

"Good. Do what I tell you and we'll get ice cream after,"

Rolly and his family lived in a house near the school. It was small but well-maintained. Blue-collar. The truck out front had a Teamsters bumper sticker. I scanned the street for anybody who looked like they might recognize me, but no one seemed to be around. It was already half dusk and more than a few of the windows were lit by the flickering blue light of a television.

Still, I pulled the hood of my Botanic Gardens sweatshirt over my head to hide my hair—just to be safe.

"Go on up and ring the bell," I told the Girl Child, stopping at the foot of the steps, well back from the door. The last thing I needed was for Rolly's folks to see me on their doorstep and call the cops.

"Do I hafta?"

"Yes. Tell them you wanna see Rolly 'cuz I'm making you apologize."

Dragging her feet every step of the way, Girl Child stumped up the concrete steps and stretched to reach the doorbell. A silhouette darkened the windows on the door and it opened to reveal a dumpy-looking woman in a sweatshirt and socked feet.

"Hello?" Her gaze traveled over Girl Child, then me, then back to Girl Child. "Everything alright, honey?"

Girl Child scuffed a toe. "Is Rolly home?" she mumbled. "I'm 'sposed to 'pologize."

"Oh, honey," the woman's urge to invite the Girl Child inside warred with her desire to keep me out. She took a step back into the entryway and called into the house: "Rolly—come to the door."

Girl Child looked back at me and I nodded to her.

Rolly appeared at the door. He was a sullen nine-year-old with skinned knees, probably the biggest kid in the fourth grade by weight, if not volume. I was doubly impressed.

If Girl Child had knocked this kid down, she would make a helluva wrestler.

"What you want?" he demanded.

I could see Girl Child's little hands ball into fists. She looked at me again and I could feel her wretchedness.

"M 'spose to 'pologize," She mumbled, barely audible.

"What was that again, honey? I couldn't hear you," the mom asked in a voice as drippingly sweet as poisoned candy.

"Speak up, Girl Child," I told her. "Say you're sorry."

"I'm. Sorry," Girl Child said, loudly but not meaning it.

"Sorry for what?"

"Sorry for pushing Rolly," she said, miserable.

"And?" I prompted.

Girl Child looked confused.

"For calling him—"

"And for calling him a fucking bitch," she said. A fat tear rolled down her burning cheeks and her lip quivered.

"Aww, thank you, honey," the woman said, melting at the sight of the tears. "Aren't you sweet? Rolly? What do you say?" Rolly shrugged. "Rolly says apology accepted," she said.

"Good," I said. "Now it's Rolly's turn."

The woman's syrupy face froze. "I beg your pardon?"

"It's Rolly's turn to apologize," I repeated.

"My son will do no such thing."

"So, he *didn't* call Girl Child's mother a slut and a welfare ho?" I said.

"What?!" The woman turned on Rolly who cowered back a step under her gaze. "Rolly, how could you say such things?"

"But Mom—"

"Don't 'but Mom' me."

"But *you* were the one who called her a—"

Once a narc, always a narc.

It was the woman's turn to blush. "Rolly go to your room."

"No, Rolly needs to apologize to Girl Child," I insisted. "Though I'm sure he's just calling things like he sees them, right, Rolly? You know what a ho is, right?"

Rolly glanced at his mom. If he did know, he wasn't about to admit it.

"How 'bout a slut, Rolly. You know what a slut is? See a lot of them in the fourth grade? How'd you like it if I called *your* mom that?"

"Okay, that's enough of that," Rolly's mom started to close the door.

"What the hell's going on out here?" A man who was evidently Rolly's father stuck his head into the foyer. The woman saw a chance to get the upper hand.

"He's saying awful things about me!" She pointed out the door to me.

"What did you say to my wife?" He demanded. He pushed in front of the woman to confront me, filling the doorway from side to side like a wall. He was a big dude: bald, with a goatee. He looked like he worked with machines and rode a Harley in his spare time. His eyes strafed over my face and hair and, for a minute, I was certain I was going to get my ass kicked but then he flinched and his eyes widened in recognition. I realized he was wearing a t-shirt from Ozzfest and I relaxed slightly. Where there was smoke there was smoke on the water.

"I was asking Rolly how he'd like it if the Girl Child called his mom the same things he called hers," I said, emboldened.

The man looked down and realized, probably for the first time, that there was a five-year-old girl on his front stoop in tears. He looked at his wife and then at his son.

"Rolly, what did you—"

"Slut. Welfare ho," I supplied.

"Cunt," Girl Child added.

The woman's eyes bulged as the man looked at her.

"You know," she said. "She's the daughter of that...that..."

"Dancer?" I supplied.

"That *stripper*," she managed to sound gleeful and scandalized at the same time.

"Yeah, that stripper," I said. "Who happens to be a single mom. Who works nights so she can see Girl Child to school every goddamn day."

"Every goddamn day," Girl Child reiterated.

"Don't repeat that, Girl Child."

Rolly's dad suppressed a laugh but the woman's eyes narrowed. She opened her fat mouth and I waited for the words 'decent folk' to trot out like show ponies but the big guy stopped her. "Okay, honey, I got this," he said. "Go on back to your show, I'll be right there."

Rolly's mom smirked at me victoriously, then retreated into the house with Rolly in tow. Girl Child scurried back to me and hid behind my leg as Rolly's dad opened the storm door and came out onto the stoop.

"Sorry 'bout all that," he said in a low voice. "Carol—she gets goin' sometimes. I haven't had a great history with strippers." He stuck out a hand. "Frank."

"Damen."

"Yeah, I know, I recognize you," he said. "Didn't know you had kids."

"I don't," I said. "I'm just the babysitter. And the bad influence, I guess. I was the one who told her to knock down anyone talking smack about her mom. Right, Girl Child?"

Girl Child glared at Frank. "I'm not a narc," she said.

Frank laughed. "You teach her that too?"

"She's like a fucking sponge," I said, then quickly added. "*Don't* repeat that, GC."

"Rolly's the same," Frank said. "Little pitchers have big mouths an' all. That's no excuse, though. Can I make it up?"

"Girl Child needs her lunchbox back," I said. "Think you could do that?"

"I can try," Frank scratched his neck but looked doubtful. "The school took it—kids aren't s'posed to bring metal ones anymore but I'll give them a call. Hey, you think maybe I could get an autograph or something?"

"I'll trade you one for the lunchbox. I'll throw in a t-shirt too if Rolly cuts out the slut-ho shit and steps up like a man the next time someone tries to pick on a kindergartner."

"You got it, man," Frank looked relieved. I bumped fists with him and started to walk away. "Hey," he called after me, looking embarrassed. "Any chance you could—I dunno, make it seem like I chased you off?"

"Sure," I said. I made my way to the sidewalk, then turned around and screamed. *"Fuck you with a donkey-dong, motherfucker! Fucking cocksuckers!"*

"You ever come back here I'm callin' the cops!" he shouted back, giving me a surreptitious thumbs up.

In the front window, Carol twitched the curtains to peek out at me. I gave her the finger.

"Yeah, cocksuckers!" Girl Child also gave the finger.

I'd created a monster.

12

CLICKMACHINE

MELODY HAD to admit—grudgingly—that I'd done a good job of solving the Rolly dilemma. She laughed when I told her about Carol's mortification, and let me stay the night even though the Girl Child was home. We made love furtively in the dark; whispering and fumbling like a pair of teenagers, then fell asleep tangled up in each other.

In the morning when we walked Girl Child to school, we found Rolly waiting for us by the entrance to the schoolyard with her lunchbox in his hand. Girl Child stopped when she saw him, pulling me up short.

"Is that the kid?" Melody asked.

"Yeah, that's him." I squeezed the Girl Child's hand to reassure her. "Don't worry, he's not going to give you any trouble." The Girl Child nodded but didn't look convinced. I knelt in front of her and handed her a balled-up t-shirt. "Okay, here's how this is going to work: he's going to give you your lunchbox and you're going to give him this t-shirt, okay? Don't give it to him till he gives you the lunchbox though, got it?" The Girl Child nodded solemnly, and I gave her a gentle shove. "Attagirl. Go on."

"You're good with her," Melody said as I regained my feet.

"Of course I am. I'm extraordinary," I said. I watched as the Girl Child trotted up the sidewalk to Rolly and stopped in front of him. He proffered the lunchbox without hesitation. The Girl Child took it and then looked back at me.

"Okay, give him the t-shirt," I called to her.

Girl Child handed over the t-shirt and Rolly grinned shyly as he took it from her. His front teeth were huge and crooked in his mouth.

"Whoa, cooooool!" he breathed as he unfolded it. It was a design Carol was sure to disapprove of but wasn't likely to get Rolly kicked out of school.

"That one's for you. Go ahead and put it on," I said, approaching. "This one's for your dad." I held up a second shirt in a larger size.

Rolly shed his jacket and backpack and pulled the t-shirt over his head. He looked down at it, grinning from ear-to-ear, and tugged at the hem like he never planned to take it off. Good. Carol would hate that.

"D'you think you could, you know, sign it?" he asked, shyly.

"Sure," I said. "But on one condition. You're gonna watch out for Girl Child from now on, you got it? Anyone messes with her; they're messing with you. Understand?"

Rolly nodded, embarrassed. "Sorry 'bout that stuff I said, I din't mean it," he said. His eyes flickered towards Melody and he blushed. "You're really pretty."

Melody gave a tight smile but seemed mollified by the compliment.

"That's a big thing, apologizing," I told him. "It's good

you're taking responsibility for your words like that, but you can't say 'sorry' and think it's all gone. You gotta be bigger than those words now. You know what I'm saying?"

He didn't but he nodded anyway.

I produced a silver marker and held it up to him. "Okay— you sign mine, and I'll sign yours," I pointed to my own t-shirt, under the collar.

"You want me to sign it?"

"We're making a deal," I said. "Right?"

Rolly nodded.

"What's our deal?"

"No one messes with Vico," he said. "Or they're messing with me."

"Good man," I said. Rolly stood a little straighter. He took the pen and scratched ROLLY onto the front of my t-shirt awkwardly. "Good," I pronounced when he held the pen out to me again. I took it and signed my name across the front of his shirt in giant letters—big enough that Carol couldn't miss it. The bell rang and the other kids started to file into the building. Rolly picked up his bag and put a hand on Girl Child's back.

"C'mon," he said. "I'll walk you to class."

"Okay. Bye, Damen," she said with a wave in my direction. "Bye, Mama!"

"Have a good day, baby," Melody called after her as she started towards the school, hand in hand with Rolly.

"Hey! Girl Child!" I called after her.

"What?"

"No more calling Rolly a fucking bitch."

✳ ✳ ✳ ✳

I expected Judge to be pissed about the Oddkat. Here he'd finally gotten me the piano I wanted and I'd shown my gratitude by kicking her over like I was Chuck Norris. Knocking her flat may have made me an internet sensation but also derailed any momentum Tombstone and I had built up in our songwriting. The Oddkat wasn't much damaged from the fall—she was built like a tank—but the impact had knocked all eighty-eight keys out of tune and it was going to take a professional to put her to rights. I bit the bullet and asked Judge to hire a piano tuner, and when the tuner showed up, Judge showed up with him.

"Congrats, Crustbucket, you're famous now," he said by way of greeting. He slapped an envelope against my chest and let it drop into my lap when I failed to react in time to take it.

"What's this?"

"Open it."

I unsealed the flap and peered inside to find myself staring at Andrew Jackson's arrogant smirk. Cash. A lot of it. I ran my thumb along the top of the stack, hearing the bills flutter against the envelope. It was easily a couple grand.

"Again, what the hell is this?"

"Think of it as a bonus," Judge said. He thumped down onto the couch across from me and settled his bulk into a comfortable spread across the cushions like Jabba the Hutt. "Not everyone's got the knack for going viral but *you* are burning through social media like herpes in a frat house."

"First of all, *ew*," I said. "And second, since when does that translate to cash money?"

Judge had an enviable talent for procurement and was typically happy to provide us with anything we asked for but that had never translated into cash until now.

"Since you took up with Phoenix," Judge stuck his feet on the coffee table and lit a cigarette, wafting it through the air as he spoke. "Trust me, Crustbucket, you wanna get rich? Phoenix is the horse you wanna bet on. Her site is a fucking goldmine. Millions of hits every day: people tuning in to get their little dose of dirt—*pay dirt.* Clicking. Linking. Sharing." Judge jabbed the glowing end of his cigarette towards the wad of cash in my hands. "I guaran-fucking-tee there's more where that came from. Think of that as an incentive. You earned it. Split it with the guys or keep it all for yourself, I don't give a shit. It's your money. So long as you keep makin' noise on *B@d Beh@v!or,* the world is your fucking oyster."

I stared at the money in my hands, still struggling to understand where it had come from and how Phoenix's website played into it. *Don't borrow trouble,* I told myself. *Money is money.* But I couldn't shake the feeling that I was missing something important.

An oath echoed out from the direction of the Oddkat as the piano tuner muttered a string of curses into the resonant strings. Judge watched him work, untroubled by the abundant evidence that our work had stalled.

"So, you're not mad?" I hazarded.

"Mad? Why would I be mad?"

"About the album? Time is money and all that?" I waved towards the drum kit and guitars and amps all sitting silent.

Judge brushed it all aside with a gesture. "It doesn't matter."

"Wait, what?" I understood the words but they failed to make any sense to me. I'd definitely missed something. "I thought making an album was the whole fucking point?"

Judge rolled his eyes. "No, the *point* was, is, and always will be, to make money."

"And how did you think that was going to happen if we didn't record a new album?"

"Listen, Crustbucket, there's no money in music anymore—hasn't been for years. Who goes to the record store and buys albums, anymore? I'll tell you who: hipsters. Fucking. Hipsters. And fucking hipsters do not represent a significant market share. Everything's on the internet now. Everybody wants music for free. Let me tell you this: the real money's in data metrics. Algorithms. Advertising. Websites track every click and companies will pay big bucks to get a peek under that skirt. All you need to tap into that is a developer savvy enough to monetize their site—that's Phoenix—and someone who can drive traffic to it. That's you."

The picture was starting to make sense in my head but I wasn't sure I liked it. "Okay, so how the hell do you expect me to drive traffic without an album?"

"I don't need an album, I need content."

Nobody makes music anymore, they make content.

I remembered the disdainful curl of Phoenix's lips as she said it and I bristled.

"I'm a musician," I snapped. "I make *music.*"

"Sure," Judge said, as if this were a given, "but more importantly, you are a fucking click-machine. Everybody loves a natural disaster and you, my friend, are the perfect fucking storm. Everywhere you go, chaos follows. People love watching you implode. The more you trend on *B@d Beh@v!or,* the more we can cash in."

I sat back stunned as the revelation sank into the dense matter of my brain. I wasn't a musician: I was trash. Clickbait trash. Barnum-and-Bailey-You-Won't-Believe-What-Happens-Next trash.

Worse, I was *content.*

Judge must have seen this play out on my face. He softened his tone:

"Listen," he said. "I'm not asking you to do anything you're not already doing. You wanna keep making music? Fine. I'll front your studio costs. I'll produce your album. Hell, I'll even put you on stage—the Aragon? House of Blues? Wrigley Field? I got connections. All you gotta do is keep the dumpster burning." His eyes flickered once again towards the Oddkat and he smirked. "It shouldn't be hard for you. You're a natural."

I stared down in the envelope while I chewed this thought down to bite-sized pieces. It was the easiest money I'd ever made. I once again ran my finger over the stack of bills, thick as the pages of a paperback, while Phoenix's words played back in my head: *You wanna be in it for the music? Fine, starve to death for all I care. Otherwise, get off your tiny little high-horse and join the viral revolution.*

I would still have the music. I could still record the album. I could still perform on stage. No one got famous without a little notoriety, and if I wanted to claw my way back out of obscurity, I was going to need all the help I could get. And having some cash on hand to smooth the way certainly wasn't going to hurt.

It was too good to be true.

It *had* to be too good to be true. There had to be a downside but with that cash in my hand, I sure as hell couldn't see it and I didn't want to try.

I shoved the envelope in my pocket and stuck out my hand. "Fine," I said. "You got yourself a deal."

13

HOT DATE

RETURNED TO the Cursèd Place to find Gorey preening himself on the front porch with his chest puffed up like he was prepared to leap a tall building in a single bound. Everyone was smoking cigars.

"What's goin' on?" I asked.

"Gorey knocked up his wife," Jojo said.

"I'm gonna be a dad!" Gorey was grinning so hard his eyes were watering. He brushed away the tears before I could see him cry as Tombstone slapped him on the back and ruffled up his topknot until the tufts of hair stood on end in every direction. Kilroy handed me a cigar.

"No shit? When?"

"May sometime—maybe June," Gorey pulled a black-and-white sonogram print out of his pocket and proffered it to me, shyly. "Ma says her cards say it's gonna be a boy...I'm gonna have a son—" His voice quavered on the verge of breaking over the emotion of it all.

The ultrasound might as well have been an ink-blot for all the good it did me. A light blob hung suspended inside a slightly darker blob. There might've been a flipper.

"Cute," I said, handing it back to him. "Congrats."

Gorey sensed my indifference and reined in his enthusiasm.

"You mad, bro?"

"No, I'm happy for you. It's a big deal."

"Don't be like that," He cradled the print in his palm and stared at it lovingly. "I just...I never thought it would be like this..."

Tombstone put an arm across his shoulders like he understood, but then again, he probably did. Fatherhood had landed on him while he was still in high school and he now had two teenage daughters that he loved to distraction, even if it meant handing over every cent he made to his ex-wife in the form of support payments. Fatherhood was as much a part of Tombstone as his stutter or his red hair and I was used to it but it was something new for Gorey. I couldn't help but feel like it signified one more step he was taking away from me along a path I couldn't follow.

I escaped to the kitchen and helped myself to a drink. Jojo stood in the back doorway, with one arm stuck out the door so she could smoke.

"Gorey as a dad," she said, as much to herself as to me. "You believe it?"

"Didn't think I'd live long enough to see it," I said.

"I know, right?" She took a drag on the cigar and blew the smoke out the back door, her mind someplace far away. "End of a fucking era."

I nodded, not sure what to say to this. She shook her head. "You want kids?" she asked after a long minute.

"Hell no. Can you imagine me as a father?"

She shrugged. "If Gorey can do it, anyone can. Why not?"

"What about you? You want kids?"

Her mouth twitched in a way that said she was thinking about something that hurt too much to say. "Anything could happen," she mumbled. "I put a sample in ice, you know, in case but...I dunno. It's not like I can get pregnant." Jojo had undergone every surgery known to man to mold herself into the woman she wanted to be but there simply was no surgery known to man that could give her a womb. She wanted to pretend she didn't care but her voice cracked and went deep and she looked out the door, embarrassed.

"There's always adoption."

"Yeah." She took another bitter sip of smoke. "Cuz that's the same fucking thing."

"Whatever, dude—you'd make a great mom," I said. "And adoption is in these days. I mean, you might have to fight off Angelina Jolie with a goddamn stick but you could take her."

Jojo snorted a laugh in spite of herself.

"Fuck you," she said. "You made fucking coffee come out my nose." She flicked her middle finger at my crotch but it missed the mark and it glanced off my hipbone. I danced away easily and retaliated with a tit punch.

"Ow! Fuck you!"

I slung an arm over her neck, trapping her head in my armpit. "B'sides, you'd have to give up drugs to be pregnant: and caffeine and booze and cheese and sushi and—"

"Alright! Alright, I get the fucking picture." She wrapped an arm around my chest to give me a titty twister.

We were such grown-ups.

"Oh, hey, guys," Kilroy's voice floated into the room. I looked up to see him in the doorway watching us roughhouse. "We're goin' to the club to celebrate. You comin'?"

Jojo and I reached a mutual, silent truce. I felt her grip ease up on my nipple and I loosened my arm around her neck. She stood, breathless, and smoothed her hair.

"Yeah, we're coming," she said.

✳   ✳   ✳   ✳

"What do you know about metrics?" I asked Gorey as we cruised towards the club in the GTO. He was the only person in the band who was likely to be tech-savvy enough to understand Judge's money scheme.

"What do you want to know about them?"

"How do they turn clicks into money?"

"Depends on the platform. Ad revenue. Data mining. Algorithm training—you know..." He shrugged. "Why you asking?"

"Judge says if we want to get studio time for the album, we're gonna have to keep creating *content* for him. For sites like *B@d Beh@v!or*. He says the money's in clicks now."

Gorey scanned the air over my head as he considered this, then he shrugged. "Yeah, sounds legit," he said. "Streaming's changing everything. You know Pandora?"

"Like the box?"

"Like the radio."

"Sure."

"Pandora's where it's at. They're blowing the traditional formats outta the water: people gettin' to pick the kind of music they wanna listen to? I mean, who wouldn't? Regular radio just keeps playing the same stuff over and over; who the hell wants to listen to Adele forty-bazillion times—" He reached over to turn on the radio and tuned the dial to The Mix where Adele was setting fire to the rain. He flipped it to KISS FM where Adele was rolling in the deep. He flipped to B96 where Adele was chanting on about rumors to the beat of a club remix.

"I get the picture," I said, switching the radio off as we arrived at the club.

Club Lure was an asymmetrical shard of a building embedded in the middle of a nondescript neighborhood. The front of the building shimmered like a mirage against the gray surroundings as a luminous display of color-shifting LEDs signaled to the rich and libidinous that this was a place where they could seek the uncomplicated company of the nude and nubile.

The interior was a fantasy of smoke and mirrors that hinted at illicit delights hidden out of sight in every corner. Stages rose out of the floor at intervals, where lithe dancers twisted and twirled above the crude masses, all wearing the same suggestive smile that seemed to say: *if this is what we do in the light, imagine what we might do in the dark.*

We were regulars at the club by now, and the ticket girl waved us through the door without charging us a cover. Word had gotten around that this was one of our usual haunts, and the tables and booths were full of hopeful Legion fans lying in wait in case we decided to make an appearance. And they didn't mind paying for some company while they kept their vigil. The Legion were our most dedicated fans. They followed us like sharks follow-ing chum: consuming everything in their path and leaving only a trail of destruction behind.

The club didn't seem to mind: butts in seats meant more money for the dancers, even if it did mean breaking up fights on a nightly basis. I felt the Legion's thousand-eyed stare follow me across the room but no one emerged from the shadows to accost me. We washed ashore at our usual booth by the stage and the girls began a game of musical chairs on our restless laps.

The girl who landed on my lap wasn't an idiot but she knew how to play one on TV. She must have been new—everybody else knew I belonged to Melody—but Melody hadn't materialized yet and I wasn't going to sit around with an empty lap while I waited. I listened to Heather or Ginger or Brandi upspeak a steady stream of crystal-gazing psychobabble for almost twenty minutes before someone came to my rescue.

A blonde emerged out of the darkness and slid her hands over my shoulders to knead my neck. "Damn, Destinee, you sure know how to make a man hard," she said, digging a knuckle into a knot between my shoulder blades. "Go on now—let the rest of us have a crack at him."

Get lost.

Destinee might've been new but she knew how to take a hint. She rose off my lap far enough to pivot her hips onto Kilroy's knee and immediately began to twist his goatee around her finger. "What's *your* name?" I heard her say, and like magic, I was forgotten.

"Thanks for the assist," I said.

The blonde slid onto my lap in a sinuous movement and twined an arm across my shoulders to toy with my hair. "You looked like you needed it," she said.

Her name was Camille. Like Melody, she was a dancer at the club, and like Melody, she was someone that I'd been known to hook up with any time I got the chance but that was where the similarities ended. She was a bombshell blonde with lips like honey and a mouth as smooth as oil, and she reveled in her sexuality like a Sybarite, making no demands, setting no limits, and feeling no apparent shame—as warm and easy-going as a sunbeam.

"I heard the big news about your friend. I'd congratulate him but I think he's pretty well covered." She nodded towards Gorey, who was so tangled in a dog-pile of tits and ass that the only part of him I could see was his topknot sticking up like a turnip top. "I guess I'll have to make do with you instead. What do you say? You want to be my daddy tonight?" Camille winked and bit her lip then picked up my hand and pressed it to her thigh below the elastic strap on her garter belt. It was a gilded invitation, and any other night I would've jumped at it but tonight my mind was elsewhere. Camille seemed to sense my reticence.

"What's the matter, honey?" she asked. "Aren't you celebrating?"

"Yeah, no it's great," I said. "Gorey wants kids. Mission accomplished."

"So, what's wrong?"

"I dunno. I don't know I feel about it. Looks like hell to me."

Camille stroked the side of my face sympathetically. "Well, then, let me take your mind off it. C'mon, let's have some fun." She got to her feet and pulled me up after her with a nod towards a nearby mezzanine. I cast another look around the room for Melody but there was still no sign of her. Camille caught my wandering eye.

"Ahh, I see," she said, sliding a hand around my waist. "'S okay, you're fair game tonight. Melody's not working. She's got a date."

A date. That caught me up short.

"A what?"

"A date. You know. Piña coladas and getting caught in the rain. That kind of thing," Camille pulled a face like this was nauseating to her.

A date. I felt agitation rise in my guts. Melody and I had never made any pretense of being exclusive but we'd fallen into the routines of a relationship without discussing it, and she'd never mentioned she was seeing anybody else.

"She didn't tell me she was dating anyone."

"*A* date, not dat*ing*," Camille clarified as if this made any difference. "It's 2012. No one does *dating* anymore. You tell her every time you hook up with someone?"

Hook up. My mind caught on the word and flashed to an image of another man's hands on Melody's body—another man's hands peeling off her clothes, another man's hands making her squirm and moan. My thoughts must have shown on my face because Camille heaved a sigh.

"Don't even go there, honey," she said as if she were reading my mind. "It's not a big deal. Dinner and a movie or something—nothing serious. It's one of her regulars. The guy is married, he just likes having a beautiful woman on his arm,"

It wasn't his arm he wanted a beautiful woman on.

"C'mon honey put it out of your mind. So, she's out tonight—let me keep you company instead." Camille crooned. She bit her lip and leaned in until her cheek brushed against mine. "I can't stop thinking about your cock..." she breathed in my ear, her voice heavy with suggestion.

I pushed her away and held her at arm's length, struggling to be rational. "No, hang on—she can afford to take a Friday night off for a date?"

"She can when it's with Ranier."

"Ranier?"

"He covers the cash she would've made working."

"There's a name for women who get paid to go on dates," I said.

"Yeah? And there's a name for married men who fuck other women behind their wife's back. But that's none of my business—" With one hand she traced the tattoos on my forearm with the tip of a finger. With the other, she reached down to stroke the front of my jeans.

"Wait, hang on—they're fucking?!" I caught her wrist and pushed her hand away, trying to be gentle but not sure I was succeeding. Adrenaline surged through my body from head to toe as my mind played a video of Melody naked and spread-eagled; Melody writhing in pleasure, impaled on a stranger's cock; Melody's head thrown back in the ecstasy of orgasm.

Stop it!

"I don't know what they do on their dates, okay?" Camille said, annoyance cracking through her alluring façade. She leaned back and cocked her head as if realizing something. "Why are you so surprised? Don't *you* pay her?"

"No."

"Really? Nothing?"

"Babysitting and breakfast," I said. "Festival passes."

Camille raised an eyebrow. "Wow, she must really like you."

"Well, she's sure as hell got a funny way of showing it!"

"Okay, let's take a breath," Camille was suddenly no-nonsense. She pressed a hand to either side of my face and forced me to look her in the eye. "C'mon, I mean it—deep breath. Right now." She took a deep breath in through her nose and let it out through her lips, waiting until I followed suit. It helped but not much. She reached into her purse and tipped out a pill into her hand. "Have a Valium. Take the edge off."

I let her put it between my lips and gulped it down with a swig of water from a bottle on the table that I hoped Jojo hadn't touched.

"Listen," she said. "Melody's got her guys. They're rich and lonely and looking for company for a while. It's good money—easy. Nothing serious. A date now and then. I don't know what all they do but you know what she's like—doesn't like being touched? Right? You think a normal guy's got better game than you got?"

That was true. I remembered Melody's insistence on *no hands* and my rational mind grabbed onto it like a lifeline. I took another breath and nodded.

"She's a maneater—and I *don't* mean it like that," Camille said, stopping me before my mind could suggest what part of the man Melody liked to start with. "Trust me, honey, she's not gonna let some guy tell her what to do. Certainly not fucking Ranier. These other guys have got nothing on you. You're something special."

"Uh-huh."

"Don't 'uh-huh' me," Camille said. "She doesn't talk about her other guys like she talks about you. The nights you don't come in she spends her whole shift with one eye on the door."

I didn't know if it was true. I didn't want to know. I forced myself to take yet another breath and felt the Valium start to soften the edges of the world. Camille ran her fingers through my hair until I managed to get a grip.

"There—that's more like it," she purred, slipping seamlessly back into the role of seductress. I let my hands slide down the soft skin of her back to her ass and she smiled. "C'mon, forget about her, let's have some fun. What d'you want? Blonde? Brunette? Redhead? Have it all." She gave a wave of her hand and I suddenly found myself surrounded by a host of eager dancers prepared to worship me with their supple flesh until the sun came up. but I didn't feel like paying for half a dozen strippers to tease me with carnal delights while the one woman I wanted was out being paid for by someone else.

"Sorry," I mumbled, peeling eager fingers off my arms and shoulders before I could be swept away. "It's just not happening tonight." I turned toward Tombstone who was sitting nearby watching me with the wary expression of someone expecting to have to break up a fight and nodded toward the door. "I'm headed out."

Camille looped an arm through my elbow. "I'll walk you out."

"I'm fine, I promise." I tried to shake her off but she held on.

"Don't go doing anything stupid, you hear me?" she said. "You're not gonna try anything with Melody tonight, are you? Cuz those guys who hang out in front of her building? They're not there for show."

"Good to know," I said, pretending like I hadn't been planning to show up on her doorstep and make a scene until she came out to talk to me.

Camille pressed her body against me again. "C'mon, stay," she murmured. "Everyone loves you here. You can have anything you want."

She wasn't wrong. I could feel that every eye had settled on me: the dancers hoping for a lucrative night and the Legion hoping for a picture or an autograph. Around the corners of my vision, I could see faces emerging from the darkness with the bright light of their interest shining out of their eyes in glowing pinpoints.

"C'mon forget about Melody, stay here and be the king..."

I couldn't say that I wasn't tempted but the hot, bitter ember of betrayal was still burning its way through my guts. "Another night," I said. I gave her a peck on the cheek and peeled myself out of her arms to head for the door.

Up until now, the Legion had kept to the edges of the room in a formless, faceless mass but now it turned its thousand eyes in my direction and pressed in closer for a better look.

"Hey! Damen! Damen Warner!"

"Hey! Can we get a picture? Sign something for us? Imma big fan—"

I ignored the chorus of voices trying to get my attention over the pounding music of the club and waded out across the crowded dance floor with my head down. I immediately regretted my choices. The crowd on the floor was like something out of a nightmare: hands reached out from every direction trying to touch me as I passed. They pawed at me like the hands of lost souls, grabbing at my clothes and arms to drag me down into the world of their avid fantasies. I wasn't sure what would happen if they succeeded.

I hauled myself towards the main entrance where Rocco was manning the door hoping to scrape off a few of the more wild-eyed fanatics at the bottleneck. There was a short flight of stairs leading up to the door and as I gained the high ground, I made the tactical error of looking back at the roiling horde behind me only to collide with the swole chest of a Dudebro who was on his way in.

"Watch it, simp," he sneered, shoving me aside without a second glance. He planted himself at the top of the stairs surveying the club through a pair of mirrored Oakley sunglasses while the rest of his squad wafted in behind him. I pressed myself against a wall, hemmed in on all sides by a fug of arrogance and cologne. The newcomers stood in the doorway like a clot, blocking traffic in both directions: a group of bros with their girlfriends out for an evening on the town. The guys were all wearing sunglasses and Ed Hardy shirts and loudly thumping their chests at each other while their girlfriends looked bored and annoyed and not nearly drunk enough for this to be considered 'fun'.

"Omigod, this is a *strip club!*" One of the girls protested, averting her eyes as she realized the stages were all featuring dancers in various states of undress. "You said we were going clubbing! This isn't any fun!"

"Don't be so goddamn *vanilla*, Bethany." Oakley scoffed; his attention occupied with the encroaching crowd of Legion fans. "Jesus Christ, what is this, Hot Topic night?" One of his buddies brayed a hoarse laugh that cut through the music, which seemed to encourage him.

"C'monnnnn, guyyys." Bethany's friend looked like she'd been sipping on wine coolers on the sly and was ready to graduate to something stronger. She hung on Oakley's arm trying to hold him back from fronting up against a wiry dude with gauged earlobes. "Don't be a douche."

"Dude! Can I get a picture!? Can I get a picture?!" Gauges pled to me over Oakley's shoulder. He stuck his camera in Oakley's face and took a burst of photos with a strobing flash.

"Get your camera outta my face, faggot." Oakley told him, shoving him backward. The press of Legion fans swirled like a swarm of angry wasps.

"We wanna go," Bethany whined hanging on Oakley's arm, trying to tug him back outside but Oakley didn't budge.

"So, go if you wanna go," he said, shaking her off.

"We can't—we don't have a ride!" Bethany protested.

"Then I guess you're gonna have to stay, huh?"

"What the fuck is your problem, man?" Gauges demanded,

regaining his feet and fronting up against Oakley's chest with a vehement gesture in my direction. "I just want a fucking picture," he said, pleading his case loudly enough for me to hear but his eyes were fixed on Oakley: a fight would be a good consolation prize.

"And I said, get outta my *face*," Oakley spat, shoving him again, this time with enough force to knock him to the ground. The Legion surged towards the door with a collective howl of anger and wounded pride as the Douche Brigade fist-pumped their way into the club.

It wasn't clear who threw the punch but the crowd suddenly became a brawl of elbows and fists. I saw Rocco say something into his wrist and the other floor hosts emerged from the various VIP alcoves. Tombstone and Kilroy climbed up onto their chairs for a better view of the mayhem while Gorey, true to form, came screaming out of a back room and launched himself onto the backs of the Legion to take a swing at one of Oakley's buddies.

"Yeah, bitches! That's what I'm talkin' about!"

I felt a hand grab onto my arm and looked down to see Bethany clinging to my bicep like she was afraid she was going to drown. She looked up and realized with a start that she'd grabbed the wrong person. "Shit—sorry!" she said, letting go.

"You're cool," I told her. The melee had opened up a path to the door and I lunged for it, dragging Bethany along with me to the relative safety of the front vestibule. A valet stuck his head in the door, trying to get a look at the excitement taking place inside. I caught his eye and gestured for him to bring the Goat around. He nodded and withdrew.

"You wanna get out of here?" I asked Bethany, "I'll give you a ride."

"No, I'm good—" she started to say with a disdainful curl of her lip but before she could finish there was a smack as one of the Legion members was shoved against the glass by Oakley's crew, still shouting my name.

"Damen! Over here! Can I get an autograph? I'm a huge fan, man—" There was a squeal of fingers on glass as Rocco peeled him off the window and tackled him into a headlock.

"Wait, are you—?" Bethany realized, maybe for the first time, that I was a somebody. She squinted at me until recognition dawned. "Oh, shit! You're that piano guy!"

You kick over one goddamn piano...

"That's me," I said.

"Hang on—you're in a band or something, right? You're *famous!*"

"I'm Damen," I said, winking at her as the Goat arrived at the curb, idling magnificently in the cool night air. I opened the driver's side door and looked back at her. "C'mon and party with me. Ditch the douchebag. Bring your friends if you want. Now or never,"

Bethany didn't need to be asked twice. She tagged each of the other girlfriends in turn and tripped out the door after me without a backward glance.

"Bethany, what the fuck?!" Oakley burst out the club door in time to see the girls piling into the passenger side door. Bethany tilted her head and smiled at him.

"You said for me to go, so I'm going," she told him. "*We're* going. Have fun with your friends. Byeeeeeeee!"

"What?!" Oakley spluttered, staring at her with his mouth hanging open. "Bethany, *wait!*" But it was already too late. Bethany climbed into the Goat and slammed the door behind her with a definitive *thunk.* I rolled down my window.

"Don't worry, bro," I shouted to him over the roar of the engine. "I'll take good care of her." Then I gave him the finger with both hands and roared out of the parking lot into the night, consoled by the knowledge that at least one person was going to have a shittier night than I was.

14

DEALBREAKER

I DIDN'T GO back to the house. The girls wanted to party, so I drove them out to Rosemont and got a hotel room near the casino. Then, I summoned Goose to be our Stepin Fetchit for booze and condoms and cocaine and anything else we needed to keep us fucking, fucked up, and feeling no pain. I wasn't sure how long we stayed there— time had no meaning in Rosemont—but it was daylight when I woke up alone with a head-splitting hangover to find a Polish woman in a housekeeper's uniform standing over me.

"What day is it?" I croaked.

"Ehm, is Tuesday?" she said, discreetly averting her eyes from the fact that I was sprawled out naked on the bed. "You want I should come back?"

I squinted at the wreck of the room, still struggling to put reality in focus. "No. Pretty sure my work here is finished. Gimme a second and I'll get outta your hair."

I pulled on my clothes, aware that the housekeeper was watching me furtively out of the corner of her eye, and threw a wad of cash down on the bed as an apologetic tip.

"Sorry 'bout the mess," I mumbled. I staggered past her out the door and went in search of something to eat.

My bender had lasted for three solid days and now I was going to pay for every minute of it by having the unbearable roar of sunlight drilled through my skull. I felt like shit, and I was still too fucked up to drive, so I sent Goose to go get one of the guys and then huddled in the darkest corner of a casino bar with my t-shirt pulled up over my head until Tombstone showed up to drive me home.

I slumped against the cool glass of the passenger side window in his pickup truck feeling the morning sweats evaporating off my skin like a reeking miasma. Tombstone pulled to a stop in front of the Cursèd Place and nudged my shoulder.

"Bu-brace yourself," he said as he pulled to a stop in front of the Cursèd Place. He pointed out the window to the front porch where Melody was sitting on the front steps, lying in wait. Suddenly, everything I'd been trying to forget came back to me in a rush.

Melody's not here. Melody's on a date.

"Where the fuck you been? I been callin' you?" she demanded as I made my way across the scorching wasteland of the front lawn through the agonizing radiation of autumn sunshine.

"Yeah," I said. "I know. I turned off my phone."

"Why you gotta be like that?" Melody followed me in the front door to the soothing darkness of the living room.

"Like what?" I said. "So, I didn't answer your calls. Big fucking deal."

"Fine, be a little bitch about it." Melody blocked my path

and stuck her hands on her hips. I stepped around her and made my way into the kitchen. "Excuuuse me for caring. Vico was worried. I was worried."

"Yeah, well you got a funny way of showing it," I snapped, chewing on a fistful of aspirin while I searched the cabinets for baking soda or Alka-Seltzer or sidewalk chalk; anything to soothe the boiling acid in my guts.

"What's that supposed to mean?"

"Who's Ranier?"

I found an ancient tablet of Alka-Seltzer, probably leftover from one of the squatters, and dropped it into a cup of water from the tap. I gulped it down like it was the water of life.

Melody's expression turned cold. "None of your goddamn business, that's who."

"I came by the club. You weren't there. Camille said you were out with this...Ranier," I persisted. I leaned on the counter, blocking Melody into a corner so she couldn't avoid answering the question.

"I was."

"She said he's one of your regulars."

"He is."

"You fucking him too?"

Melody drummed her fingernails on the counter, her lips drawn into a tight, bloodless line. "Imma give you a chance to think 'bout whether you want the answer to that question."

"Well, then I guess I already fucking know," I spat back at her.

"What part of 'I don't belong to you' are you too *estupit* to understand?" she shouted back, prodding into the middle of my pounding forehead forcefully with the tip of her finger. "I. Don't. Belong. To. You. You don't tell me what to do, you hear me? *Never ever.* You don't like it, you can fucking leave."

"Oh, I'm fucking *estupit,* alright," I snarled at her.

"Don't make fun of me."

"Make *fun* of you?! I spent a whole night defending you to the woman who called you a slut and a welfare ho and she was fucking right all along!" I threw the empty cup into the sink and heard something shatter. I turned and shoved my way back out of the kitchen and started up the stairs to the bedroom.

"Don't you walk away from me!"

Through the haze of my rage, a thought occurred to me and I turned on the staircase to face her again. "Were you out fucking someone the night you needed me to fucking *babysit?!*"

"No. I told you—Avi made me come to the club—"

"No, you *told* me Avi said you had to give him a weeknight. Are you fucking him too?!" I could feel paranoia starting to set in but I couldn't seem to stop it.

"I was at the club. You can ask Evie."

"That still doesn't answer my question."

"Well, it's all the answer you're gonna get, cuz it's none of your business."

I couldn't look at her anymore. I stormed up the remainder of the stairs to the bedroom and slammed the door, locking it behind me to shut her out. I collapsed onto the mattress listening to the sound of Melody pounding on the door and calling me a litany of names in Spanish that required no translation. I pulled the pillow over my head to block out the sound and let sleep overtake me.

✳   ✳   ✳   ✳

The room was dark and quiet when I woke up again. I felt slightly less like walking death but it still took a supreme effort of will to force myself upright and to stagger down the stairs. Kilroy was in the living room doing yoga on the filthy shag carpet under the supervision of a girl with dreadlocks knitted into her hair. She was adjusting the position of his hips as he held a warrior pose, not that he needed the help. He did yoga every day.

"You're so tight," she murmured as she pressed her thumbs into the taut muscles near his spine. Every word she spoke came out in a yoga voice.

"That's what he said," I croaked as I passed.

Kilroy didn't turn his head; he rotated one wrist and shifted his hand into the mudra of the Flipping Bird, and continued with his asana. He had this routine down to a science: the yoga would turn into a massage which would turn into whatever tantric, vegan form of sex he was practicing that week, which would be followed by a Meeting. It sometimes seemed like he'd swapped one addiction for another: heroin for holism but if it kept him off the pale horse, then he could *Namaste* his way to fucking Narnia for all I cared.

I flopped down onto the couch and caught my breath, still feeling like a shit sandwich.

"Hey Bro," Kilroy rasped, tottering slightly as his concentration wavered. "You look the way I feel."

"Unnnggh," I acknowledged, wordlessly.

Out of the corner of my eye, I saw Goose's head pop out from the kitchen and then disappear in a flicker. He appeared a moment later with a can of beer in his hand, still cold from the refrigerator, which he cracked open in a hiss of foam and handed to me.

"Car's here," he said in an embarrassed mumble.

"Cool," I said. I didn't have the slightest fucking clue what he was talking about. I took a sip of the beer and waved him off. Goose took a few steps back but continued to hover around the edges of my vision.

"*Car*'s here," he insisted again.

"Yeah, I heard you," I said. "Thanks. Get lost."

Goose twisted his hands anxiously but didn't budge from the end of the couch.

"He means the car Judge sent," Kilroy clarified, moving into a new pose and arching his back with evident anguish.

"What car Judge sent?" I asked, already knowing I wasn't going to like the answer.

"I dunno what you said to your Melody," Kilroy managed between gasps as he struggled to take deep healing breaths through clenched teeth. "But she was fucked up when she left here."

"Good."

"Nah, bro, not good. Judge is some kind of pissed about it," Kilroy pushed himself upright, his face running with sweat from beneath his beanie, and managed to align his crooked chakras. "You better talk to him tonight before he—argh! Fuck!"

Kilroy wrenched something out of alignment with a yelp

of agony and fell against Yoga Girl's shapely body to steady himself. He gave up on whatever pose it was he was trying to contort himself into and collapsed onto the floor, pulling her down with him.

"What did he say?" I asked.

"Does it matter?" Kilroy shrugged. "Just go an' talk to him before he unleashes hell."

Going to the club and talking to Judge about Melody was about the last thing I felt like doing, then or ever but avoiding it wasn't going to solve my problems. I gulped down another fistful of aspirin from the kitchen and went outside to find a limousine with a Club Lure decal on the door waiting at the curb.

"You Damen?" the driver asked.

"Yeah."

"Get in."

"You taking me to the club or am I gonna end up on my knees in a construction site?" I asked, only partly joking.

"I do what Judge tells me to," the driver said, opening the passenger door. "He said to pick you up an' bring you to him. I'm not getting paid to clean up blood."

This was not reassuring.

I climbed into the limo and sat as far away from him as I could without looking like I was scared shitless. By the time it pulled up to the club, I was about ready to crawl out of my skin. I charged through the club's doors, buoyed along on a surge of adrenaline, but I'd barely made it onto the club floor before I was knocked sideways against the wall.

"I told you not to fuck with Melody." Judge loomed over

me, his face blank and cold. He removed his reading glasses in a slow deliberate motion, folded them, and put them in his breast pocket. Then cracked his knuckles in a businesslike way and took a step towards me. I felt the bottom drop out of my stomach as animal terror overtook my brain.

"Judge, listen to me—" I took a step back, and then another one staggering backward in an awkward retreat. Judge walked me backward down the hallway towards the bathrooms to a door that I knew led to a storage room, and shoved me inside, locking the door behind him.

"Judge, listen—" I managed as limbic, animal terror tried to overtake my brain.

"Fuck you, Crustbucket. I warned you what would happen if you hurt her," Judge said, shoving me with enough force that I stumbled against the bank of refrigerators.

"Me hurt *her?"* I snapped. "I've been her bitch for weeks: driving her home, watching her kid—she snaps her fingers and I fucking jump like a goddamn trained poodle." I kicked over a stack of boxes in frustration sending a rain of promotional postcards cascading over the floor. If I was going to go down, I might as well go down in flames. "And what? She's off boning any dude who waves a wad of cash at her? Fuck that. Fuck her. Fuck you."

"I told you..." Judge repeated; his voice was quiet and grim. "Not. To fuck. With her. You didn't listen. And now there are fucking consequences." He curled his hand into a fist the size of a grapefruit, and I swallowed with difficulty.

Dear God, pray for me now in the hour of my death...

"Not the throat," I begged in a choked voice as he raised

his arm. Closing my eyes, I braced myself for the inevitable blow.

"Oh. Hey guys, what's goin' on?" A voice spoke from somewhere overhead. I cracked one eye open to see a youthful brown face smiling down at me mildly from beneath the crest of a tall spiked mohawk: Father Jesse.

I allowed myself the tiniest spark of hope.

Father Jesse was a paragon of contradictions. The only outward indication that he was an actual Catholic priest was the clerical collar pinned to his t-shirt. Everything else about him looked like it belonged in the mosh pit at a Bad Religion concert. He was all of maybe twenty-six and still dressed like he was pissed at his dad. His face was riddled with piercings, his neck was tattooed with flaming skulls on both sides, and the tall crest of his hair nearly brushed the tiles of the drop ceiling overhead. I didn't need to see the rest of him to know he was almost certainly wearing a Utilikilt.

But he was actually a priest. By day, he served at the convent next door where the diocese, in its infinite wisdom, had placed him—no doubt hoping that the nuns there would set him straight on matters of appearance and comportment. There were no obvious signs that they'd made any progress on that front. But, despite his appearance, he was a gentle earnest soul who just wanted to do some good. He spent most nights wedged into the back corner of the room hearing the confessions of patrons and dancers alike through a glory hole that had been clawed through the wall of a discarded dance booth. As far as I knew, 'confession' wasn't a euphemism for anything: it was actual

Bless-me-Father-for-I-have-sinned confession with actual *Go-forth-and-sin-no-more* absolution on offer. As Father Jesse himself had once joked: *Come for the titties, leave with the Holy Spirit—one-stop-shop!*

"I couldn't help but overhear," he said, leaning on the top of the dance booth wall like a casual next-door neighbor about to ask for a cup of sugar. "There some kinda trouble here?"

"No, no trouble, Father," Judge said, taking a discreet step away from me. The club may have been Judge's domain but this particular corner of it was Father Jesse's dominion. Judge wasn't religious but he was smart enough to know that he didn't want a priest as a witness to the kind of beat down he had in mind for me.

"Heckuva night, eh?" Father Jesse's tone was conversational as he took out a pack of cigarettes from the side of his kilt, then reached overhead to nudge open the air vent. He stuck a cigarette between his lips then looked back at the two of us sheepishly. "Bad habit, I know. I only got one vice left. Gotta take it where I can, y'know? Gives me an excuse to, you know, take a break? 'S good to take a break sometimes. Think things over. Get my head on straight before I do somethin' stupid. You got a light?"

Judge stared at him like he'd asked for a left-handed smoke shifter. I fumbled in my pocket for a book of matches and handed it to him.

"Really, bro? Matches?"

"I like the smell of the sulfur."

Father Jesse considered this then shrugged. "Right on," he said, focusing his attention on the end of the cigarette for a moment as he lit it, then handed the matches back to me. "You ain't a smoker, of course, I mean...gotta protect your voice, right? But Judge, I know you do. C'mon, man, have a peace pipe." He held out the cigarette to Judge and settled in like he was preparing to wait as long as it took for Judge to decide to take it. There was a long moment of smoky silence as the tension curled its way toward the vent in the ceiling, and then Judge took the cigarette and took a drag.

"I gotta go change the rotation," he muttered at last. He turned to me and stuck a finger in my chest, still holding the lit cigarette. It was so close I could feel the heat from the ember. "You make this right," he said. "Make up or break up. It's your choice. You got twenty-four hours," He handed the cigarette to Father Jesse with a terse nod and stumped out of the room slamming the door behind him.

"Shit, man, he *pissed,* huh?" Father Jesse jumped down from where he was standing on his folding chair and came around the wall of the booth to talk to me. I deflated into the threadbare seat—limp with relief.

"You know, he's kinda protective of Melody."

"Yeah, I gathered." *Thank you, Father Obvious.*

"He's 'bout the only family she got—been lookin' out for her since back when she lost her folks. He stood by her all through the drama with her Baby Daddy. For a long time, she din't have anyone else. I kinda thought the two of you were gettin' along. You and Melody, that is. What changed?"

"D'you know she dates her regulars?" I asked.

"I know a lot of things but that's kinda her business."

"Oh, it's a fucking business alright."

"Yeah? Okay, well, you're datin' a stripper, my friend. Men're gonna pay to spend time with her, 's kinda part of the package." Father Jesse smiled to soften the blow. "I mean, here at the club, guys're buyin' dances—payin' for her company three minutes at a time—you care 'bout that?"

I thought about it. "No."

"Guys pay her to take off her clothes, y'care 'bout that?"

"I don't love it."

"C'mon, get your head out of your ass."

"*My* head?"

"Yeah, *your* head," Father Jesse said. "It's her *job,* man. She's just tryin' to make a living with what she's got. B'sides, how many women have you chased down 'cuz it excited you? 'Cuz it felt good? 'Cuz you been bored or angry or alone? I mean, you picked up, what, three—four girls here on Friday."

"That's different."

"Is it?"

"That didn't mean anything, it was just sex—" I said, wincing as the words came out of my mouth. Father Jesse raised an eyebrow, and let me stew in my hypocrisy.

"Fuck you, Father," I mumbled.

"I ain't judging."

"That's literally your job."

"Nah, man, it *literally* ain't. Judge not, lest ye be judged, right?" Father Jesse said. "I'm not the referee in this sport, I'm like a team medic—everyone out there knockin' against each other tryin' to get to the other side. I'm just here tryin' to keep everyone in the game..." He seemed to think over this analogy for a second then added: "An' maybe I, you know, *nudge* folks a little bit to point them in the right direction but they've gotta run their own plays."

I ran my fingers over my forehead and buried my face in my hands. "The fuck am I going to do?" I asked rhetorically.

Father Jesse took a final drag on his cigarette and blew a streamer of smoke towards the vent in the ceiling. "So, you fuck other women. Melody fucks other men. If it's a deal-breaker you gotta tell her. Judge's got it about right, though: make up or break up. You gotta make a choice. You can't keep goin' round being butthurt an' takin' it out on her. She just bein' her bad self." He stubbed out the cigarette on a discreet place on the cinderblock wall then climbed back up on his folding chair to close the air vent. He looked down on me from on high and seemed to take pity on me. "Go see her," he said. "Talk to her. Direct. Face-to-face. You'll know what you can handle when you're lookin' her in the eye."

Father Jesse gave my shoulder a slap then left me alone to think about what he'd said. I sat in the broken booth stewing over my troubles until I heard the familiar riffs of *Yankee Rose* signifying that it was the last call. I emerged from the storage room to find the club floor deserted. The last few patrons scurried towards the door as if they were anxious to make their escape before the lights came on. Camille was leaning on the bar nearby wearing street clothes. I got the feeling she'd been waiting for me.

"You talk to Jesse?" she asked.

"Yeah."

"You pay him?"

"He didn't fix anything."

"Pay him anyway." She plunked a coffee can in front of me and held it there until I dropped a wad of cash inside.

"Good," she said. "It was my big mouth that got you bent all out of shape, so I feel like I gotta be the one to put things right. I don't want Judge messing up that pretty face." She put a hand on either side of that pretty face and forced me to look her in the eye. "You want to see Melody again?" she asked but it was more of a statement than a question: she already knew the answer. I nodded anyway.

"Then come with me, I'll take you to her."

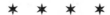

"What's *he* doing here?" Melody demanded through the crack in the door, still bound shut by a security chain. All I could see of her was the dark, shining iris of one eye, sizing me up.

You'll know what you can take once you're lookin' her in the eye, Father Jesse had said but now that I was here, I still didn't know what it was that I wanted.

"I brought him to talk to you," Camille told her. "Open the door, honey. C'mon, hear him out. He's on borrowed time b'fore Judge...well, you know." Somehow, whatever she wasn't saying was worse than anything she could have said.

Melody opened the door a fraction wider and forced herself to meet my gaze. Her face had a fragile, kitten look about it that I sometimes saw when I watched her sleep but rarely got to see when she was awake. She looked vulnerable. She wasn't wearing any makeup and her face was swollen and puffy like she'd been crying.

Fuck.

I'd hurt her. I hadn't meant to. I'd been so angry and upset about the fact I wasn't the only man in her life that I'd lashed out. She hadn't seen it coming. She didn't even know what she'd done to deserve it. "I'm sorry," I mumbled. "Can we talk? Please?"

Melody closed the door and I heard a rattle as she undid the chain but the door stayed closed.

"Your move," Camille told me.

I let myself into the apartment. The front room was empty: no sign of Melody and no sign of the Girl Child either. I found them both in Melody's room burrowed in a nest of blankets. The Girl Child was asleep, tangled up in a tight ball, with Melody curled around her protectively.

"Melody, I—"

Melody pressed a finger to her lips and pointed to the Girl Child, gently stroking her hair with one hand. "She didn't sleep all night," she whispered. "Kep' on waking up screaming cuz of bad dreams. Kep' asking where you were at."

It must have been bad. Melody was strict with the Girl Child about staying in her room: sleeping in the big bed was reserved for emergencies only. I felt a surge of protectiveness for the two of them. The Girl Child didn't have night terrors when I stayed in the apartment. When her fears conjured monsters out of the darkness, I would stay beside her bed to keep guard until she fell asleep.

I forced myself to look at Melody, who was still looking up at me steadily: waiting for me to speak. Her threadbare t-shirt had been washed so many times the fabric was sheer against her skin. I wanted to touch her. I tried to remember the rage that had gotten between us: Melody dating other men, Melody with her legs spread, Melody with another man's hands on her body but now I felt like a dipshit for even thinking about it. She wasn't trying to make my life miserable: she was just an ordinary woman in an over-washed t-shirt, trying to carve out a living in a world full of assholes like me. I sank down on the edge of the mattress and put my hand on top of Melody's, feeling her fingers curl around mine automatically.

"I'm sorry," I whispered. "I've been a shithead."

"Yeah. You have," she said, still coiled with tension like a watch-spring. I put a hand on the Girl Child's head and didn't say anything else.

"Do you hate me?" Melody whispered. I realized she was waiting for me to turn on her. She expected me to cut her down with names and accusations and to walk away like everybody had before.

I shook my head.

"This's my life. Imma do what I gotta do for Vico. She's not gonna grow up scared or hungry," she said.

Like me, she didn't say.

I nodded again.

"You can leave me," Melody continued. "You don't gotta stay."

"I'm not going anywhere," I said. I sighed and looked at my hands in my lap. "I'm not anyone to judge. I do what I want. You can do what you want. Nothing serious, right?"

Melody nodded.

"Just don't...you know...rub my face in it?" I risked a glance at her and Melody nodded, her head resting on the blankets in a wild tangle of her hair. A whisper of a smile brushed across her lips, and I bent over to kiss her, realizing how much I'd missed the taste of her mouth. She put a hand on my throat and let it rest there until I came up for air. I felt relief settling over me and I bit her nose gently.

"Also, I'm not gonna babysit so you can fuck other guys. You can pay for a goddamn sitter," I told her. Melody caught my lip ring between her teeth and bit down.

"And I'm not gonna watch you go 'round picking up other bitches in front of me," she said through her clenched teeth. "You take that shit out of the club, okay?"

"Except Camille," I said. "Cuz, I mean, c'mon…"

Melody struggled to suppress her smile.

"Fine," she said. "But then you gotta babysit when *I* get with Camille."

"Fuck, woman, you are cruel."

Melody released my lip ring and kissed me again. "We got a deal?"

It wasn't perfect—not even close but I could live with it.

Or, at least, I knew now that I couldn't live without it.

"Yeah," I said. "We got a deal."

15

STATE STREET BRIDGE

THE CITY had turned cold during the night and dawn poured in off the lake as a pale lightless gray. By now everybody else in the band would have retreated to the Cursèd Place to go to ground before the sun came up but I was wide awake and sober and not yet ready to plunge back into the shambles of my life.

I left Melody's place and took the L into downtown where I drifted through the Loop searching for direction that I wasn't sure was going to come. The drumbeat of morning commuters had not yet started and the city seemed to be holding its breath. I wandered out to the middle of the Wabash Avenue Bridge and stared down into the green water below. The morning chill had cast a shroud of mist across the river, and ghostly fingers swept over the water in a come-hither gesture.

Jump whispered a voice in my head, and with a certain, grim satisfaction I let myself imagine it. I imagined my body falling through empty space until I hit the water and it closed over my head, soft and warm like a bath. I imagined sinking to the bottom and never coming up again. I imagined letting go of the world and all my troubles; imagined breathing them out of my body in a stream of silvery bubbles trailing upwards toward the receding light as the rest of me sank into the comfort of the final, elemental darkness below.

Some days, the river looked pretty inviting.

I tore my eyes away from the beckoning water and looked around at the city instead. The rising sun blazed against the tops of the tallest buildings, throwing them into sharp relief against a flawless blue sky. At ground level, the streetlights glowed on shadowy streets where twilight still pooled between the buildings. Below that ran the Riverwalk; a narrow park where a monument commemorated the Vietnam War. I realized then that I wasn't alone. A man stood beside the wall of names with a bouquet of grocery store flowers in his hand. He ran his fingers along the letters inscribed in the stone until he found a name that meant something to him, and he bowed his head, moving his lips in words I couldn't hear. Once he'd said his piece, he set the flowers at the foot of the wall and then took a step back to snap a salute.

Then he took off his shoes.

I somehow knew what was going to come next and felt my breath catch in my throat. I'd never seen somebody attempt suicide before. I'd never seen anybody die in real life, only on TV. It occurred to me that I should call for help, and my fingers closed around the phone in my pocket but then I stopped as indecision overtook me.

Maybe it's not what it looks like, a voice in my head argued, trying to sound reasonable.

IT'S WHAT IT LOOKS LIKE! another voice screamed. *He's committing suicide! Call for help! Save him!*

He doesn't want your help—maybe he's got a good reason—you don't know his life...Do you really want to get involved? He'll be angry if you get in his way.

Since when do you fucking care?

I stood rooted to the spot with my phone in my hand, utterly unable to move as the voices in my head warred with one another. The man took off his jacket and folded it neatly, checked the pockets, and laid the bundle on his shoes. He took out his phone, laid it on top of the pile, and turned his back on it. He didn't want help. Maybe he was afraid it wouldn't come for him anyway. Or maybe he was afraid it would.

I didn't know what to do but I also couldn't look away; compelled by morbid curiosity to be a witness in this otherwise private tragedy. The man climbed the steps that led to the bridge directly across from me and made his way along the span. He stopped where the two halves of the drawbridge met in a narrow seam and climbed over the railing, standing with his heels on a ledge so narrow that his toes dangled in the air over the whispering waters below. He gripped the railing with both hands, his arms stretched wide like a crucifix as he turned his face upward to pray. His eyes met mine for a minute and held my gaze without fear: without emotion of any kind. His mouth made the shape of an 'amen,' and then he let go.

His body pitched forward and he fell toward the water headfirst, disappearing beneath the surface in a plume of white froth. The sound of it came to me a minute after the water closed over his head and I flinched as if it had been the sound of an explosion.

Splash.

"Hey!" There was a shout from the riverbank. Down on the Riverwalk, another guy was urgently shedding his jacket and shoes. "Call 911!" he shouted to a woman who was with him as he broke the glass on an emergency life ring. He pitched the life ring into the water and dove in after it, bobbing to the surface a moment later. He swam toward the dwindling ripples in the middle of the water, towing the life ring behind him, and once again plunged beneath the surface.

The woman must have called for help. Within minutes, a police launch cruised up the river fast enough to scar a wake across the surface of the water, and the sight of the flashing lights snapped me back to reality. Help had been called. Help had arrived. I had failed. I had stood and watched and done nothing.

Nausea quivered in my stomach.

Good, my mind said, magnifying my guilt until it filled my whole body. *You deserve to feel like shit, you fucking asshole. It'll happen to you someday and when it does you won't need to wonder why no one tries to stop you: you'll already know.*

I retreated to the far end of the bridge and began to run: fleeing from the scene of a crime I'd committed by doing nothing.

✳   ✳   ✳   ✳

I found myself at the Big House without knowing how I'd gotten there. I stood panting on the sidewalk at the foot of the front steps and leaned my face against the cold metal of the iron gate while I struggled to catch my breath.

"Damen?"

I looked up to see my mother standing at the top of the front steps like a gray ghost. She was dressed in soft layers: a silk scarf, a long sweater, a pair of wool pants, all in the muted colors of autumn rain. It was a departure from her usual icy-crisp tailoring. Her hair wasn't done and she wasn't wearing any makeup but somehow this only emphasized the spare elegance of her features which were currently arranged in an expression of astonishment.

"What are you doing here?" she asked.

"I'm...just...I dunno," I stammered.

"Mmm." Mom made a noncommittal sound and descended the front steps to retrieve a plastic-wrapped newspaper from the front walk. She opened the gate and gestured me inside. "Alright, well you'd better come in. You're looking worse for the wear." She ushered me up the steps to the front door without giving me time to protest, and let it fall shut behind me.

The house was quiet and dim. Mom's influence was evident everywhere I looked. The front rooms were now arranged with a cool elegance that was orderly to the point of being sterile. The artwork and furniture and heirlooms and curios had all been cleared away and replaced with ornamental floral displays. Through the doorway to the living room, I could see the piano cowering beneath a arrangement of orchids that was bigger than it was.

"Is Dearie here?" I asked.

"Still asleep," Mom spoke in a hushed voice and gestured

me toward the door of the kitchen, where we could speak freely without our voices carrying to the rest of the house.

The kitchen smelled of burned toast and brewing coffee. On the counter, a coffee pot dripped and gurgled beside a breakfast tray half-assembled with toast and honey. Milk. A dish of colorful pills. A white calla lily. Over the sink stood a large stained-glass window depicting the Archangel Michael in all his resplendent glory. Morning light filtered through the colored glass suffusing the room with the warm buttery glow of God's relentless judgment.

Mom pointed to a chair: "Sit."

I sat.

The coffee pot finished brewing with a gurgle and Mom filled a mug and set it on the table in front of me. Then she turned her back to fill a mug for herself. Seizing her moment of distraction, I snagged a bottle of cooking brandy off the counter beside the stove and poured a hasty shot of it into my mug.

"Early for that, don't you think?" Mom said without turning.

"You're one to talk," I said.

"Yes. I am," she said. "Because I know,"

I took a defiant slurp of coffee without breaking eye contact, expecting her to scold me for the booze, the slurping, or the insolence but she stared back evenly until the coffee burned my tongue and I was forced to look away.

Mom didn't press me further, just turned her attention back to her coffee. She unlocked the cabinet where Dearie kept her silver and took out a sugar bowl. Lifting the lid, she pinched out a single cube of sugar between two fingers and dropped it into her cup.

"You take sugar now?" I asked in surprise. I'd never known Mom to like sweetness of any kind.

Mom looked embarrassed. "Something new I'm trying," she said. "I started a new treatment after my procedure. The side effects are less...strident. Less...'straight lines and hard edges' as you call it," Her tone was pointed. I'd criticized her ruthless perfectionism by describing it as a 'life under glass,' and she hadn't forgotten it. But she did seem softer somehow. Separating from Michael had done her some good. I thought back to the day she'd announced their separation and remembered a strip of photographs I'd been meaning to ask her about.

"D'you remember that time we went to Great America?" I asked. "I was, like, thirteen, I think? You came and got me from the school?"

"No, should I?"

"You were there," I told her. I reached into a pocket and took out my wallet where a strip of photo-booth photos was tucked in the billfold. I handed it to her.

"Obviously." Mom stared at the photos with her forehead furrowed in thought as she contemplated her younger self but nothing seemed to surface in her memory. She shook her head. "Doesn't ring a bell."

"We went to some diner up in Wisconsin? Sam showed up—you seemed pissed when he did...You asked if I would go with you to California—" I prompted.

She shrugged. "I remember being very drunk. I was drunk a lot in those days." That much was true: she'd been the one pouring alcohol into her coffee back then. "It was right before I went to treatment. You remember me going to treatment?"

"I remember you being gone," I said. "And then coming back different. No one ever told me where you went or why."

"I did eventually tell Edward and Evelyn," Mom said. "I assumed you'd figured it out on your own."

I had but that wasn't the point. The real question had never been where she had gone but why.

"Was it because of me?" I asked.

"Was what because of you?"

"I dunno—treatment? I was the one that called Michael to come to get us and you said I 'didn't know what I'd done."

"I don't remember that." Mom's eyes went blank for a moment as she searched her memory and came up empty.

"You kept saying it: 'You don't know what you've done. You don't know what you've done,'" I persisted but her expression stayed blank. I couldn't tell if she was obfuscating. Mom wasn't a liar but she'd been known to bend the truth to her liking, and she wasn't above outright stonewalling if she didn't want to share something.

"Sorry. Nothing," Mom shook herself to shrug off the effort, and changed the subject. "Have you eaten?" she asked. She went to the counter and busied herself by pouring coffee into the cup on Dearie's breakfast tray.

"I'm fine," I muttered, annoyed but my stomach piped up to contradict me.

"There's plenty of food: bread and honey. Help yourself." Mom picked up the breakfast tray and headed for the door. "I'll let Dearie know you're here."

I stowed the photographs back in my wallet then got to my feet to survey the counter where everything was still laid out. A discarded slice of toast lay beside the toaster oven, blackened around the edges. I dropped it onto a plate and drizzled it with honey from a jar on the counter from Dearie's hives.

"That's the last of the honey, I'm afraid." Dearie's voice floated to me from the doorway to the back staircase. I turned to see her standing behind me wearing a quilted bathrobe over a full-length nightgown. Her hair was wild around her head and she looked frail and old for the first time but she was still wearing her pearls, so all was right with the world.

"Sorry! I didn't mean—" I dropped the spoon back into the jar with a clatter.

"Oh! No, no!" Dearie looked alarmed. "Please, help yourself—you're more than welcome to it. I only meant we're not going to harvest the hives this year since the queen is in decline. They will need the stores to survive the winter." She coughed delicately and licked the corners of her lips. "Excuse me," she said. "This...medication makes my mouth dry."

"You should sit." I ushered her toward the kitchen table and pulled out a chair for her.

"Thank you, I can take it from here." Dearie rested a hand on my arm as she sank into the chair. It seemed to take more effort than it used to. Mom returned to the kitchen with the breakfast tray still in her hands. The questioning look on her face resolved into understanding when she saw Dearie at the table. She brought the tray over to Dearie and began to set breakfast dishes on the table in front of her, piece by piece.

"The pharmacy will be open by now," she said. "I should go pick up your prescriptions while it's early. Will you be alright here without me?" Her tone was neutral but I could hear the real question underneath: *Will you be alright here with Damen?* I flinched at the sting of it. Dearie reached out and patted my hand reassuringly

"Yes, of course. I'll have Damen here for company. I shan't be lonely." She smiled up at me and meant it.

"Very well." If Mom had an opinion about this, and she probably did, she kept it to herself. She set a small dish full of multicolored tablets on the table beside Dearie's elbow and caught me eyeing them. "Don't get any ideas," she said. "They're *vitamins.*"

Dearie threw her head back and laughed. "Yes, alas, I am not on the so-called 'Good Stuff,' yet," she said. She put one of the tablets between her lips and chased it with a sip of milk from her glass then grimaced. "Oh my, that has turned."

"Oh. I'm sorry." Mom collected the glass and gave the milk a perfunctory sniff. She wrinkled her nose at the smell and moved toward the sink to pour it out but Dearie stopped her.

"No, no! Save it, please—" she insisted. "It's good for the roses."

Leave it to Dearie to find a use for spoiled milk.

"Just pour it at the roots on your way out. Damen can get me some water—" She turned her attention to me as quickly as she said it: "*Would* you get me some water, please? From the tap is fine."

"Sure." I went to the sink where a fresh glass stood in the drainboard and filled it from the faucet. Mom shouldered up beside me to pour the bad milk back into the jug.

"Make sure she eats something," she murmured to me conspiratorially. "Some of that medication shouldn't be taken on an empty stomach."

"Okay."

Mom gathered her keys and purse off the counter. She let herself out the back door with the jug of sour milk in her hand, leaving Dearie and me alone.

"You should eat," I said, returning to the table. Dearie looked down at the toast on her plate and sighed.

"I have so little appetite anymore," she said warming her hands around the coffee mug. She took a single tentative sip of coffee as if hoping it would be enough to placate me.

I gave her a Look. "C'mon, Mom says you shouldn't take your *vitamins* on an empty stomach." I nudged the dish of tablets toward her pointedly. Dearie pursed her lips in a smile.

"Ahh, I see you and your mother have joined forces against me."

"I ain't no dummy. I know better than to defy her," I said. "C'mon, have a bite."

Dearie laughed and took a small bite of her toast for my benefit and chewed it laboriously. I took a bite of my toast in solidarity. The burned edge crumbled bitterly against my tongue.

"Will you be joining us for Thanksgiving?" Dearie asked.

"Yeahhhhh, no," I said. "I don't think that's a good idea." I hadn't been home for a family holiday in more than a decade. My command performances were typically reserved for special occasions: weddings, funerals, graduations, all of which inevitably ended in a fight.

"Will you at least try?" Dearie put her hand on mine. "For me? It will be my last..."

"Please don't talk like that—" I begged. The words *my last* stabbed me in the guts and made me want to vomit.

Dearie looked sympathetic. "I'm sorry," she said. "I find I'm becoming rather more direct these days. Time is precious; I don't have the luxury of being circumspect anymore if I want to enter Elysium with a clear conscience."

"Dearie, please—" I begged. I could hear my voice shaking. I couldn't bear to think about death right then. I thought again of the man at the river leaving his cell phone on the tidy heap of his clothes, convinced no one would answer his call. A fist tightened in my throat and I swallowed hard. Dearie seemed to sense my distress.

"What's troubling you, Blue?" she asked. "Tell me what's on your mind."

"It's nothing. It's not important."

Dearie reached out a hand to smooth the hair at the nape of my neck. "Tell me anyway. Get it off your chest. I'm listening."

What you say to me, you're sayin' to God.

I had a sudden, absurd memory of Father Jesse listening to confessions through a glory hole in a strip club and I laughed in spite of myself. It came out teary and hysterical.

"Sorry," I said, feeling my tongue free up at last. "I saw something— it might've been someone...in trouble," *Why couldn't I say suicide? Maybe it wasn't.* "And I didn't do anything—I know I should've called for help but I just... just watched," I said. "Now, I can't stop thinking about it."

The feelings rose inside me like a tide and I struggled for breath, staring up at the angel window to keep my eyes from streaming—not in front of Dearie.

"Oh, Blue," Dearie took my hands in hers. "You have such a good heart."

Did I? It was news to me.

"I'm going to hell."

"Come now," she soothed. "We stumble, we fall—we struggle—these aren't sins. 'Heaven knows we need never be ashamed of our tears for they fall upon the blinding dust of the Earth, overlaying our hard hearts.'" Leave it to Dearie to quote Dickens over breakfast. "Whatever you've done, I forgive you," she said.

"It's what I didn't do."

"I forgive you for that too," she said as if it was that simple. Maybe it was. I took another bite of my burned toast, this time tasting the honey over the bitterness.

"Better?" Dearie asked.

"Better," I said, then nodded to her plate. "Have some. Try it, you'll like it."

Dearie poked the toast on her plate but didn't pick it up. "You still haven't answered me about Thanksgiving."

"And you still haven't eaten anything," I said. "If I say I'll come to Thanksgiving, will you eat your toast?"

"Not just say it, Blue, promise me," she said. "And I promise I will eat as much of this toast as I am able." It was a game, and not a subtle one. We both knew she was going to win.

"All of it," I insisted. "And all your vitamins."

"Very well, then. All of it," Dearie agreed. "And Thanksgiving?"

"I'll be there," I said. "I promise."

16

TEMPER TANTRUM

"So, THE good news is you're trending again," Phoenix cued up a video on her laptop and turned the screen to face me before pressing play. At first, the video was little more than colored lights and blurry shapes but it quickly resolved into the hazy darkness of Club Lure. The camera wobbled and shook as it pressed forward then found its focus on me like it had acquired target-lock.

"Damen! Damen Warner! I'm a huge fan!"

My on-screen doppelganger turned its head towards the camera at the sound of the voice calling his name and promptly rebounded off of Oakley, who had stepped in the door.

"What is this, Hot Topic night?" Oakley shoved me away and, for a moment, my on-screen self disappeared from view as it was swallowed up by the thicket of t-shirts glowing radioactively in the club's blacklight. The image blurred and shook, then snapped back into focus as a burst of brilliant flashes illuminated the growing scuffle.

"Dude! Can I get a picture!? Can I get a picture?!"

"Get your camera outta my face, faggot."

Oakley shoved the camera back into the crowd of the Legion now howling with wrath. The footage froze for a moment as the camera found Tombstone's pale face in the crowd and a bright yellow arrow called him out by name, in case anyone failed to recognize him. It resumed filming in time to capture Gorey diving into the crowd with his fists flailing, before once again sweeping through the darkness to find me. It found me with one foot out the door as I was beating my retreat with Bethany and her three friends in tow.

The final image was of me giving Oakley the finger with both hands.

Phoenix halted the playback, leaving my grinning face frozen on the screen. "Ugh. I hate you," she groaned. "You're too damn good at this."

"Uh, thanks?" I hazarded. "And is there bad news?"

"The bad news is it's already yesterday's news. Last *week's* news. These things don't have much of a shelf life. Someone caught a video of this yahoo jumping off the State Street Bridge and that was that. If it bleeds it leads." She scrolled to the top of the page and the video from the club disappeared and was replaced by a high-angle view on the Chicago River. The camera was punched in close on a figure standing in the middle of the bridge with his head bowed. I didn't need to watch it to know how it ended.

"Turn that shit off," I told her, feeling guilt surge in my guts. I reached into my pocket for my one and only comfort object: my pocket watch. My fingers closed around its leather case, and I breathed a sigh of relief as I felt the comfortable weight of it settle into my palm.

There weren't many things in my life that I held as sacred but the pocket watch was one of them. It was an heirloom: an antique timepiece in a silver case with the emblem of the Chicago Columbian Exposition engraved on the lid. Michael had bestowed it on me sometime around my twelfth birthday—back before things went bad between us. It had been his before it had been mine. It had belonged to Grandfather Enoch before that, and to his father before that. It had passed hand to hand in an unbroken chain for more than a hundred years. I carried it with me wherever I went. It was the first thing I reached for when I woke up and the last thing I touched before falling asleep. It was the one thing I couldn't live without.

I flipped the cover open to check the time. The hands stood frozen at ten and two like a sixteen-year-old taking their drivers' test, and I frowned. It was neither ten nor two. AM nor PM.

The watch had stopped.

It had never stopped before. *Had I wound it?* I couldn't remember for sure but I thought I had: winding the watch was as much a part of my morning ritual as the daily shit n' shave. I tilted the crystal watch face towards the light and nudged the winding pin with a fingertip, testing the tension, then held it up to my ear like I was listening for a heartbeat. If it was ticking, I couldn't tell—I couldn't hear anything over the sound of Phoenix's strategizing.

"We got a *little* runway left," she was saying. "That ruckus you kicked up at the club turned into a brawl and the cops got called. A bunch of people got arrested. Disorderly conduct. Disturbing the peace. Apparently, there's a convent next door?" She snorted a laugh through her nose, "I couldn't make this shit up if I tried. Anyway, the regular news ran a segment on it, so we can still get some mileage out of it. Brawls are good for a quick hit but if you want to stay at the top you're gonna need to step up your game. Escalate. Take it up a notch—are you even listening to me?" Phoenix asked at last, annoyed.

"Uh-huh. Escalation. Got it," I said, parroting back her words to her although in truth I hadn't heard much of them. She rolled her eyes and folded the laptop shut with a snap.

"Okay, fine. Well, I guess I'll leave you to it then," she said sourly, grabbing her satchel off the end of the couch and shoving the laptop inside. "If you want to stay on the front page of the internet, get me something I can work with."

"Kay."

I looked up long enough to watch her leave, feeling a whisper of satisfaction at the fact I'd been able to piss her off then turned my attention back to the watch.

Tictictictictic...

The second hand was moving again, tripping around the face in tireless laps like a carousel horse. *Had I imagined it?* For a second, I wasn't sure but it still wasn't ten and it still wasn't two. Whatever internal mechanism it was that had stopped had somehow managed to right itself. I didn't know why. I didn't know how.

I wasn't sure I wanted to.

"Fuck my life." I shook my head and pressed the watch back into its leather jewelry case and tucked it back into my pocket and checked my phone for the actual time. A notification pinged reminding me that it was Lily White's weekend with the Girl Child and I was due to meet Melody for moral support. And I was late.

Shit.

✳   ✳   ✳   ✳

"This is where you live?" Lily White's lip curled in disdain as he took in the crumbling façade of Melody's apartment building. It was a far cry from his cozy abode in Gentryview Acres. The street consisted of a stretch of rundown houses made of crumbling brick and faded vinyl siding interspersed with crude blocks of low-income project housing. Melody's building was a four-story brick walk-up that occupied the last parcel of blighted land before the street dead-ended in a chain-link fence overlooking a freight corridor.

Home, sweet home.

"Don't be fooled," I told him. "It's not just ugly, it's also dangerous." I nodded toward a streetlamp where a flashing blue light announced the presence of a police camera. As far as I could tell, it was just there for decoration: I'd never seen a single cop car turn down the street.

"I wasn't talking to you, Rockstar," Lily White snapped but his eyes slipped past my shoulder to the front steps of the building. I didn't need to turn my head to know he was sizing up the cluster of round-shouldered homies gathered there who, I now knew, were *not* just there for decoration. I was on nodding terms with most of them by now. I'd come around often enough that they'd stopped puffing themselves up every time I approached and instead had started calling me *'Azul',* like a pet gringo. In return, I called them *'Jefe'*, one and all, pronouncing it 'Jeffee' to their general amusement.

"You don't get to judge where I live," Melody snarled at him. "Some of us don't got rich parents to buy us a house."

Lily White looked like he wanted to protest but instead, he said: "Fine. Whatever. Is Victoria ready?"

"She's getting her things."

"Can I come in?"

"No."

From the steps, the Jeffees had been watching the unfolding drama like it was a telenovela and now gave a gleeful chorus of "oohs" at Lily White's expense. He glared at them but then softened his voice into a croon.

"C'mon, baby, can't we talk? Like we used to? Please? I'm sorry. I miss you. I hate seeing you like this."

"Well, I don't miss you," Melody hissed. "We are *over*. I don't wanna talk to you. I don't care what you gotta say. An' you got no right to judge me after what you did."

"And I said I was sorry! I'm trying to make it right! I'm paying my support, aren't I? I want to be part of our daughter's life—"

"—that doesn't mean you get to be a part of mine," Melody cut him off. I got the feeling that the gate between them was the only thing keeping her from taking a swing at him. Lily White looked like he wanted to say more but then his eyes moved past Melody and his expression softened into a smile.

"Hey, Punkin!" he beamed, waving both hands.

"Dada!" The Girl Child labored her way down the walkway dragging her overnight bag behind her like an anchor.

Melody seized upon the excuse to distance herself from Lily White and went to help her but Girl Child pushed her away. "No! I can do it *myself!*" she insisted.

"Look at you, big girl!" Lily White enthused. "Strong like your Mama!"

Melody glared at him but said nothing. Lily White crouched down to Girl Child's level and held up a hand for a high-five. "Good job, Punkin. Hey! What d'you think about maybe coming by my place for Halloween?"

The Girl Child squealed in delight and turned to Melody with her eyes sparkling with hope. "Can I, Mama—"

"No."

The Jeffees made a chorus of sympathetic sounds. Melody put up a hand to silence them.

"Not for the whole night, just a couple hours to go Trick-or-Treating..." Lily White persisted.

"No."

"Pleeeeeease?" Girl Child begged. "I wanna go TrickTreating, pleeeeeease?"

Melody gave Lily White a glare that would have reduced a lesser man to cinders. *"No,"* she said, somehow managing to stretch the word into three dimensions. "I gotta give you your court-ordered weekends. I don't gotta give you NUH-THING else."

The Girl Child dissolved into tears and let out an angry shriek signaling the start of a temper tantrum. This was a new trick. Melody's tolerance for bad behavior was vanishingly small and the Girl Child knew it. But now that she had Lily White on her side, she was prepared to pull out all the stops.

"I wanna go tricktreating!" she screamed. *"I wanna go tricktreating!"*

"I can take her up by my folks—it's a safe neighborhood—c'mon, just for one evening? Just be cool..." Lily White soldiered on over the Girl Child's wails, determined he wasn't going to take 'no' for an answer. I got the feeling he'd failed to take 'no' for an answer more than once in his life. "I mean, it's not like you're not gonna take her 'round here."

"Who says I'm not?"

Lily White gave a jerk of astonishment and looked around the street as if that alone should have been enough to make his point for him. *"Here?!* It's way too dangerous! She shouldn't even be living here! And with you working all hours, doing who knows what, and with who knows who at your place all the time..." he cast a glance at me and then to the Jeffees, lumping us together in the category of 'who knows who' before soldiering on: "My neighborhood's way safer. The schools are better—there're private schools even. She's got her own room at my place..." He wasn't talking about trick-or-treating anymore. I didn't like where it was heading, and Melody didn't either.

"So, what're you saying?" Melody asked, crossing her arms over her stomach as if to prevent herself from flying apart. "Vico, *be quiet!"* she snapped.

The Girl Child stopped screaming and slumped down on the sidewalk, crying like the world was about to end.

"I'm saying I want more custody. Joint. Maybe even full. My lawyer thinks I got a case," Lily White said.

"You think you're gonna take my baby from me?!" Melody

screamed. I caught her in a bear hug and picked her up off the ground as Lily White dodged back, laughing nervously at the fury he'd unleashed. The Girl Child stopped crying, looking frightened. The Jeffees surged down off the steps in a swarm and surrounded Lily White in a tight knot in the unmistakable shape of an ass-kicking.

"Be cool, Jeffee!" I shouted to them. "Be cool! There's a kid—*uno chica!*"

The Jeffees looked at the Girl Child, then at me, then resumed staring at Lily White with unvarnished hostility but didn't touch him.

"It's okay," I murmured into Melody's ear, holding her tight. "He's just running his mouth. He's got nothing, don't worry— don't give him anything to use against you. Be cool," I put an arm around her waist and pulled her against my chest where she wilted slightly as she lost steam. "It'll be okay. Judge won't let anything happen to the Girl Child. *I* won't let anything happen to Girl Child. We'll handle this," Melody's clenched shoulders unraveled slightly in my arms.

"He wants to take my baby..." Melody protested. Her anger was tipping toward despair and I could hear the tears in her voice. "He can't take her away from me—"

"Shhh, I know."

"He doesn't get to have her—not after..."

"We'll take *care* of it," I promised. "We'll get through this. Together. I'm here for you,"

"'*Ey, 'Monita, todo bien?*" one of the Jeffees asked.

Melody scrubbed at her face with a hand and nodded. "'*stoybien,*" she mumbled, barely audible. The Jeffee looked to me for confirmation and I nodded.

The Jeffees backed away from Lily White and resumed
their place on the steps without taking their eyes off of him.
Lily White swallowed hard as he watched them disperse
but stood his ground.

"C'mon, Punkin, time to go." Lily White told gestured the
Girl Child to her feet and handed her a piece of Kleenex
through the gate. Melody shrugged off my arms and
wrapped the Girl Child in a frantic hug, clinging to her as
if she thought she'd never see her again.

"I'm sorry, Mama," Girl Child sobbed into her shoulder.
"I love you—I'm sorry."

"'S okay, Vico," Melody told her. "I love you too. You be
good, okay? I love you—"

The Girl Child nodded then wriggled out of Melody's
arms to open the gate and take Lily White's hand. Melody
choked on a sob and fled back into the building, unable to
watch as Lily White climbed into the Corvette and drove
away, taking the Girl Child with him.

17

HALLOWEEN

I WAS NO longer welcome at Club Lure.

The brawl between the Legion and Oakley's douche-brigade might have made for top-notch clickbait but it had also given the nuns next door the exact excuse they'd been looking for to file a lawsuit. Father Jesse did his best to intercede but everybody knew it was a losing battle.

It wasn't really my fault: the Sisters of Agony had been trying to shut down the club long before I arrived in town. If it hadn't been my ruckus, it would have been someone else's ruckus: really, it had always been a matter of time. I hadn't thrown a single punch and I'd been gone long before the cops arrived but that didn't matter to Melody who still held me Personally Responsible. She was salty about it for several days until she realized that the fact I wasn't allowed to go to the club meant I could watch the Girl Child in the evenings instead of having to pay a babysitter while she worked extra shifts to rake in as much cash as she could before the club shut down.

"Boo!" the Girl Child shouted when she opened the door on Halloween. Her face was painted into a wide, grinning skull. "Boo! Damen! I scared you!"

"Ahhh! A monster!" I exclaimed, scooping her up in my arms and turning her upside down. "This is the Girl Child's room. Monsters aren't allowed in here." I tickled her until she squealed and then bounced her onto her bed.

"It's me!" the Girl Child protested. "It's me! Vico!"

"Don't be silly, Vico isn't a skeleton," I insisted. "You're a monster. Get back under that bed where you belong," I chased her around the room until she fled shrieking into the kitchen to hide behind Melody.

"Vico, don't *yell*," Melody snapped. She too had painted her face to look like a skeleton and had piled her hair on top of her head and twined it with ribbons and flowers like a proper Mexican death-goddess but she didn't look like she was planning on having any fun. Beneath the painted smile, the lines of her face were tight and angry as she tried to smooth on her lipstick with the Girl Child tugging on her arm.

"Mama, I wanna go tricktreating!"

"No."

"But Mamaaaaa," the Girl Child whined "it's Halloweeeeeeeeen! I wanna go tricktreating!"

"I said, *no*," Melody told her with the finality of a single mother.

"Dada would've let me."

"Well, you're not with your dada, you're with me," Melody snapped, "and I gotta go to work." She hauled the roller bag across the floor to the back door and heaved the wooden bolt out of its brackets.

"I wanna go tricktreating!" the Girl Child screamed.

"You're mean! I hate you! I wanna go live with Dada!"

Melody froze and turned around slowly, like a leopard about to pounce. The Girl Child realized she'd pushed too far and fell quiet.

"You wanna go live with your dada?" she growled. "Fine. Go live with your dada. You'll never see me ever again and I'll be here all by myself, crying every night until I die."

The Girl Child's eyes got wide.

"No more hugs. No more kisses," Melody continued. "I'll be dead. And it'll be your fault because you wanted to go live with Dada instead of me."

"Jesus, Melody—" I said but Melody held up her hand to silence me.

The Girl Child's face crumpled into tears and her whole body trembled as the first hitching sobs bubbled up.

"Don't die, Mama!" she begged. "I'm sorry—"

Melody was not going to give in so easily. "No, no," she said. "You don't want me; you want your fucking dada. Go live with your dada."

"I don't wanna live with Dada, I promise! Please!"

This was going to cost her a fortune in therapy someday.

"You gonna listen to me?" Melody asked her. "You wanna stay here, you gotta listen to me. You gonna behave?"

"Yes, Mama!"

"You wanna go live with your dada?"

"No, Mama."

"You promise me?"

"I promise."

"I forgive you, then," Melody said. "Come give me a kiss. I'm going to work," She held out her arms and the Girl

Child ran to her and buried her face against Melody's coat, still sobbing. Melody wrapped her in her arms and kissed the top of her head, holding onto her until a car horn honked somewhere in the alley below.

"That's my ride," she said, straightening up and once again grabbing her roller bag. She brushed a distracted kiss across my lips and then headed toward the door. I scooped the Girl Child up in my arms and followed her out onto the fire escape.

"Hey, I can take her," I said.

"Take her where?"

"You know, *ickortray-eatingtray.*"

"In this neighborhood?" Melody's disdain was palpable.

"I'll take her over to the school—they're doing a funfair on the playground," I'd seen the flyer for it in the heap of paperwork from the Girl Child's backpack one day while looking for her lunchbox. "C'mon—you'll be able to work, she'll get some Halloween fun, and her dad won't have anything on you."

Melody weighed this for a moment then gave a curt nod. "Fine, whatever," she said. "Home by eight, and bring me something chocolate."

I wrapped an arm around her waist and pulled her close to bite her ear. "With or without nuts?" I asked and felt her smile against my cheek.

"Stay out of trouble," she said, and then she walked out.

✱　✱　✱　✱

The schoolyard was a festival of Halloween fun. A group of parents had pulled their cars onto the crumbling asphalt of the basketball courts and parked in a wide circle with their trunks all pointed towards center court: 'trunk-or-treating' they called it. Kids in costumes and moms with strollers ambled from car to car in a steady clockwise whorl collecting candy from each vehicle. Armed with a pumpkin-shaped bucket in one hand and a plastic flashlight in the other, the Girl Child darted gleefully from car to car, procuring a hoard of sugary loot.

"Can I have some?" she wanted to know, holding out a fist full of fun-sized candies toward me.

"Let's get some real food first, kiddo," I told her, aware she hadn't eaten anything all evening, and if I let her eat candy for dinner, I'd be scraping her off the ceiling when I got her back to the apartment. At one end of the circle, a food truck was doing a lively business selling sausages and tacos, and other carnival food on a stick. "How 'bout a taco?" I asked her. "You want a taco? Taco first, then candy."

"Okay," she said as her attention settled on a Day of the Dead procession that was making a circuit of the playground and scattering yellow flower petals in its wake.

"Stay here," I told her. "I'll be right back."

I made my way toward the taco truck keeping one eye on the Girl Child even from this loose distance. A trio of guitarists took up a position in the middle of the circle and threw down a hat before launching into a serenade in Spanish to the delight of the crowd.

"'Ey, what I getchu?" The food truck owner asked through the food truck window. He was dressed like a pirate, complete with an eye patch that looked like it might be real.

"Uhh, sorry—" I glanced at the painted menu board. "A taco and a Chicago dog. Two drinks."

"Chu wan' fries?"

"Sure."

The pirate droned along with the song as he worked, swaying from foot to foot and missing most of the words until it came to the chorus, which he sang with gusto:

Malagueeeennnuuhhhhna salerosa...

He slapped a hotdog into a paper wrapper with a theatrical flourish and dumped a fist full of fries on top before wrapping it all up together.

"Twenny dollar," he pronounced.

Highway robbery.

I dug into my wallet for cash as one of the singers hit a high note and strung it out for an impossibly long time, until the guitars fell silent and the crowd applauded and cheered. Even the pirate stopped what he was doing to clap his hands and whistle through his teeth appreciatively. The singer, at last, stopped for breath and the rest of the band resumed playing to a round of cheers.

My fingers closed on the correct change and I slapped it down on the food truck window as an ear-splitting shriek dragged my attention back to the basketball court. It was the Girl Child who had shrieked—I recognized the sound by now. My eyes went to the place where I'd left her but she wasn't there. Barbed wire coiled around my heart and began to tighten as I scanned the crowd in a panic.

Where the hell was she? There was another shriek—a different shriek, a different kid, scared by a woman dressed as a witch. All the kids were shrieking—another over-sugared kid on a jump-scare holiday. But the Girl Child's scream had been different and my nerves stood on end in alarm.

A movement on the edge of the crowd caught my eye. A teenager in a hoodie had grabbed the handle of Girl Child's candy bucket and was pulling her toward the edge of the car-circle while she bashed his knuckles with her flashlight.

"It's mine!" she screamed in five-year-old rage. "Mine!" She dug in her heels and wailed.

"Girl Child!" I dashed toward her but found myself tangled in a crowd of slow-moving strollers and waist-high hobgoblins like something out of a nightmare.

"Let it go, Girl Child!" I screamed at her, pushing through the crowd. "Let go of the bucket!" But the Girl Child was not prepared to relinquish a single piece of her hard-earned candy. She sat on the pitted pavement and wrapped her arms and legs around the pumpkin bucket in defiance.

"Mine!" she screamed. "Miiiiiiiiiineeee!"

The kid in the hoodie lifted the bucket into the air, Girl Child and all, but no one in the crowd seemed to be giving him a second thought—a teenage asshole stealing candy from a little kid. He was short and slender and dressed in a hooded sweatshirt over a Joker mask: the perfect embodiment of a Halloween trope.

But the Girl Child was putting up a fight—too much of a fight to be worth it for some free candy. There were smaller, meeker kids to steal candy from but the teen in the Joker mask hadn't moved on to any of them. He'd chosen the Girl Child, and he wasn't letting go. I saw him wrap an arm around her chest and pick her up off the ground. He began to carry her toward the gap in the fence, toward the street beyond.

Fuck!

"Let her go!" I screamed at him, still trapped in the crowd. "Put her down! Let her go!" The Joker kid ignored me. He was nearly at the fence when a kid in a blue wig hurtled out of the crowd and charged at him with his head lowered.

"Hey! Pick on someone your own size!" The kid in a blue wig hollered, colliding with the teen at waist-level and knocking him back a step. I shoved aside a woman pushing a stroller the size of a Zamboni and broke free of the crowd in time to see the handle of the bucket break, spilling Girl Child to the ground in a shower of loose candy. The teen staggered to regain his balance and rounded on the blue-haired kid, who kicked him in the shins.

The teen swiped at the blue-haired kid but then saw me bearing down on him. His body language flickered from anger to surprise, to fear, to *oh shit!* and he turned on his heel and beat it down the sidewalk like a raped ape. I chased him for a few steps until I lost sight of his figure against the glaring headlights of a Corvette pulling a U-turn in the middle of the block and roaring away into traffic.

"Yeah! You better run!" the blue-haired kid shouted after him. "An' donchu come back!" He turned around and I found myself staring at a miniature doppelganger of myself: blue wig, OBNXS t-shirt, hands heavy with gaudy plastic rings, arms painted with magic marker tattoos. The t-shirt had my signature on it. Big letters. Big enough his

mother wouldn't be able to miss it. The kid grinned showing a familiar-looking mouthful of oversized teeth.

"Rolly?"

"Damen! You see that?" he asked. "I scared him off!
Like you said! No one messes with Vico or they're messin'
with me."

I gave him a slap on the back, not trusting myself to
speak, and turned my attention to the Girl Child. She was
on her hands and knees, sniffling as she gathered her
spilled candy.

"He broke my pumpkin," she whimpered, holding up
the torn handle.

"You should have let it go!" I snapped, realizing only
after I opened my mouth my voice was shaking.

"It was *my* candy," she protested.

"He didn't care about the candy, Girl Child, he was trying to grab *you!* There's more candy." I sat on the ground,
suddenly shaking all over, and put my head in my hands
trying to hear past the roar in my pulse in my ears.

Girl Child scuffed a sneaker on the ground contritely.
"M'sorry," she mumbled; bucket dangling forgotten from
one hand. I took a deep breath and felt her arms go around
my neck. "M' s-sorry!" she sobbed.

"Hey, it's okay. You're okay." I put an arm around her
and held on for a minute until she stopped crying. "It's not
your fault, you hear me? I'm sorry I hollered at you—I was
scared. I thought he was going to take you away from me."
She nodded against my shoulder and pulled her face away.
Her face paint was smeared into a blurry gray mush—a
melting sugar skull.

"Let's go home, okay?" she said.

"Okay."

I let the Girl Child eat whatever she wanted out of the Halloween bucket on the walk back to the apartment building, then dumped the rest of the candy into a grocery bag and stowed it on top of the refrigerator. I washed the paint off her face and put her to bed, building her a makeshift tent out of a bedsheet and a broom handle to help her feel safe. Then, I retreated to Melody's room and flopped down on the bed to stare at the ceiling, trying to make sense of the attack.

I hadn't gotten a good look at the Joker: probably a teenager, probably a dude. That was all I knew. The mask had covered his whole face and the hoodie had covered everything else. He'd targeted the Girl Child for some reason. My mind kept circling around the thought, kicking its tires and trying to figure out how it worked. There had been other kids on the street—other moms, easier targets—why pick on the kid with the six-foot blue-haired tacklebox? I didn't exactly look like a pushover.

Who would want to snatch the Girl Child?

My mind answered the question almost before I asked it—*Lily White* but I dismissed the thought out of hand. He couldn't possibly be stupid enough to try to kidnap her... could he? He had to know he'd be the first person Melody would point her finger at. Kidnapping the Girl Child wasn't going to do much to help his custody case.

Your neighborhood's dangerous; she shouldn't even be living there.

And then it clicked: he didn't have to kidnap the Girl Child to get full custody; he just had to make it look like Melody couldn't keep her safe.

My neighborhood's way safer. Better schools—private school even...

I could see it now: a handful of cash to a local teenager to nab the Girl Child's candy and try to make it look like an attack. Give her a scare. Make me look like an irresponsible shithead. Make Melody look like a bad mother. Give him a lever to pry apart the family.

The fucking weasel. I couldn't prove any of it but every molecule in my gut screamed Lily Weasel was behind it.

I was going to fucking kill him.

18

WHISKEY AND
GALLOWS HUMOR

KEPT MY suspicions about Lily White to myself over the next few weeks, but the thought was never far from my mind. Work on the album had once again stalled: creating enough chaos to feed the *B@d Beh@v!or* click machine was turning out to be a full-time job, even for me. As our internet notoriety grew, privacy became a thing of the past. I couldn't go anywhere anymore without having a camera shoved in my face, and it was just a matter of time before I lost my shit and punched someone.

I did my best to lay low but after ten days of rattling around the Cursèd Place like the bead in a can of spray paint. I was prepared to seize any excuse to get out of the house, come Baptists or Baphomet, even if that meant getting up at the crack of damn dawn to watch Club Lure shrug itself out of existence.

I sat in the parking lot outside the club watching the last few patrons filter out the club's doors as the sun dragged itself above the horizon. A cluster of dancers gathered on the frosty asphalt of the parking lot to watch Judge switch off the undulating LED displays and lock the doors for the final time. In the blink of an eye, the shimmering neon fantasy transformed into an unremarkable block of commercial architecture—as gray and dull as November.

Evelyn emerged out of the pack and approached the car. I rolled down the window, letting in a frosty blast of November air to hear what she had to say.

"Everybody's going for breakfast," she said. "You coming?"

I glanced over at Melody who was in the process of folding herself into the passenger seat. "We going to breakfast?" I asked.

"We're going," she told me.

"We're going," I told Evelyn.

✳   ✳   ✳   ✳

The entire Club Lure entourage descended on a Pancake House, filling the booths with the boisterous, over-bright laughter of the newly unemployed.

"What are you going to do with yourself now that you only have two jobs?" I asked Evelyn over coffee and eggs.

"I'm down to one job. Faire was just for the summer," she corrected then she sighed. "I really don't know," she admitted. "The club was the only thing keeping me sane."

"The *club* was keeping you sane?"

"Yeah...you wouldn't understand."

"Try me."

"Trust me," she said, with a bitter breath of a laugh. "You don't know what it's like. You get to live this amazing, crazy life doing whatever the hell you want—you spend your days writing music and your nights partying and you don't give a crap about what anybody thinks of you. It's like magic! I don't know how you do it—"

"Whiskey and gallows humor."

"—and meanwhile I do everything right—everything anybody asks of me—college, grad school, honor roll, day job, night job, *weekend* job, and I'm barely scraping by. I'm working away every minute of my life just to pay rent and buy groceries and I never get to *live*. I'm suffocating."

"So, don't do it."

"Don't do what? Eat? Live in a house? I'm not exactly doing this for pin money. I don't want to go to Mom and Dad for money—it's got too many strings attached. They gave us money for the wedding all, like, 'no strings attached' but that's turned into a nightmare, because of course. And the Gardens isn't paying me what I'm worth—I've got a master's degree in Botany for Pete's sake but they don't want botanists, they want horticulturists—"

I snickered. "*Hor*ticulture..."

"Oh, please." Evelyn rolled her eyes. "When I tell people I work at the gardens they're all like 'Oh, so you're right where you want to be' but I'm basically doing data entry. I've been doing data entry for *years* now. They don't even have a real title for what I do—they call me a 'Social Outreach Administrative Associate,' whatever that means. Mostly it means doing all Harold's work—he's got one foot in retirement. He keeps promising it'll lead to something better but it never does." She stopped to catch her breath and massaged her temples with the tips of her fingers as if she could rub the frustration out of her brain. "Every day it feels like my life is getting written for me. I don't know how to break out of it. Having the club was like...it was nice knowing I had a secret that was...dark, and kinda interesting. Sexy. Exciting. It was nice to think I was more than just the nice white girl with rich parents."

"Hey, at least you *got* a job for next," Melody said, elbowing her way into the booth on the tail end of the conversation. Camille squeezed in beside her, giggling around a ring pop she had stuck in her mouth.

"Still haven't found another club?" Evelyn asked.

Melody shook her head. "Vico's gonna be in all-day school soon. Maybe I needa get a daytime job." She grabbed Camille's hand and stuck the candy jewel of her ring pop in her mouth; the band still wrapped around Camille's finger.

"I'm gonna go back into law," Camille said. "I got a lead: some firm downtown. I met one of the partners in the Viagra triangle. Turns out he knew of a position that needed filling," She licked the candy jewel on the ring suggestively and winked before holding it out to me. I kissed the ring, tasting cherry candy and the strong skunky sharpness of cannabis underneath.

"Ohmigod..." Evelyn pinched her eyes shut and sighed as Camille laughed again.

"Who do I gotta fuck to get a nice cushy office job?" Melody demanded. She was joking. I hoped. Camille pulled her close and kissed her on the lips.

"Don't worry, *mamacita,* you'll find yourself a nice sugar daddy."

"I'm sitting *right here,*" I protested.

Melody hugged my chest and snuggled under my arm. "Yeah," she pouted with an apologetic simper. "But you don't perform anymore." She sank her teeth into the flesh of my side and laughed when I jumped.

"I perform just fine and you know it." I wrestled her across my lap with a playful spanking. Camille joined in with enthusiasm and let her hand linger on Melody's ass. She leaned over my lap to murmur something into Melody's ear, burying me beneath a stripper dogpile.

"Should I give you some privacy?" Evelyn asked with a hint of acid in her tone.

"Don't mind me, just living the dream," I said. "In a Pancake House. At five AM. With two ex-strippers. For my next trick, I'll shed my skin and transform into Kid Rock."

Evelyn smiled but it didn't reach her eyes. I remembered what she'd said about her life of suffocating perfection and it made me think of Mom living her sterile, colorless life in a world of hard edges. Suddenly, I understood her pain.

Evelyn sighed wearily. "I should get going."

She counted out the right number of bills to cover her food and slid out of the booth, grimacing as her bare legs peeled off the sticky vinyl. I squeezed out from under Melody and Camille and followed her to the door.

"Hey, don't go—" I reached for her hand but Evelyn didn't stop.

"I gotta get some sleep," she mumbled. There was rain in her voice. "Might as well, right? It's the only thing I get to do on my own time. Sleeping my life away..."

"Hey! Stop picking on my sister," I ordered. I pulled her against my chest in a hug and dug my fingertips into the knots twisting up between her shoulders. Evelyn's breath hitched in a laugh—or maybe a sob—and she settled against me, allowing herself to be held. We stayed like that for a long moment until Evelyn pulled away.

"Thanks," she said, scrubbing at her face self-consciously.

I bent my head to look her in the eye. "Listen," I said. "You ever want to get in touch with your dark side, I'll take you as far down the abyss as you want to go, okay? But don't think you don't have something special up here in the light."

Evelyn snickered but she was smiling again. "You're such a weirdo, Blue."

"You know it,"

She straightened her shoulders and wiped her face one last time. "Thanks, though. It helps. See you around."

"Go get 'em, Tiger." I sent her on her way with a sports-manlike butt-slap and then waited by the door until she was safely in her car before turning back to the restaurant. Judge caught my eye from across the room and gestured me over with two fingers that I didn't dare ignore. He was sitting in a corner booth with Rocco and Father Jesse, carrying on a conversation in a low voice that stopped as soon as I approached.

"I come in peace," I said, holding up my hands.

Father Jesse got to his feet and gave Judge's shoulder a slap. "You two should talk," he said. "I gotta go check in with the girls. Rocco?" He gave a jerk of his head and the two of them cleared out, leaving me to face Judge alone.

"Sit," Judge commanded.

I sat.

"This fan club of yours—"

"Hey, if this is about the club closing, I didn't tell them to start that brawl—" I protested but Judge silenced me with a sharp look. I got the feeling he still would've liked to kick my ass into my throat but the fact he had called me over for a sit-down meant he needed me for something.

"We all knew the club's days were numbered," he said. "Your fanboys moved up the timeline. But now that it *is* closed, I'm looking for a new investment opportunity."

"Okay..." I glanced around, still unsure where this was leading.

"I'm thinking of putting up some pop-up concerts. Underground venues, word-of-mouth promotion."

"Gorilla style."

Judge's eyes narrowed as he tried to determine if I was being a smartass but he nodded. "These fanboys of yours— if you put out a call out to 'em would they come?"

"The Legion? They show up whether we tell them to or not."

"Good."

I felt a pang of longing at the thought of getting back on stage. I missed the rush of standing in front of a crowd hearing thousands of voices calling my name. Nothing else made me feel half as alive. But I still had my doubts.

"You want to get into concert promotion now?" I asked.

"That's right."

"Christ, you really are in the business of losing money, aren't you?" I said before my brain could catch up with me.

"So?" Judge said, neither confirming nor denying the remark. I felt my stomach drop like a stone into a well, listening for it to hit the bottom. I'd always suspected Judge was engaged in the kind of creative bookkeeping that involved a lot of *Money, People,* and *Dirt* but I'd never gotten up the nerve to ask him about it outright. He was funding our album, after all.

"So, you sure as hell picked the right business," I said.

Anyone who knew anything about the music industry knew that concert promotion was a quick way to go broke. The big headliner acts typically had contracts with major media conglomerates whose entire live performance departments constituted a single line-item on a balance sheet hundreds of pages deep. But for anybody who was not a billion-dollar global heavyweight, live performance was a sucking black pit of lost revenue and Murphy's Law. Promoters regularly got hosed by weather, unions, protests, canceled dates, sick performers, lawsuits, and property damage. Ticket prices were arbitrary, and the profits, if any, came from booze and merchandise—all of which were typically marked up to the limits of market tolerance.

If ever there were a way to lose money, then live performance was it.

In Chicago.

In the winter.

"If I do this for you, I want something in return," I said.

Judge leaned back with a creak of the vinyl seat and glared at me. "You mean *besides* getting paid? *Besides* getting your asses back on stage to play whatever the hell you want? *Besides* all that?"

I dug in my heels. "You got another disgraced band with a cult following in your hip pocket for command performances designed to go the right amount of broke?" I demanded. He wouldn't have come to me with this unless he had to, and I was going to leverage it for all it was worth. "I don't know where you're getting your money—and I don't want to know—but if you're going to use us as a front for your little fluff-n-fold operation, I want something in return."

Judge blew a sigh of air out through his nose and settled into an attitude of grudging respect. "Fine. Whaddya want, you fucking ballbreaker?"

"Melody's baby daddy."

Judge jerked in surprise. "What about him?"

"He's gonna try to sue for custody—Melody tell you?" I asked and Judge nodded. "How far you think he'll go to make his case?"

Judge considered the question for a moment. "I think he's got more money than brains and he doesn't like to be told 'no.' Why?"

"There was a thing on Halloween—some teenager tried to snatch the Girl Child. I told Melody he was trying to steal her candy but I think there was more to it than that. He didn't just grab for the candy, he tried to carry her out of the schoolyard. My gut says that baby daddy was behind it—trying to make Melody's neighborhood look dangerous to help his case...?" The longer I went on, the more paranoid it sounded and I faltered. "I can't prove any of this, I just..."

I waited for Judge to call me an idiot and laugh me out of the booth but he seemed to be considering what I'd said seriously.

"If that's all true, what d'you want me to do about it?" he asked at last.

"I don't...I just..." I searched for the right words. "I wanna make sure Girl Child's safe. Listen, I know I was a shit about the...thing with Melody last month. If you still wanna kick my ass, then fine but help me keep this twatwaffle from taking her kid."

Judge seemed to approve of this and gave another curt nod. "Fine," he said. "You help me by getting your minions to come out for some events, and I'll find out what I can about this Halloween kid. We got a deal?" He held out a hand and I shook it.

"Deal," I said. "Let's put on a fucking show."

19

MOVES LIKE JAGGER

"I NEED YOU to watch Vico after school. I got a job, maybe." Melody was wearing only her bra and panties as she sifted through the heap of clothes in search of something she wasn't finding. She pulled on a grayish dress that hugged her curves and came down to her knees.

Mostly.

Halfway.

"Another club?"

"No, a daytime job." She turned this way and that to inspect herself in the mirror. "Does this look like an office dress?"

"Sure. On Cinemax."

Melody smacked me in the chest with the back of her hand. Hard. It hurt. But she let me slide my arms around her waist. I bit her neck behind her ear and grinned at her in the mirror.

"You should wear it," I told her. "I guarantee whoever's interviewing you will be putty in your hands." I slid a hand down the outside of her hip to where the fabric ended and then stroked upward on the inside of her thigh. Melody gave a little sigh of pleasure then snapped back to business.

"I gotta go," she said. "Wish me luck."

"You don't need luck. You got dat ass." I gave her a little spank as she passed me towards the door.

Melody didn't come back for the rest of the day and into the evening. I took that to be a good sign. I fed and watered the Girl Child and was putting her to bed when Melody walked back in the door.

"How did it go?" I asked.

"I got the job," she said, kissing my cheek then whispering in my ear: "You were right about the dress."

"I know," I said.

"Meet me in the bathroom when you're done."

The only room in the apartment that had a door that worked. And locked.

"Yes, ma'am."

We celebrated her victory until we were weak-kneed and breathless, and then collapsed onto her bed, exhausted. Melody fell asleep almost immediately, snoring gently in the darkness beside me. My body ached with weariness and my limbs were heavy with residual warmth from our recent exertions but sleep eluded me. I stared at the ceiling for an hour or two, praying for sleep while my brain ran like a hamster in a wheel—getting nowhere and spinning faster the harder I tried to make it stop. The harder I tried to sleep, the more awake I felt, and after a while, it wasn't just my mind that was racing—my heart was racing too, and there was a sheen of sweat on my skin despite the chill in the room.

I forced myself to take a deep breath but it didn't

help. I was too keyed up. All my senses were dialed up to eleven. Overhead I could see a crack in the popcorn ceiling cutting across the ugly yellow stain of light from the streetlamp below. It was late enough to be early but the neighborhood was never truly quiet, even at this time of the night. The apartment was crowded with the din of sirens and dogs and the grumbling of low-end engines, all muddled together with the sound of a high-pitched squeal coming from somewhere inside the wall. I thought it might have been the plumbing but the sound came and went and hovered maddeningly near the frequency of my tinnitus so I couldn't tell if it was coming from inside my head or outside it.

And then my traitorous mind began to play Maroon 5's 'Moves Like Jagger' on endless repeat. I gave up on trying to sleep and got out of bed.

I'd had episodes like this in the past. I wasn't sure why but every so often I'd find myself surging with bottomless energy, like my brain was plugged directly into the sun. I wouldn't sleep. I'd forget to eat. I'd make a lot of questionable choices. And then I'd wake up a few days later with a hangover from hell and a lot of 'splainin' to do. But that was pretty much par for the course for my life: situation normal, all fucked up.

I paced the four square feet of floor space beside the bed trying to burn off some of the nervous energy that was spinning up inside of me but it didn't help. The more I moved, the more energy I seemed to have.

Melody shifted in her sleep, reaching for the spot I'd left. "'S'matter, baby?" she mumbled into the pillow.

"Can't sleep," I muttered. "Can't sleep. Can't think. Just trying to think—gotta get some blood to my brain." The room was too small. Suffocatingly small. I had to get out. I pulled on my clothes and knelt on the mattress long enough to press a kiss by her ear. "I'm gonna go out for a bit. I'll be back," I whispered but Melody didn't respond, once again submerged in sleep.

Picking up my shoes, I tiptoed through Girl-Child's room and I let myself out the front door, letting it lock behind me.

It was still full dark outside. Low clouds pressed against the tops of the crumbling buildings with a cold, damp wind. I needed to move—needed to walk. Run! Jump! Climb!

Moves like Jagger, got the moves like Jagger, got the moooooooves like Jagger.

I started to run. I had to run. I didn't know where or why. My feet pounded along the broken sidewalk past barking dogs and early morning delivery trucks. A cop car cruised past and caught me in the beam of a searchlight. I gave them the finger but the cops didn't stop. I wasn't the droid they were looking for.

My lungs were on fire after less than a block but I didn't stop. I *couldn't* stop. My mouth was coppery with the taste of blood and I could feel my pulse in my face but all I wanted to do was laugh and cry and howl at the moon. And run until I puked.

I made it as far as the train yards where I was forced to a halt at a crossing. A slow-moving freight train was making lazy passes back and forth, collecting tanker cars from a siding with a horrific shriek of metal-on-metal as its flanges navigated the curve. I leaned on the crossing signal and retched onto the gravel, sobbing for breath.

Moves like Jagger, got the moves like Jagger.

My thoughts were drowned out by the diesel engines grinding past. I let the roar of them wash over me, feeling the sound on every inch of my skin until it swallowed me up. Now that I'd burned off some of my excess energy, my thoughts began to regain some semblance of coherence, and I tried to figure out what to do with myself. I couldn't run forever, even though my brain seemed to think it could, and I shuddered at the thought of returning to Melody's place with the walls closing in.

I pointed my feet in the direction of the Gray Area and began to walk.

The sky was beginning to lighten by the time I arrived but the streets were still empty and quiet. I figured I'd have the place to myself, but no sooner had I elbowed my way inside than I heard a murmur of voices. I ducked out of sight in a shadowed alcove as a pair of round-shouldered dudes in work jackets rumbled past rolling a hand truck full of file boxes between them. They labored along the narrow creaking hallway, muttering off-color jokes to one another in strong Chicago accents as they made their way toward a door I recognized as one that Judge had told me never to open.

Thwump.

"Aw, shit."

A wheel on the hand truck had caught on an uneven floorboard and the load toppled to the floor, the lid of the topmost box cracked open and spilled a sluice of paper across the floor near my feet. I recognized the seal of the

City of Chicago and glimpsed the word "Affidavit" and was suddenly certain I didn't want to know anything else.

"Did it open?"

"Just one."

"Get the rest into storage and we'll come back to clean it one up."

There was a litany of swears as they collected the spilled boxes and rumbled the rest of the way down the hallway. I waited until they turned a corner and retreated before anybody could know I'd been there.

No music today.

With the last of my phone battery, I called Gorey for a ride. The sun was low in the November sky, and when it peeked between the clouds, it threw a ray of warmth down to the wet streets as Gorey pulled a second-hand Honda to the curb in a cloud of questionable emissions and squealing brakes. He looked like he might've still been half asleep.

"Late night?" I asked him.

"Dude, it's *early*," Gorey protested as he scratched an unshaven cheek, cracking his jaw with a yawn. "Where's your car, anyway?"

"Melody's."

"Fuck, dude, how'd you get all the way out here?"

"I ran."

"Jesus. From Melody's?"

"My feet are pretty tore up."

Gorey yawned again. "I need coffee," he managed through an open throat. He pulled the car into an open space in front of a Ukrainian coffee shop. "You want?"

I was ravenously hungry. I nodded.

"Cool," Gorey said. "You're buying. Two sugars. Two creams. None of that soy shit. And a donut."

"Get your own damn donut."

"Get your own damn car."

"Fuck you."

"Fuck you."

I climbed out of the passenger seat. I was too jumpy to sit still much longer anyway. Caffeine probably wasn't going to help but my stomach was clenching with hunger and the smell of pastries was hard to pass up. I returned with two coffees and two dozen donuts to find Gorey sitting on the hood of his car, now blocked in by a bread truck making a delivery.

"How many donuts did you get?"

"I'm hungry. Shut up," I shoved a donut in my mouth with a middle finger raised. Gorey helped himself to a jelly-filled. I climbed onto the car beside him; in the cool fall air, the warmth of the hood felt pleasant.

His gaze suddenly went past me and his face darkened. "That's shit," he growled.

I followed his gaze toward a scrapyard full of junk cars and scrap metal fenced in with dilapidated chain-link. A burly dude with a shaved head was teasing a mottled, white pit bull on a short length of chain, holding a food bowl out of her reach. The pit bull growled and danced, barking pleadingly. She could smell the food but not reach it. She sat. She stood. She turned in circles trying to figure out what magic combination would please her master. The man holding the chain laughed, barking insults at her.

"Stupid bitch. Who's a stupid bitch? Yeah, you are."

A pair of rough-looking guys approached the fence and called out something indecipherable in a tone of familiarity. The man holding the leash let it go and put the food bowl on the ground to go talk to them. The pit bull lunged for it, afraid he would change his mind but the chain was secured to the side of the building and it snapped taught, pulling her up short within inches from the bowl. I felt Gorey tense beside me and caught his arm before he could do anything stupid.

"He can't fucking do that," Gorey growled.

The pit bull owner exchanged a system of hand-slaps with the newcomers that suggested a transfer of goods. The pit bull, unaware, continued to struggle toward the food bowl, tongue lolling, whining pitifully.

"Shut it, bitch!" The owner rounded on her with a shout and the pit bull cowered, flat on her belly, ears low against her head and tail limp on the asphalt. She stared longingly at the food, pleading with her eyes for her master to take pity on her.

The two thugs retreated to a Cadillac on rims, and the yard owner headed back to the building, pit bull forgotten and ignored. Seeing him move, she sprang to her feet and bounded after him, hopeful and begging, only to be caught in the side with a swift kick of a boot. Subdued, the pit bull retreated to her crate to lick her wounds.

Gorey was past me in an instant. "Hey!" he shouted across the lot at the closed door. "Hey, motherfucker—come out here and feed your fucking dog!" He grabbed the chain-link fence and shook it until it rattled. The pit

bull came out at speed, all snarls and angry growls ferocious enough to raise the hairs on the back of my neck, but
Gorey was undeterred.

"Fuck you, you fucking shitdick!" he screamed, almost
inarticulate in his rage. "Get your ass out here before I call
the cops on you!"

The threat of the cops opened doors. The junkyard owner
charged out of his door like a freight train and fronted up
against Gorey on the far side of the fence, red-faced with
indignation.

"The fuck did you say, *chuj?*"

"I said feed your fucking dog, you diseased pig-fucker!"

The lot owner stuck a hand under his coat to his waistband. I scrambled off the hood of the car to pry Gorey off
the fence.

"Yo, get your crazy friend out of here," the lot owner
shouted to me. "Retard gonna get himself killed!" He made
a feint with the hand under his coat: enough to show the
butt end of a semi-automatic pistol tucked in his waistband,
aimed, unwisely, at his family jewels.

I pulled Gorey off the fence and flung him behind me,
pressing myself forward so I could stare the lot owner
down through the grid of wire. All the unburned energy
of the night before flowed through me like white-hot light.

"Listen to me, you shithead," I said in a surprisingly steady
voice. "You're not gonna fucking shoot me and you're not
gonna shoot my friend. You're gonna walk away from this
fence and you're gonna feed your goddamn dog, or I'm
gonna call down such a shock-and-awe show of force there
won't be enough of you left in the smoking crater to send

to your mother in a Ziploc snack baggie." The more I ran my mouth, the crazier I sounded. I was grinning—why was I grinning? All my teeth were showing. I started to laugh. It was only slightly hysterical.

"Just who the fuck do you think you are?"

"You don't wanna find out."

The lot owner sized me up for a moment longer through narrowed eyes as uncertainty bled the edges off his anger. He glanced at Gorey over my shoulder and flinched. Following his gaze, I realized Gorey was filming the whole exchange on his cell phone.

"Smile, bitch," he said.

The lot owner glared back at me, fuming. With extreme reluctance, he took his hand out from beneath his coat and backed away until he was even with the pit bull. Catching her by the collar he flexed his thumb over the clasp on the chain and unhooked it from the collar.

"Get 'em."

The pit bull launched herself at me, ferocious and snarling, and smacked into the wire with the full force of her weight but she couldn't reach me through the mesh. I stood my ground, staring down the lot owner trying to pretend my balls were not performing a tactical retreat to somewhere behind my navel.

The junkyard owner threw up his hands and stalked back to the building, giving us the finger all the way. At the sound of the slamming door, the pit bull faltered. She gave a questioning bark toward the building, then trotted cautiously to her bowl and wolfed down the food before he could change his mind. I sagged against the fence, suddenly weak. I wasn't one-hundred percent certain I hadn't shit myself.

"Dude!" Gorey's eyes were alight. "That was fucking *money!* Judge wants clicks? We'll get him fucking clicks. We're gonna be so fucking rich."

20

THANKSGIVING

THE BIG House was tastefully decorated for fall with gourds and pumpkins. Every window was brightly lit. I rang the bell, staring into the button eyes of a pair of decoratively quaint ragdoll pilgrims dangling in the center of a wreath of mums. The thought of spending the evening with the whole fam-damnly hung over my head like the autumn gloom. And I was going to have to do it alone. Melody and the Girl Child were celebrating the true American holiday, Black Friday, by staking out the doorbuster bargains for as much loot as they could carry.

"Damen!" Raffi opened the door wide and greeted me with outspread arms. Turkey scented air wafted out around him in a warm puff. He had swapped out his aloha shirt for a tarpaulin of a bowling shirt in brown and yellow.

I held up a hand. "How."

"Very funny." He took a step back to let me inside and accepted a one-armed hug, slapping me on the back hard enough to knock the wind out of me.

"Oh! You made it!" Dearie appeared in the entryway, looking frailer than ever. She was wrapped in a cable knit fisherman's sweater and a festive scarf to hide how thin her neck was. I could feel her bones when I hugged her and my stomach knotted but I kept my mouth shut.

She stood back to look at me, a sad smile on her lips. She'd put on lipstick and pearls but her time was running out and she knew it. She ran her hands over the front of my shirt, smoothing it out.

"Don't you look nice," she said, and she meant it. I was wearing a shirt with buttons and jeans with no holes in them. Black on black. I looked like I was going to a funeral. I felt like I was going to a funeral. Thanksgiving at the Big House was a business function as much as it was a family gathering. The front rooms of the house had been transformed into a kind of open house for Metron uppity-ups in button-down shirts and cashmere sweaters. Somebody, Mom, probably, had hired a caterer and a crew of waiters in black uniforms with starched white collars. The one guarding the liquor looked particularly humorless.

Dearie looped her spidery hands through the crook of my elbow and guided me into the house. "We shan't be very formal tonight," she said. Even her voice was weaker now. I had to stoop to hear her over the hubbub of small talk. "Dinner will be buffet style—please help yourself to anything you like." She gestured to the dining room, where tables groaned beneath platters of food. I turned to follow her gesture and bumped into a grandiose fall floral arrangement made of dried seedpods and artful twigs.

"Sorry—"

I was apologizing to a floral arrangement.

The cascading monstrosity of dead flora tottered but I managed to catch the vase and steady it, showering myself in confetti of bittersweet berries in the process. Some kind of thistle made out of murder scraped my cheek, drawing blood.

"Ow—Christ..." I muttered, touching the scrape. "Sorry, Dearie." I'd been in the house for all of five minutes and I'd already picked a fight with a flower arrangement. It was going to be a long night.

Dearie laughed gently and brushed the berries out of my hair. She held the dried-up husks cupped in the palm of her hand until a waiter offered her a trash can.

"Oh, Blue, I'm so thankful you're here." Her smile was genuine and I warmed myself beside her pleasure.

Dearie let me escort her through the house and into the living room, making polite nods towards the people she recognized. She refused to use a cane so moving around the house now involved a constant, ritual touching of objects as if trying to memorize the feel of them before she was gone. When she ran out of furniture to hold onto, she took my arm and we both pretended that I wasn't holding her up. Her hands were cold now.

She led me into the front room where Mom and Michael were bent over a chessboard. Mom had captured most of the pieces but Michael seemed to be winning. The piano was occupied by a Korean woman skillfully playing a deconstructed modern piece with all the emotion of a dial tone. Another hired hand. She might as well have been a robot. I escorted Dearie to her wingback chair and fetched a knitted afghan for her lap without her asking.

"Damen."

I straightened to find Michael standing over me, leaning on his cane. He held out his free hand toward me. "Thank you for coming," he said.

"Yeah, well…" I mumbled. I could feel Dearie's eyes on me and I struggled to think of something to say that wouldn't cause a fight. "Happy Thanksgiving," I managed, glancing around the room so I didn't have to look him in the eye. A small knot of Muckedy-Mucks had formed, preparing to petition for Dearie's favor. One of them set a glass on the piano: scotch on the rocks. The glass was beaded with moisture from the chill, leaving a wet ring around the base of the glass. The pianist fixed him with a glare. Suddenly I liked her a lot more.

"Hey, asshole—it's a piano, not a bar," I snapped at him.

The Muckedy-Muck sized me up contemptuously. "I'm sorry, *who* are you?" he asked in a tone that made it clear he didn't care.

I didn't answer him. Instead, I picked up the glass and downed the contents in a gulp without breaking eye contact. A single malt. Expensive. The flavor ruined, thanks to the ice. I was about to spit the ice cubes in his face when Michael caught my arm.

"Don't. Start," he said in an undertone that reached only my ears. "Dearie isn't strong. We're all gathered here for her. Because it's what she asked of us."

I looked to Mom and found her watching me sharply from across the room. I realized she wasn't wearing her wedding ring anymore. Neither of them was. Mom was playing nice with Michael tonight too, for Dearie's sake, and if she could do it, then so could I. I took a deep breath and spat the ice cubes back into the glass.

"I'm not here to make trouble," I said.

"Good." Michael gave a curt nod and plucked the glass from my hand, depositing it on a nearby bussing tray. "Keep your head on straight. Your mother has told the bartenders not to serve you tonight."

I opened my mouth to protest but was interrupted by a general hallooing from the direction of the front door as Evelyn shuffled inside. There was a general commotion of polite cheek kisses and exclamations of greeting. Seizing the distraction, I skulked out of the room to check out the food, glad for any excuse to get out from under Michael's uncompromising gaze.

The dining room was lined with tables, all of them heaped with artful platters of cheese and crackers and fruit and meat. Clean, polite people drifted around the tables, picking at the glistening flesh of various dismembered animal carcasses with silver forks and decorative wooden toothpicks.

"Not sure there's *quite* enough food here." A furry Greek fellow sidled up beside me, laden with dishes covered in plastic wrap: sweet potatoes, ambrosia salad, and what appeared to be half of a spiral cut ham. He grinned at me and leaned in conspiratorially. "Good thing I brought my own." He nodded towards a decorative centerpiece made of wax fruits and I lifted it off the table to make room for his offerings.

"Thanks." He unburdened himself of the dishes then stuck out a hand. "You must be Damen. I'm Markos."

Evelyn's fiancé.

"So, you're the guy banging my sister," I said, shaking his hand. Markos laughed, resonantly.

"She warned me about you," he chuckled. "You can try to shock me but I work at the Renaissance Faire—my mind lives in the gutter."

I didn't expect to like him, but I did. Here among Michael's bloodless, featureless, tedious people, Markos looked as out of place as I felt. He was dark-skinned and stout with curly hair and a pair of tortoiseshell glasses. His goatee and his mustache were curled at the ends into small waxy loops, and even in street clothes, he looked like he was ready for the Renaissance Faire, wearing a vest that looked like it had been made out of pheasant pelts.

"Alright, what've we got here?" he asked rhetorically, turning his attention to the feast on the table and rubbing his hands together in anticipation. He scanned the abundance and gasped with sudden delight at something he saw. "Ooh! Manchego!"

This was evidently a type of cheese. Markos swept up a plate and began to fill it with gusto.

"How can you still be hungry?" Evelyn asked arriving in the room with a dish of fruit salad in her hands. She looked at me and shook her head. "We already had one Thanksgiving dinner. You would not *believe* how much food is involved at the Markos abode." She unwrapped the fruit salad and tried to find room for it next to a tray of cheese and crackers.

Markos shrugged, unphased. "What can I say? I'm Greek. My whole family is in hospitality. We know how to put up a good spread." He filled a plate and handed it to me before turning to fill one of his own.

"Okay, well, don't make yourself sick," Evelyn told him. "And play nice."

It was unclear whether her last comment was directed at me or at him.

"Trust me, I'm a professional." Markos put an arm around her waist with an easy familiarity and kissed the side of her head before releasing her back into the crowd. When she was gone, he glanced around furtively then reached into his vest to pull out a flask.

"Ouzo. Want some?" he asked offering it to me.

"God, yes." I took a swig, feeling fumes of anise invade my sinuses. Good stuff. *Strong* stuff. "Holy shit..."

Markos grinned. "Right? My Yia-Yia makes it. I think it's mostly rubbing alcohol. I got more in the car if you need it." He nodded toward the window and the street below.

"Oh, I'm gonna need it," I assured him. "No way I'm getting through this sober—" A movement outside the window caught my eye and I stopped short. Through the dark silhouette of my reflection, I could see the GTO parked in the street below. A dark figure lurked beside the driver's side door, doing something with the door handle. As I watched, the figure pulled the door open and ducked inside.

"The fuck?! 'Scuse me."

I shoved my way through the crowd to the door and burst out into the cold November night. The GTO's hood was open now, obscuring the figure from view.

"Hey!" I shouted. I winged my plate in his direction and it smashed against the hood in a spray of ceramic shards and scraps of food. The figure's head popped up and struck the open hood with a thunk.

"Ow!"

I recognized the voice. A sheepish face appeared around the edge of the hood, illuminated by the glow of a street-light nearby: Edward.

"Oh, hey." He grinned

"Don't 'oh, hey' me, Edebevic, what the hell are you doing to my car?" I demanded.

"Don't be mad," he begged. "I wanted to...you know, check the oil. Make sure it had enough." He waved the dipstick at me, the ring still wrapped around his forefinger. He had a paper napkin crumpled in his other hand and a bottle of winter oil upturned in the oil intake.

"Check the oil," I repeated, stupidly.

"Yeah, you know..." He put the dipstick back and cleaned his fingers with an anxious wringing gesture. "Hey! You know I got the money now. To buy it. I want to buy it."

"Yeah? Where'd you get the money, Captain Custodian?"

Edward blushed. I picked up the empty bottle of oil and thrust it into his stomach before slamming the hood closed. I saw him flinch at the noise.

"I'm not..." he said. "I'm in the office now, with Dad."

"Uh-huh. Good to know nepotism is alive and well."

"Who's nepotism?"

"Christ..." I fought the urge to smack him.

"It was Dearie's idea," he insisted as if he'd read my mind. "I been tryin' to learn how it all works. Boards and stuff. All the people. I'm not good with paperwork but I'm good with ...you know...other stuff." He made a tinkering gesture. "Anyway, the pay's good, so I been saving—I got the money now."

"Okay, hand it over." I stuck out my hand.

"I mean, I don't have it right *now*, now."

"Big talk there, Ed. All hat and no cattle," I told him, yanking my hand away. I headed back toward the house, seething. Edward trotted to keep up.

"But I can buy it, right?"

"Get me the money and I'll think about it," I said. I kicked myself inwardly. I'd promised to sell him the car when he had enough money because I never expected him to come up with it: all his life he'd skated by on borrowed grace. He'd made it through a few semesters of night school, and sometimes did some odd jobs on the side but for the most part, he lived at home and mooched off the family fortune. He went through life doing Dearie's bidding like he had nothing to prove and no one to prove it to. Somehow, that had now translated into real money, and no matter how much I hated it, I'd be damned before I broke my word.

I stumped back into the house and retreated to the back stairs off the kitchen to stew in private. It was almost an hour before Evelyn found me there, doing my best to kill Markos' flask of Ouzo.

"I was wondering where you disappeared to," she said. "Staying out of trouble?"

"Trying."

"Markos wants his flask back," she said, wrestling it out of my hands, and shoving a plate of pie into them instead. "Here. Eat this so I can watch you,"

"What is this? A new kink?"

"Not eating sugar, remember?" She nibbled on a piece of cheese, staring longingly at the succulent apple slices glistening with sugary glaze beneath the crumbling buttery crust. A globe of rich ice cream was melting down the side.

"Just *have* some. No one has to know." I speared an apple slice and held it out to her. "C'mon, you know you want some."

"Not today, Satan."

Evelyn warded me off with a fork until I gave up on teasing her and made room for her on the step beside me.

"Dearie's so happy you came," she said.

"That makes one of us."

"*I'm* happy you came," she insisted. "Who knows how much longer..." Her voice cracked and she couldn't finish but I knew what she was saying. I pretended not to see the tears slipping down her cheeks in long silvery stripes. She wiped them away and changed the subject: "How's Melody liking Metron?"

"What?"

"Metron. How's she liking it?"

"What do you mean, 'liking it'?"

Evelyn leaned back to look at me. "Her new job," she said.

"How the fuck did she get a job at Metron?"

"Through Camille, I think," Evelyn said. "She's working for Sam now."

I met one of the partners at a firm downtown. He knew of a position that needed filling.

"Hell. Guess we know how she got that job."

"She *does* have a law degree," Evelyn said, only slightly acidly. I gave her a Look.

"Uh-huh."

"Oh, please."

"Tell me I'm wrong."

"Not my business," Evelyn held up her hands. "Anyway, she put Melody in touch with Edward and he got her a job there—"

Who do I gotta fuck to get a nice cushy office job?

Fuck.

"Something to do with filing documents—"

You should wear that dress. They'll be putty in your hands...

Fuck, Fuck, *FUCK.*

I tried to shut down the thought of Melody and Edward but jealousy twisted in my guts all the same.

"That motherfucker..."

"What?" Evelyn seemed to sense she'd poked a bear and reached out to take the plate out of my hand.

My mind tuned to an adult channel and played office gangbang fantasies. I shook my head, trying to clear it but it was too late: the image of Melody's legs spread across a photocopier dumped endless, close-up copies into my mind.

"That MOTHERFUCKER!" I shouted suddenly, slamming my hand into the wall.

"Damen, calm down!" Evelyn grabbed my arm, trying to hush me. "Who's a motherfucker? C'mon, talk this out with me—"

I shook her off and charged through the kitchen door to the astonishment of the catering staff like a runaway train. There was no stopping me now.

"Ohgod—Please don't do anything stupid!" Evelyn pursued me but I ignored her. I stormed toward the front of the house making it as far as the front entryway before the ouzo caught up with me. I groped for something to lean on for balance and managed to get a grip on the banister. The floor pitched and rolled beneath me like a ship on the high seas and I knew if I let go, I'd end up on my face. It was late enough now that the front rooms were all sectioned off with pocket doors turning the entryway into a dim cloister. From the dining room, I could hear laughter and voices from the handful of remaining guests corralled inside for after-dinner drinks.

"EDWARD!" I roared, at the faceless walls around me. My voice reverberated from every surface. Echoing through the house like thunder.

The dining room door opened a crack, letting a golden beam of laughter and voices spill out into the hallway. For a moment I could see into a world rosy with beautiful people where I didn't belong and never would, and then Edward appeared, blocking my view.

"Damen? What's wrong?"

"You hired my girlfriend?" I demanded.

Edward looked blank. "Who?"

"Melody. My girlfriend. Evelyn says she's working for you now," I held up a hand at about Melody's diminutive height and recognition bloomed on his face.

"Oh, yes!" Edward grinned, pleased to have figured out who I was talking about.

"Why the hell would you do that?!"

"Uhhh," Edward frowned, the scar on his forehead puckering as he tried to figure out why I was upset. "She said she needed a job? Sam heard I was looking and said she was good?"

"Did she blow you to get the job?" I demanded.

"What?"

"Did you sleep with her?"

Edward looked affronted. "God no! I would never—"

"No?" I was building steam; I could hear the blood rushing in my ears. I was going to blow it. One night. I couldn't even handle my shit for one night. "What, then? "She must've done something—or is Metron hiring strippers now?"

"She's a stripper?"

Christ, he was naive.

Does this look like an office dress?

Sure, on Cinemax.

Goddamn, *I* was naïve.

"It's just an office job!" Edward protested. "Scanning and filing—sometimes she reads stuff for me."

"Reads stuff."

"Yeah, you know, out loud 'cuz I'm so slow at it."

"Nothing else? No 'special favors'?"

"No, never." Edward put a hand on each of my shoulders and forced me to look him in the eye. I wanted to shake him off but I didn't. "It's just an office job. A boring, paper-work office job."

"*What* is going on out here?" Michael appeared in the door-way, filling it from wall to wall. He saw me and grimaced. Stepping out into the entryway, he slid the door closed behind him, hiding our private drama from his professional colleagues. "Do we have a *problem?*" He asked in a low voice.

"No, no problem," Edward said with a smile like he meant it. "Just a misunderstanding. Damen's girlfriend works for me! Did you know? I didn't know. Small world, huh?"

Michael's eyes flickered from me to Edward and back to me again. "I told you to be on your best behavior—"

"Don't fucking start with me, Michael—" I growled.

Michael's jaw clenched. "You're drunk, Damen. You're causing a scene—"

"Oh, you think this is a fucking scene?" I snarled, surging toward him but Edward stepped between us.

"Debussy!" he exclaimed, coughing the word into the middle of our argument, apropos of nothing. Both Michael and I stared at him in confusion.

"What?"

"It's free. The player is done. We closed off the room... she'd like it," Edward was tracing a pattern in the air with his free hand as he struggled to assemble the thought, then looked at me expectantly like I was supposed to know what the hell he was talking about.

"I don't know what you're saying to me."

"The piano." Edward made a piano-playing gesture. "It's free. The player is done. We closed off the room cuz everyone's in the...eating place...

"The dining room?"

"Yes! Dining room," Edward said. "She'd like it if you played. Dearie would. She likes when you play—"

"Debussy."

"Debussy," Edward grinned. "You want to play?"

He was giving me a second chance. I'd done nothing all evening but get drunk and pick fights but there he was, standing between me and Michael, throwing me a lifeline.

"You want me to sit by myself and play Debussy while everybody else parties in the dining room," I translated.

"Yes."

I glanced at Michael who was watching me, waiting to see what I did. I hated the idea but I didn't *hate* the idea: I'd still be there for Dearie but I wouldn't have to deal with anybody else. And I'd have the piano.

"Fine," I said.

"Oh, good!" Edward took my arm and guided me towards the living room door. I tried to pretend I didn't need the support to keep me upright.

Michael hesitated, no doubt disappointed that he wasn't going to have the excuse to kick me out. Evelyn tugged him gently toward the dining room.

"C'mon, Dad, your guests'll be wondering where you went," she said. Michael nodded reluctantly and allowed himself to be led back to the promised land.

Edward gave me a thumbs up and released me into the dim solitude of the living room where the piano stood waiting in the corner. I slid onto the bench and opened the lid, stroking the smooth ivory of the keys to calm myself.

"I'm glad you're here."

A sudden voice broke the silence, and I flinched, striking a discordant note on the piano.

"Holyshit!" I gasped.

I turned to see Dearie sitting in her wingback chair, contemplating her reflection in the darkened glass.

"Sorry, Dearie, I didn't know you were in here," I managed.

Dearie shook herself and turned her head to look at me. She looked tired. Exhausted. Her gaze lingered on my face like she was trying to memorize it and suddenly I regretted that she was seeing me drunk. I felt my face get hot.

"Please don't apologize," she murmured. "I know this is difficult for you. I know you are trying." She licked the corners of her lips and rested her head against the side of the chair. "The piano will be yours when I'm gone. It's not much of an inheritance, I'm afraid but nobody loves that piano like you do."

I looked at the piano's gleaming surface and swallowed hard.

"Please don't talk like that," I begged. Dearie smiled distantly.

"I'm afraid it's past the time for pleasant fictions, Blue. I don't have much time left. I must get my affairs in order," she said. "And it comes with a condition." She rose with an effort and shuffled to a wooden secretary on the far wall and retrieved an envelope.

"This is for you to give to Michael," she said, placing it in my hands. The paper was thick and velvety and Michael's name was written on the front in her elegant, cursive handwriting. "It's...rather sensitive. I need you to give it to him when the time is right."

"How will I know the time is right?"

"It's not sealed."

I turned it over and realized this was true.

"Why me? Why not Edward? Or Sam?" I asked, feeling panic rising in my throat. The envelope seemed to weigh a million pounds in my hands.

"It has to come from you, Blue." Dearie put her hand over mine on top of the envelope. "Will you do this for me?"

I wanted to say 'no' but I knew I'd never be able to, and I knew if I said 'yes' I'd never be able to go back on it. I didn't trust myself to speak, so I nodded instead, and Dearie kissed the top of my head. I put the envelope on the music stand and pulled off my rings one by one, trying to focus on anything besides my pounding heart and knotted chest.

Debussy.

I let my fingers find the music, conjuring up gentle echoes of peaceful moonlight even as panic was built up around the edges of my awareness like a storm. Dread tightened around my chest, crushing my heart and filling my mouth with the taste of blood until I couldn't breathe, couldn't see, couldn't hear over the flood of darkness overtaking my brain.

I came to without realizing I'd passed out. The room was now impossibly bright. The pocket doors had been flung wide and everybody left at the party was gathered around staring at me. Raffi stood over me holding something that smelled like ammonia under my nose. I shoved it away woozily.

"—the hell?" I mumbled. I was still sitting on the piano bench with Raffi holding me upright. My forehead hurt. I rubbed it, feeling a groove where I'd planted my face against the music stand. Dearie's envelope was in my lap.

"What happened?"

"You fainted, dude," he said, closing the container of whatever it was he'd used to revive me. "You feeling ok?" He crouched until his head was level with mine and checked my eyes. "You might've hit your head pretty hard—your pupils are different sizes." His eyes flickered back and forth as he compared them to one another.

"That's normal for Damen," Michael spoke for me from somewhere over my shoulder. "Left pupil should be larger."

Raffi glanced over my shoulder at him for confirmation and seemed to accept this. I heard him turn and address the room at large: "He's okay—just fainted. Make some space." Then he lowered his voice to a murmur that only I could hear. "I think you had a panic attack."

I nodded and closed my eyes and struggling to catch my breath. With shaking hands, I reached for my rings, fumbling to put them on one by one while the other guests shuffled out of the room. There was a satiny grumble as the pocket doors slid closed and the hush seeped back into the room.

"Are you alright?" Michael asked. His low voice seemed to fill the space.

I nodded without looking at him and picked up the envelope off my lap, glancing at Dearie as I did. She nodded encouragingly.

Just one condition. It has to come from you.

All I had to do was hand it to him and the piano would be mine. Here. Now. While we dangled together in the uneasy truce of Dearie's last Thanksgiving.

"Michael—"

"Damen."

I smoothed the envelope on my chest and stood but was still too dizzy and disoriented to stand. I leaned on the piano for balance, waiting for my vision to clear before I spoke but Michael spoke first.

"I think it's time for you to go."

His words sank into my flesh down to the bone and took

my breath away. I nodded, fighting back the urge to cry, and slipped the envelope beneath the lid of the piano before pulling the quilted cover down over the top. Dearie watched me sadly from a few feet away.

"I'm sorry, Dearie," I mumbled.

"Say your goodbyes," Michael said. "Quetzalez will drive you home."

21

BORSHUN

THANKSGIVING HAD been an unmitigated disaster. Quetzalez drove me home and waited in the car while I staggered to the front door and made my way inside. No one else was home: Goose and Mary May were the only ones there. Everybody else had someplace to be. I left them in the living room, both picking over leftovers from the fridge in front of the television and retreated to my bedroom to where I could wallow in self-pity in private.

December came to Illinois as a flat faceless gray, reminding me of all the reasons I hated the Midwest. Frost formed on the windows at night, and the furnace smelled like burning hair whenever the heat kicked on. The wild, unstoppable energy that had sent me tearing through the night-lit streets had burned itself out for good now, leaving only a dull lethargy in its wake. I laid low for several days, staring at the walls like a burnout until my phone rang with a panicked call from Melody. The boiler at the Girl Child's school had given out and classes were canceled for the day. Now that she was working at Metron, it meant commuting into the

Loop each morning on the L, making it impossible for her to get to the school in the middle of the day on short notice.

"You'll owe me one," I told her.

"I'll owe you one," she promised.

I drove to the school and collected the Girl Child but I didn't have a key to the apartment, so I took her downtown to the Kristkindlemarket to see Santa Claus instead. Even on a weekday, the line for the Santa coiled around a series of metal barriers in the granite expanse of Daly Plaza. The Girl Child didn't care. She skipped along beside me, giddy with excitement at being out of school and surrounded by holiday cheer.

"You know what you're gonna ask Santa for?" I asked her to pass the time while we waited.

"Yes!"

"What is it?" I asked.

"It's not for me, it's for Mama."

"Yeah? What's your Mama want?" I asked. Maybe I could surprise her. A damp wind blew in off the lake making the Girl Child shiver. Her coat was too thin—Melody had been right about that but she still hadn't bought her a new one, so I took off my scarf and wrapped it around her neck and shoulders until she looked like a mummy.

"Borshun!" Girl Child said proudly, muffled beneath layers of scarf.

"Borshun?" I repeated, trying to understand. "What's 'borshun'?"

"I don't know..." Girl Child admitted. "Mama always says she wishes she'd gotten a borshun but Dada wouldn't help her get one so she got me instead."

Abortion.

Fuck.

I glanced around to see if anyone else had heard this.

"Your Mama told you that?"

"No, but I heard her tellin' other grown-ups."

"Okay listen, you can't be asking Santa for a borshun," I told her as the line shuffled forward and we turned a corner only to be met by another length of the barrier.

"Why not?" The Girl Child looked at me with big dark eyes. "It's bad, isn't it?"

"What makes you say that?"

"'Cuz Mama got mad when I asked what it was."

"Yeah, it's not very nice."

"But what is it?"

We were standing in front of the Nativity crèche and I glanced self-consciously at the empty manger where a divot was molded into the straw in the size and shape of a Baby Jesus, not yet arrived. Mary was half kneeled over the empty manger with her arms outstretched as if to ask the empty straw 'What did I do to deserve this?' Nearby a sad-eyed Joseph looked on with gloomy acquiescence: resigned to his role as the stepfather to the bastard son of God.

"D'you know where babies come from?" I asked her. As a kid, I'd believed for an embarrassingly long time that babies were delivered by train thanks to the story of my own birth which was always told in the same rote words like a catechism:

The Blue Line El was stopped on the tracks. The storm came in and the power went out and the train got stuck just past Division. The heavens opened and the waters broke and there wasn't a doctor on board. Mom was wearing a sundress and a raincoat and I came out head first and blue and Michael caught me. He turned me right side up and smacked me on the back until the water came out and the air went in and I started to cry. And then the train began to move and the voice said: 'This is Damen' so that was who I became.

"Mama says the stork brings babies but Rolly says it's when grown-ups do a special kind of hug when they're naked an' it takes a long time?" She looked doubtful about both explanations.

"A long time?"

"He says it has to be a lot of secs."

Sex.

Why me? I glanced at an uncaring Illinois sky wondering if giving a five-year-old The Chat while in line to see Santa Claus was a special form of hell invented just for me.

"Well, Rolly's not wrong..." I said at last. "A man and a woman do a special kind of hug and sometimes it does last for a little while but it's called sex. S-E-X, and you're too young to know about it."

"And they do it to make babies?"

"Sometimes. Mostly grownups do it because it feels good. Like scratching an itch. And if it leads to a baby, then the mama grows the baby in her tummy—have you seen a lady who was skinny but had a big tummy? It means she was growing a baby."

"So, what's a borshun?"

"It's when grownups don't want the baby to grow."

"Oh." The Girl Child looked at her shoes. I waited for the inevitable, tearful follow-up question: *Mama didn't want me?* But it never came. Instead, she said: "Maybe I'll ask for a basketball instead."

I allowed myself to breathe a cautious sigh of relief. "Good plan," I told her. "C'mon, let's go talk to the big man."

✳   ✳   ✳   ✳

"We're back!" I called when we got back to the apartment. "In the kitchen."

Melody was sitting at the kitchen table counting cash into tidy piles while Camille entered figures into a spreadsheet on her laptop.

"What's all this?" I asked, picking up one of the stacks to flip through the bills. It was nearly all twenties. There had to be a cool grand in my hand. Melody smacked my wrist and pulled the cash away.

"That's *taxes*," she said.

"It's cash," I said. "Why even report it?"

"Cuz I want a house," she said, "which means I gotta have a credit score, which means I gotta have a bank account which means I gotta have income, which means I gotta pay taxes."

"No more easy approvals," Camille explained. "The Recession fucked everyone, and not in a fun way."

"Ahh," I said, although in truth, I hadn't really been listening. I turned my attention back to Melody. "Hey, can I talk to you for a minute?" I jerked my head towards the bedroom and headed through the doorway without looking to see if Melody was following me.

"What's this all about?" she asked, leaning on the door-frame with her arms crossed. Her attention was still on whatever it was she'd been working on in the other room and she seemed annoyed by the interruption.

"Have you been going around saying you wish you'd had an abortion?" I asked, keeping my voice low. Her attention came to bear on me in an instant.

"Who told you that?"

"So, it's true," I said as if there had ever been any doubt. "You can't say stuff like that! The Girl Child hears every-thing! Even I know that."

Melody rolled her eyes. "She's *five*," she said. "She don't know nothing."

"Yeah? Well, she's not gonna stay five forever," I said, "and what's going to happen when she finds out you didn't want her? You think it's gonna be nothing then?"

Melody scowled. "You calling me a bad mother?"

"I'm not calling you anything. I'm telling you to watch what you say. You keep this up, you're gonna mess her up for good."

"Why, cuz you're such an expert? Huh? Telling me how to raise my kid like I'm some kinda idiot? I'm not gonna let anything happen to her. I love her. So what? That's not enough?"

"Love her, just don't want her."

"Whatever, I don't gotta listen to this." Melody held up a hand to dismiss me and tried to push past my elbow into the kitchen. "Who says you get any say at all, huh?"

"*I* do." I insisted. "Because I fucking *care* about her. If you don't stop this, I'm going to—"

"You're gonna what?" Melody stuck her hands on her hips and glared up at me. "She's my kid an' you don't get to tell me what to do. You don't like it; you can fucking leave."

"You know what? Fine," I snapped. "You can treat me like shit if that makes you feel like a champion, but if you think I'm gonna stay here and watch you break the Girl Child into pieces you can go fuck yourself."

"Fine!"

"Fine!" I grabbed my coat off the bed, spilling the shopping bag full of holiday cheer across the bedspread and floor. "She wants a basketball for Christmas, by the fucking way." I snapped. Then I left and I didn't look back.

*   *   *   *

I retreated to my bedroom at the Cursèd Place and collapsed onto the mattress, landing heavily on the body of somebody already lying on it.

Hurrf!

I propped myself up far enough to see who it was I'd landed on. Tombstone. I put my head down again.

"What the hell, Tombstone?"

Tombstone rolled me off his back and propped himself up on one elbow to make the sign for 'bitch' using the letter 'm' instead of the letter 'b'. Marla. I could fill in the rest: it was December. He'd missed his support payment and his ex-wife Marla had kicked him out. The weather was too cold for him to stay in the RV, so he'd moved into the house and taken over the first unoccupied bed he found. I wanted to be angry but I didn't have the energy.

Tombstone tossed his head at me: *what about you?*

"Yeah," I made the M-bitch sign back to him. *Me too.*

✳   ✳   ✳   ✳

I didn't hear from Melody for the rest of the week. The silence ached like physical pain, and the longer it went on, the worse it hurt. I kept telling myself it was a matter of time: that I'd done the right thing and that the pain would go away eventually. But it didn't.

I did my best to drown it out by plunging myself into music. Through fair means or foul, Judge had arranged for us to take the stage at the Congress Theatre as the headliner for a local band showcase for the holiday season. He'd even managed to legitimize it with the sponsorship of one of the bigger Chicagoland rock stations. Or maybe it was the station that was putting on the showcase with Judge as one of the sponsors—I wasn't clear on the details, and I wasn't about to ask Judge for clarification.

Now that I'd fucked things up with Melody—again— chances were good that he was going to carve out a pound of my flesh the next time he saw me. I would've deserved it, too. Maybe I was even hoping for it. A part of me felt certain that getting my teeth kicked in would hurt less than the crushing pain I got in my chest every time the echoes of our fight played over in my head:

You callin' me a bad mother?

Because I fucking CARE!

Mama says she wanted a borshun but Dada wouldn't get her one, so she got me instead.

It was an endless loop. It didn't matter how hard I screamed my heart out in rehearsals or how

loud I turned the television up at home, nothing seemed
to drown it out.

Nothing but whiskey.

I got drunk and stayed that way, picking fights whenever I could find them and running my mouth whenever I couldn't. *B@d Beh@v!or* weighed in almost daily with
updates about my antics, both real and imagined, keeping
our online presence surging, and I was the new sensation. I wasn't a headliner: I was a sideshow, and a low rent
one at that but I wasn't in a position to be picky.

It was soundcheck on the day of the show when Judge
appeared. I was standing in the maw of the proscenium
with my back to the house, listening to Jojo hammer out a
driving, heavy metal cadence with enough force that I could
feel it on my skin. The monitors dropped in and out as the
engineer tuned the room to our sound. I leaned on a mic
stand with my eyes closed, letting the sound pour over me
to drown out the static of my mind. Somewhere inside the
depths of my pocket, my phone buzzed. I reached for it,
cracking my eyes open long enough to look at the screen:
Mom. I dismissed the call and shoved the phone back into
my pocket.

"You got a minute, Crustbucket?"

The sound of Judge's voice in my ear shot panic through
my system. I yelped, sending a shriek of feedback through
the monitors. I wheeled around to find him standing at the
backline speaking into the talkback mic that was wired
directly into my ear.

"What the fuck?!"

–uck –uck –uck?

My panic bounced around the theatre on an echoing delay. "Give me a heart attack why don't you?" I gasped, wishing that it didn't sound so uncertain and weak.

Judge waved me over and I staggered to the edge of the stage, leaning heavily on an amp rack for support.

"You look like shit on toast," Judge said eying me like he expected me to land on my face at any moment.

"Yeah well, you are what you eat." I reached down behind the amp rack for the bottle I'd stashed there and undid the cap. "Listen, if this is about Melody, can you wait until after the show to kick my ass? I'd rather not go on stage with another black eye."

"I'm not here about that."

"She tol' you about the fight though, right?"

"She told me, alright," Judge said, stuffing his hands into the pockets of his coat and chewing over something on the inside of his lip. "But she also told me what you two were fighting about, and I'm not gonna go around kicking your ass for trying to protect Vico." Judge grimaced like the subject left a sour taste in his mouth and shook his head. "I've told her the same thing but fucked if she listens to me."

I felt a wisp of relief at having done something right for once and allowed myself to relax. In my pocket, my phone began to buzz again.

Mom again.

I silenced it, again.

"You were right, you know," Judge said.

"I know! Poor kid's gonna get hurt when she figures it out. She doesn't deserve it—"

"Not about that," Judge cut me off. "About Baby Daddy."

I stared at him blankly.

"Halloween?" Judge prompted when it was clear I didn't know what he was talking about. "The kid in the Joker mask?"

"Oh, yeah, right. Duh." I tried to pretend that I hadn't completely forgotten that I'd asked Judge to look into the attack on Halloween. Now, looking back, it seemed stupid to think that Lily Weasel was behind it all, but Judge's expression was grim.

"The kid's name is Fredrico Franco—sixteen years old, an idiot but not a bad kid. He said a white dude in a yellow car slipped him a c-note to steal a little girl's candy and try to get her off the playground. Told him it was a prank, you know, *Impractical Jokers* or whatever."

"How'd you find him?" I asked, then shook my head, figuring I already knew the answer.

"Money, People, Dirt."

"What did you do to him?"

"Nothing. Just asked him some questions. Gave him another fifty to keep his flap shut about it," he said. "The real question is: what do *you* want to do about it?"

I stared up into the lighting grid, trying to gather my spongy thoughts. *What did I want to do about it?*

"I dunno," I sighed. "The way things are with Melody right now..." I didn't need to finish the thought for Judge to understand. For a third time, my phone buzzed against my leg.

Mom.

Again.

What the fuck was so important?!

"Sorry, my Mom is blowing up my phone. I gotta take this or she's going to keep calling."

Judge nodded and stepped off leaving me alone at the back of the stage. I took a deep breath before answering the call.

"I can't talk now, Mom, I'm onstage—"

"Go to a quiet place and sit down," Mom said, cutting me off. My heart dropped through the floor. "I have bad news."

22

ROOM 7

"**Y**OU MUST be the prodigal son." The security guard looked up at me with an eyebrow raised and typed something into his computer.

"Sorry, what?"

"Your dad said they were expecting one more—blue hair and tattoos. Guess that's you. Look here—" He pointed to a camera mounted on the top of the monitor and then printed out a curling paper name tag with my picture printed on it, so dark that I couldn't see my face.

"Room 7. The rest of the family's already there."

The elevator spat me out into a dim hallway that opened onto a ward where the hospital rooms were laid out in a ring around the vast circular desk of a nurse's station. I stepped out of the elevator and then froze.

Dearie had a stroke. She's in the hospital. You should come now.

I couldn't do it. Jabbing at the elevator button, I gasped for air as panic set in. The elevator doors stayed closed. My distorted reflection stared back at me in a living replica of *The Scream*—just as silent, just as stricken. I wrenched my gaze away, searching around for someplace—anyplace—I could go to escape the panic that was quickly over-taking me.

There was a meditation room nearby: all the church but none of the God discreetly tucked away behind a wall of frosted windows. I crashed landed in the first pew I came to and put my head between my knees, trying not to pass out. The room was the size of a small conference room with rows of padded benches all facing a plain white wall with the word HOPE sketched out in gold letters. It smelled like paper and disinfectant as if even faith required a reg-ular washing-of-hands, and the only sound I could hear over my panicked breathing was the rumble of industrial ventilation.

For several long minutes, I struggled to get a hold of myself. Wishing I was sober. Wishing I had something to drink. Wishing I could be anyplace else but there right then.

"I thought I might find you here."

I turned to find Mom standing in the doorway, her face shadowy in the faint light filtering through the frosted glass. She approached and sank into the pew beside me.

"What happened?" I managed, choking on the words.

"Dearie collapsed in church. She asked Michael to take her to Readings & Carols at St James and she had a stroke during the service. It was...very sudden. The doctors say it was painless." Mom picked up one of my limp hands and intertwined my fingers with hers before resting it against one cheek. Her eyes were dry and bright and solemn.

"So, she's—?" I couldn't finish my question but I didn't need to.

"Not yet," Mom said. "Very soon, though. She is still breathing, she still has a pulse, but her final directive is very explicit not to resuscitate. The doctors have stabilized her so we could say our goodbyes. Once you've seen her, we'll take her off the machines and let her..." She waved a hand in a gentle movement of dismissal.

We sat in silence for a long moment, and then Mom patted the back of my hand.

"Come along. It's time."

She guided me out of the chapel and led the way past the nurse's station to Room 7. Someone had lettered the name ADOMNAN on the whiteboard beside the door, which was closed but not latched. Mom pushed it open silently and stepped inside closing it behind me once I too had crossed the threshold.

The room was nighttime dark, lit only by a soft, warm glow from the far end of the room. There were two beds: the nearer one was empty and the farther one was obscured by a curtain that divided the room like a veil between worlds.

I didn't want to see what was on the far side of it. *I didn't! I didn't! I didn't!*

But I had to.

I edged forward with my heart in my throat until I could see feet, then blankets, then a pair of wrinkled hands, until at last I could see her face. I stopped in my tracks. It had to be a joke. Someone was playing a joke on me. Surely, it that couldn't be Dearie lying there with a slack open mouth and shrunken yellow skin. Surely this was a joke. A prank. A leftover Halloween decoration. Surely?

Please, God...

But it was.

Dearie's eyes were closed, sealed up like an infant's. In the open gap of her mouth, I could see a crescent of teeth around the edges of the blackness that seemed to be filling up her throat. The stroke had melted her features on one side into the specter of someone I didn't recognize. And she was no longer wearing her pearls.

A sound like a sob escaped me. Edward looked up to see me standing at the foot of the bed like an unwelcome guest.

"Here—sit," Edward rose out of the chair beside Dearie's left hand and offered it to me. He was still wearing a suit. It made him look like he was dressed for a costume party. "She's not awake but...you can still talk to her. She'll hear you."

How could he possibly know?

I forced my numb legs to move forward, tripping over nothing until I fell as much as sat in the sagging vinyl of the chair. I took Grandma Dearie's hand, expecting it to be cold but it was warm and damp. Her chest rose and fell: each breath an inelegant gasp through her open mouth. Her hair was wild and thin. I reached over her face to smooth it and felt her fingers tighten around mine.

"Dearie?"

Dearie said nothing, just sucked in another gasping breath. A tube ran under her nose with a quiet hiss of air.

"Dearie?!" I said again, more urgently. My voice cracked and trembled under the word. "It's me, Damen—Are you there?"

I didn't expect a response, no matter how much I wanted one. I turned away from the light, trying not to cry and failing. Michael sat on the far side of the bed staring into the middle distance as he clutched Dearie's thin fingers between both of his big hands. Beside him, Evelyn clutched his elbow with a tiny box of tissues in her hands. She offered me one, wordlessly. Her face was red and swollen from crying. All around the room were artifacts of past visitors—an arrangement of orchids, a scattered collection of condolence cards, one lonely Mylar balloon hovering nervously in the corner as if unsure it belonged there. Outside, I could hear the murmur of voices from nurses on the night shift and a faint mumbling radio playing Christmas tunes as if life were just carrying on, indifferent to the fact that Dearie's time was running out and that soon it would be gone.

Speak now, or forever hold your peace.

"Dearie, it's me," I whispered again. "It's me, Damen, please...Don't leave me," I begged. "Don't leave me here alone—"

Say your goodbyes...

But I couldn't. Saying it out loud would crack me open and the ugly, animal thing I kept locked inside would tear me apart. Angry, scared, and alone.

And then it was too late. Dearie was gone.

I wasn't sure how I knew but I did. Her chest still rose but she didn't draw in any more breath. A pulse still fluttered the delicate skin on her neck but her heart wasn't beating. Her body was still on the bed but it wasn't her anymore—it was just an empty corpse.

I uncurled my fingers from her hand and stood feeling somehow light—as if my feet weren't touching the ground anymore; as if I'd broken loose from the last mooring line holding me to the earth. I drifted away from the bed, away from the light, away from the horrible sight of human remains, ignoring the questions flung across my path.

I walked out the door and I didn't look back.

She was gone. Nothing else mattered.

23

SPIRALING

HANDLE OF the cheapest blended whiskey cost fifty bucks at the twenty-four-hour convenience store even though it was only worth half of that. The Pakistani cashier never put down his phone the whole time I was there, tossing my change onto the counter before turning back to a soccer game on the ancient TV. I wrapped the bottle in a plastic grocery bag and was already undoing the cap before I'd even made it out the door.

Twist off. This was what I had become.

It was late now and the streets were deserted. The bars had all closed and businesses hadn't opened yet. Twinkle lights lit the empty morning darkness, unseen by anyone but me. I found a place to sit among the figurines of a Nativity crèche and rested my head in the empty manger trying to fill the empty place inside that Dearie had left behind.

"What's the occasion?" A cop stood over me with a steaming cup of coffee in his hand. I realized the top of the bottle was sticking out of the grocery bag tucked in the crook of my arm. I didn't care. I took a swig.

"God is dead," I said.

"Ain't that the truth."

I offered the bottle to him and he poured a tot into the coffee.

"You didn't see this. And I didn't see you," he said.

I nodded foggily.

"And you're gonna go ahead and get where you're goin'," he said. "You want me to call someone? Give you a lift?"

I shook my head and regretted it as the world spun around me.

"I'll take the L," I mumbled. I held out my hand for the bottle but he didn't give it to me.

"Move 'long now," he said and stalked off to find someone else to harass.

I couldn't remember how I got to Melody's place. A car door slammed somewhere close to my head and I jerked awake to find Melody standing over me. The light was grayish with early morning and she had the Girl Child asleep on her shoulder. She kicked the bottom of my boot then curled her lip disdainfully when she saw I was awake.

"He dead?" A second figure appeared beside her and resolved itself into the shape of Melody's downstairs neighbor. The hot one. She had a cellphone pressed to her ear and she snapped her gum while she sized me up.

"No, just drunk." The contempt in Melody's voice could have etched steel.

"Melody—" I reached out to her for comfort but she dodged away, disgusted.

"Ew, *no*," she spat at me. "I ain't forgotten what you said, asshole. You don't get to pretend like it didn't happen."

"Melody, please, I'm sorry—"

I got to my feet to follow her through the side gate, blocking it open with my arm when she tried to slam it on me. Reverberations shot through the bones of my arm to the shoulder and I felt my hand go numb.

"Stop following me!" Melody hissed, glaring at me over Girl Child's sleeping back.

"Yeah, creeper, get lost." The hot neighbor wedged herself between me and Melody and shoved me in the chest with both hands. I staggered backward, nearly losing my balance, and before I could regain my feet, she was up in my face, enveloping me in the gum-flavored vapor of her breath. "She doesn't want to talk to you, *hombre*," she said. "Why don't you leave her alone?"

Melody had unlocked the side door and was pushing her way inside. I pushed past the neighbor and wedged a shoulder against the door before it could close.

"Melody, please—listen!" I begged. "Dearie—my Grandma just died—"

Melody gave up on trying to close the door and dodged away. The sudden loss of resistance sent me crashing to the floor inside where I landed on my face. The neighbor put her knee on my back to hold me down.

"You want I should call the cops?" she asked.

Melody was already up the first flights of stairs. She turned the corner at the landing without a backward glance "No. No cops."

I flailed helplessly under the hot neighbor's weight, struggling to free myself. "Donchu fucking move, *cabròn*," she growled, grinding her knee into my kidney, then called up the stairs again: "You want I should call Hacksaw?"

I didn't know who that was but I knew I didn't want to find out. I stopped struggling.

"No, let him go. I'll handle him," Melody replied. I could hear her footsteps turning another corner overhead and the jingle of keys as she approached her door. Once she made it to the apartment it would be too late: if she bolted the door from the inside I'd be shut out for good, and I wasn't sure I'd be able to take it.

The hot neighbor seemed reluctant to let me go, but she took her knee off my back and spat at me as I crawled towards the stairs on all fours. I felt it hit my shoulder but ignored it, scrambling to climb a mountain of stairs that seemed to get taller the more I climbed.

I made it to the door as Melody was closing it and hurled myself at the gap but fell short. A clump of my coat wedged between the door and the frame. I couldn't force the door open but she couldn't force it closed either.

"Let go of the door," Melody's voice came through the crack. I could hear Girl Child crying in the background. I felt like crying too. I wanted someplace safe. Someplace warm. Someplace where someone would understand.

"Melody, please."

"Let go of the door or I get the pepper spray!"

"Please just listen." I *was* crying now. I tried to let go—tried to sit up—but my coat wouldn't let me.

"Let go of the door."

"I can't," I sobbed. God, I was pathetic. "I'm stuck." I stopped struggling and rested my forehead against the door. "My coat's stuck," I mumbled. "You gotta let go so I can get it out."

I could feel Melody considering her options. There was a jingle of her keys.

"I'm sorry about your grandma," she said quietly. "But you can't come in. You're drunk an' you're scaring Vico."

"I'm sorry," I begged. "I don't have anywhere else to go."

"That's not my problem," she said. "Go home."

"Okay," I mumbled. "I'll go. I'm sorry. Just...lemme out and I'll go."

I closed my eyes, waiting. Melody shifted her weight on the door and eased it open a crack—just a crack—until my collar came loose. I pulled myself free and then bashed my shoulder against the door as hard as I could, hearing the wood crack as it snapped open half a foot before being pulled up short by the security chain.

"Motherfucker!" Melody swore.

A stream of pepper spray struck me full in the face, burning on contact, invading my nose and mouth down to my lungs. I reeled back, choking as my face and chest erupted in fire. Melody slammed the door behind me and I heard the wooden bolt fall into place sealing me out.

I staggered back down the stairs, catching one wrong and falling down the remaining steps in a clatter. I came to a stop with my head pressed against the cold brick of the exterior wall, tangled in an abandoned bicycle. I tasted blood. The world went dark.

✕

I found myself on my back on a kitchen table while Melody's hot neighbor poured milk over my burning face. I couldn't tell if she was trying to help or trying to waterboard me but she evidently got what she wanted because the next thing I knew she was naked on top of me, riding hard. And the next thing I knew an enormous dude with more neck than head was picking me up out of the tangle of her bed while she stood by the doorway talking on her phone.

"You must be Hacksaw," I heard myself say before he threw me out.

✕

I found myself staring up at the painted face of a winking redhead. There was a blonde on my left side and a brunette on my right and a piano under my fingers and a line of empty glasses stacked up where the music should have been.

"Maybe you should slow down!" someone shouted over the noise.

"Maybe you should go fuck yourself," I replied.

✕

I found myself staggering along a sidewalk, borne up with a girl under each arm. Then I found myself in an unfamiliar apartment, forgotten, watching the two of them sixty-nine, giggling. I was wearing someone's underwear on my head. I wasn't sure why.

✕

I found myself at a bar called Mother's in a race of shots against a biker dude and his girlfriend.

✕

I found myself in a college dorm getting a blowjob from a dude (chick?) with a tattoo of a butterfly on his (her?)

shoulder. I wasn't about to tell him (her?) to stop.

><

I found myself in a blues club of some kind—a place so dark and smoky it could only be illegal—listening to a women's honey voice pour over me while I poured myself into a bottle of something homemade and a million proof.

><

I found myself singing alone in the harsh yellow light of Lower Wacker Drive. I felt someone take my arm, a hazy dark figure dressed in all black.

"C'mon," he said, gesturing to a van idling nearby. "Let's get you out of the cold."

><

And then, at last, I opened my eyes to find myself once again back in the land of the living. Whether I wanted to be there or not. I was lying on a cot in a homeless shelter with a bucket on the floor nearby in case I puked. It looked like I might've used it already. Someone had put a damp cloth on my neck. Squinting against the searing daylight, I saw Father Jesse sitting nearby making painstaking notes on a composition notebook.

"WhrmmI?" It came out as a single word. Father Jesse looked up.

"Welcome back," he said. "You been on a helluva bender."

I made an effort to sit up, hugging the bucket to my stomach, and reached for the pocket watch. It was stopped. For how long? I didn't know. I turned the pin to wind it.

"How long was I...?"

"Four days."

"Four days?!" I'd blacked out before but this was extreme even for me.

"Melody said she maced you in the face and didn't see you again after that. I found your phone at her neighbor's place."

Pieces of my misadventures flickered across my memory too quickly for me to catch. I wasn't sure I wanted to pursue them anyway.

"You feel like you can walk? We should get going."

"Oh, right, the show..." I didn't have the slightest fucking idea how I was going to perform when I could barely stand upright but I'd never let a hangover stop me before and I wasn't about to start now—

"Ah, no," Father Jesse caught my arm as I wobbled on my feet and held me steady. "You missed the show, buddy. Four days, remember?"

"Oh. Right." I sat back down. "So, what's the rush, Padre?"

Father Jesse licked his lips nervously. I realized he looked different. His hair wasn't spiked up into its usual mohawk; without it he looked subdued, almost normal. Almost. A wool scarf half covered the flaming skull tattoo on the right side of his neck. And he was wearing pants. Real pants. Like a real priest.

"The funeral's today," he said. I felt the breath go out of me all over again, remembering in a rush all the things I'd been trying to forget. He glanced at a clock somewhere over my shoulder. "Over now, actually but everyone's still gathering at your folks' house."

"No one told me..." I was going to cry again.

"No one could find you," Father Jesse said. "But it's not too late. You should go to the gathering. Say your goodbyes."

Say your goodbyes.

"I—I can't," I said. "I already tried...I couldn't, and then..." I trailed off.

Don't remember. Don't remember. Don't remember.

The image of Dearie's slack, dead face appeared behind my eyes and I shuddered.

"You were there when she died, weren't you?" Father Jesse put a hand on my shoulder. I didn't try to shake it off. He took my silence as an affirmation. "You don't have to be afraid. It doesn't hurt to die."

"Why, you ever died before?" I snarled at him scornfully but Father Jesse nodded.

"Once."

I looked at him and realized he was serious. A smile quirked the side of his mouth. "I got better."

I laughed in spite of myself. It was bitter and broken but it was a real laugh. I rested my forehead on the cool plastic rim of the bucket, feeling tears running down my face. My hands were starting to shake. Father Jesse put a hand on my back.

"Grieving sucks, man. There's no way around it but you're gonna have to face it sooner or later. The longer you wait, the harder it's gonna be. But you don't gotta do it alone. C'mon—let me take you to your people."

"I don't have 'people'."

"Yeah. You do, buddy," he said. "You don't have to like them but you got 'em. And they're the ones you need right now."

24

THE FUNERAL

"YOU STINK."

I'd barely stepped inside the front door before Mom caught my arm and hustled me up the stairs to the second-floor bathroom. She sat me down on the toilet and turned on the tap in the sink to let the water get warm.

"Give me your shirt," she demanded. "You can't wear that."

"I don't have anything else."

"I'll give you one of Michael's."

"I don't want anything of Michael's."

"Too bad." She held out a hand and waited until I peeled the t-shirt over my head and handed it to her. She dropped it into the trash can and thrust the washcloth into my hands. "Give yourself a wipe-down. I'll be back." She went out of the room leaving me alone, staring stupidly at the washcloth and struggling to remember why I was there.

This was a mistake. I shouldn't have come here. I didn't belong. The washcloth turned cold in my hands but I still couldn't bring myself to move.

Mom returned with a collared shirt in a dry-cleaning

bag. She found me sitting in the same position where she'd left me and made a disappointed *tsk*. Hooking the shirt on the back of the door she took the cloth from my hands and began to scrub at my face in a businesslike way. The rough cloth scraped my skin until it felt raw but I didn't resist. I wasn't going to get any sympathy, least of all from Mom.

Suddenly, my mouth watered as my stomach betrayed me. Mom must have seen it on my face because she forced my head over the side of the bathtub before I could spew all over the floor. There wasn't much to bring up, just foul, bitter, yellow fluids. I coughed and spat into the tub as Mom turned on the tap to wash away the mess.

"You get it all out of your system?" she asked. It wasn't clear if she meant the alcohol or my attitude. Probably both.

I nodded.

"Good."

She pushed my head under the spout to wet my hair. The water was ice cold. I yelped and tried to jerk away, banging the back of my head against the spout and sending a spray of icy water down my back. Mom held me down. Her grip was powerful and I was too tired to resist.

"It's f-fucking f-freezing," I managed through clenched teeth as icy water dripped across my back and neck.

"*Language,*" Mom scolded, unsympathetic to my plight. She squeezed shampoo onto the back of my head and briskly lathered it into floral scented suds. "If you don't like how I do things, you should bathe yourself. You're a grown man, after all."

She rinsed the shampoo out of my hair, then let go of my

head and stood back; waiting for me to make some move on my own. I cupped a hand and scooped some of the water into my mouth to rinse away the bile, then hauled myself to my feet with painful slowness.

Mom threw a towel over my head and began to dry my hair, her fingers digging through the deep pile of the terry cloth against my scalp. I closed my eyes in the humid darkness beneath the towel and surrendered to her will. At last, she pushed the towel back and draped it over my shoulders. With a loose corner, she dabbed at a spot on my cheek while she calculated my sobriety.

I reached for her suddenly, wrapping my arms around her waist like a child. I pressed my face into the front of her dress and held on like my life depended on it. Mom wasn't a hugger but she didn't push me away. She ran her fingers through my hair and waited until I let her go.

"When did you last eat?" she asked finally.

"I don't remember," I mumbled. My stomach clenched at the thought of food and for a minute I thought I might be sick again. I fought it back.

"You should eat while you're here," she said. "There's plenty of food downstairs. Have something with a vegetable in it."

I nodded numbly: it was easier to agree. Mom took a comb out of a drawer nearby and ran it through my hair, smoothing it back from my face. When she was satisfied, she retrieved the washcloth from beside the sink and began to scrub my body. I gasped again at the cold as she ran it over my skin—neck and shoulders, arms and chest.

"Okay! Okay, I can do it," I mumbled wrestling it away

from her with an effort.

Mom leaned against a vanity nearby with her arms crossed over her chest as she supervised my ablutions, ready to step in with extreme prejudice if I failed to meet her exacting standards. I dragged myself to my feet and made a fumbling effort to wash myself in the sink. The water turned gray as it swirled down the drain.

"I didn't see you after you left the hospital," Mom said at last when she judged the silence had gone on too long. "You didn't answer your phone."

"I lost it," I said.

"Ahh." Mom offered no further comment on this. Instead, she asked: "Will you be joining us for Christmas?"

The question smacked me in the face. "How can you think of Christmas at a time like this?!"

"It's four days away, someone has to."

"Don't you care Grandma Dearie is dead?!"

"Of course, I care," Mom snapped. "We're all hurt. We're all grieving, Damen but we don't all get to crawl in a bottle and disappear."

"That's rich, coming from you," I hurled the words at her like shrapnel but failed to draw any blood. Mom took the shirt off the back of the door and pulled off the plastic cover. She held it out to me with an expression that *dared* me to say I wouldn't wear it.

I took it. It was several sizes too big but I buttoned it up and looked at myself in the mirror. I looked like a kid playing dress-up in his dad's clothes. I turned to Mom, opening my mouth to protest but she stopped me with a chilly glance.

"It'll have to do," she said. She buttoned the top button. It felt like a noose around my neck and I had to fight the urge to tear it open with force. Taking my wrists, she arranged the cuffs in a practiced fold and pinned them shut with a pair of cufflinks, stabbing the brass studs through the fabric like she was driving the final nails into my coffin.

"I don't think I can do this," I said.

"Then don't think about it," Mom replied. She gestured toward the door with a nod of her head. "Let's go."

Together we made our way down the stairs to the gathering on the first floor. The crowd flowed from room to room with no apparent pattern, just a general hubbub of low voices and finger foods.

"Behave yourself," Mom admonished as she disappeared into the flow of mourners, leaving me alone at the foot of the stairs. There was food nearby; I caught a whiff of crab-meat and mayonnaise and my stomach turned over again. Shuddering, I slipped through the crowd toward one of the front rooms, feeling eyes on me as I passed. A ripple of murmurs followed in my wake as people took in the blue hair, the facial piercings, the tattered jeans...Mom could dress me up all she wanted but I would never fit in. Not here. Not among the sober, dark figures of Michael's world.

I snagged a glass of wine off a passing server's tray and gulped it down, abandoning the empty glass on a nearby end table. The room was spinning but I couldn't tell if it was from hunger or the alcohol. The server glared at me but the alcohol dulled the pain threatening to overwhelm me and loosened my chest enough for me to breathe.

I retreated to the kitchen where Evelyn was coordinating

with a caterer and struggling to find enough counter space to set down a casserole someone had brought. She gestured to the freezer door with her chin and the caterer hastened to open it for her but it was already packed solid with casserole dishes of different shapes and sizes.

"Goddamnit!" Evelyn swore, balancing the glass dish on one arm and evicted a store-bought bag of ice cubes to make room for it. She wedged the dish inside with an audible crunch and slapped the door closed—then seemed to notice me for the first time.

"Midwesterners," she groaned. "I told them 'No casseroles,' but see if that stops them. Take one when you go. Please, for real. Even Markos can't eat this much food. Anything leftover tonight I'm going to give to Father Jesse." She dumped the bag of ice into the sink and turned to give me a hug. Unlike Mom, Evelyn *was* a hugger. I held on as long as I could until the caterer made it clear that we were In The Way.

Evelyn gestured to the back door and we slipped into the back staircase. It was quieter here but cold. Evelyn settled herself on a step and I squeezed in beside her. Shoulder-to-shoulder, we filled the narrow hall from wall to wall.

"Where were you? I was worried."

"I dunno. Around."

"I can't believe she's gone," Evelyn managed, tearing up around the words. I put an arm across her shoulders to comfort her and she rested her head against my neck. It was the first warm thing I'd touched in four days.

"I'm sorry you missed the service," she said at last when she could speak again. "It was really nice."

"Was there a wake?"

"No, she wanted to be cremated. Dad's been carrying her around all evening."

I tried to imagine Michael carrying around an urn of ashes, expecting it to be funny but no matter how I imagined it, it was painful and pathetic. I didn't have the heart to laugh.

"You been staying with Melody?"

"No, she kicked me out."

"Yeah, she said you showed up smashed."

I shrugged. "Yeah." It was one of the few things I could remember with any clarity and all I wanted to do was forget about it.

"Evelyn?" The caterer tapped on the door gently, bringing us both back to the present. Evelyn wiped her face on her wrist and stood.

"I'm being summoned," she said, smoothing her skirts. "I'm supposed to be running this show. I need to get back."

I caught her hand and held on, knowing that if she went then I'd have to go too. She gave my fingers a squeeze and pulled me to my feet. "C'mon, you didn't come all this way to hide in a stairwell," she said, wrapping me in a quick one-armed hug. "I'm glad you're here. Just try not to...you know...set anything on fire. Okay?"

She was only half-joking.

I nodded.

She went back out into the golden warmth of the kitchen, leaving me alone again. I lingered in the comfort of the darkness but the longer I stayed there, the more I realized she was right: I couldn't stay. That wasn't why I had come. I waited until the caterers were too preoccupied to pay me any attention and I slipped out through the kitchen and back into the main rooms of the house.

It was harder to stay unnoticed here. I could feel eyes on me as I passed through the crowd in a trail of whispers. I kept waiting for someone to stop me: for an accusing finger to find me and a voice to call out: *"You! You don't belong here!"* But it never came.

"Damen—you made it." A new voice caught me up short and I flinched at the sound of it.

Sam.

"Fuck, don't sneak up on me like that!" I gasped, turning to find him leaning against the staircase with languid insouciance. I should have known I'd run into him here; he was the Adomnan family lawyer, after all.

"Language, please. This is a funeral," Sam admonished but his tone was sly. He didn't care about my language and he didn't care about decorum: he was there to revel in the wailing and gnashing of teeth, and from the looks of it, he was having the time of his life.

"Sorry. *Gee-golly-jeepers,* don't sneak the fuck up on me like that," I amended.

"Salty as ever, I see." Sam made a gesture almost too small for me to see and a server appeared with two glasses of wine. Sam took both and handed one to me, holding his glass aloft. "A cup for the dead already and Hurrah for the next that dies," he said. He clinked his glass against mine and took a sip without waiting to see if I was going to drink to this cockeyed tribute. I gulped the whole glassful down so that I wouldn't have to say anything to him, not trusting myself to speak.

Sam eyed my appearance with a grimace of distaste. "One of Michael's, I presume?" he said, nodding at my shirt. "You ought to have your own you know."

"So Mom tells me."

"Come by to get measured. I'll have my tailor make one up." Sam plucked an invisible speck of fluff off his sleeve and flicked it away with a flourish designed to draw my attention to his suit. It looked like it had probably cost him a fortune: every inch of it was sculpted to the planes of his body like a second skin, and it was cut from wool that had been dyed so dark it seemed to absorb all the light in the room. I wondered if he'd had it made for the occasion. It wouldn't have surprised me if he had.

"Yeah? With what money?"

Sam gave a dismissive wave. "It would be worth it just to see you out of Michael's clothes," he said.

Sam was the only person I knew who hated Michael as much as I did. He and Mom had once been a couple, back before I was born. Sam had loved her enough to ask her to marry him, and Mom had said yes but a few weeks before the wedding she caught him with another woman and called the whole thing off. Sam had tried to talk her around—he could talk *anybody* around—but not Mom. She told him it was over on no uncertain terms and walked away without a backward glance, which made Sam want her more. She was, and always would be, The One Who Got Away. Even now, his gaze followed her through the crowd, watching her from a distance as she stood beside Michael in an informal receiving line to see off the departing guests.

Then Sam's radar locked onto someone that he wanted to ambush and he glided away into the crowd. The hunt was on. I breathed a sigh of relief.

I stashed my empty wineglass on an empty tray and made an aimless circuit through the house, avoiding conversation and trying not to look anybody in the eye. The crowd seemed to be made up mostly of Metron associates: clients and employees and partners from the company had all come to pay their obligatory respects to the sovereign family. Words had been spoken. Wine had been drunk. Duty had been fulfilled. The edges of the crowd were beginning to bleed off into the gray afternoon, leaving the house too empty and too quiet without them.

The house was full of the smell of lilies and pine. Someone had made a subdued attempt to decorate for Christmas. There wasn't much heart in it. The Christmas tree in the formal dining room was covered in lights but otherwise undecorated. The gifts underneath were as fake as a department store window display: paper-thin holiday cheer over a box full of emptiness. I stepped on one, crushing it with my boot until it collapsed.

We're past the time for pleasant fictions.

Dearie's words drifted up in my memory and I felt my chest constrict. The room was suddenly too full and too empty at the same time. I reeled backward until I touched the comforting solidity of a wall for support. Ducking into the living room I found a cluster of manager-level drones speculating about what Dearie's death would mean for their Christmas bonuses. They kept casting their eyes towards a tasteful urn made of bone china standing on the lid of the shrouded piano: Dearie's ashes.

It was so small. Too small. Everything she'd been and this was all that was left.

My mind reeled away from the thought and I tore my eyes away. Someone had abandoned their drink on the mantelpiece. I gulped it down. Another half-empty glass stood on an end table beside the door, the rim marked with a crescent of lipstick. I gulped it down as well. Trying to drown the growing spark of anguish rising in my chest. It wasn't enough.

I reached for a third.

"Oh. My. God..." One of the women in the group caught me in the act with a disgusted sneer. I glared at her and drained the dregs of the wine in my hand, biting back the smart remark on the tip of my tongue. The room was spinning in earnest now. I probably should have eaten something. I thumped the glass down on the end table, and sank onto the piano bench, keeping my back to the empty wingback chair beside the window. Peeling back the quilted cover, I opened the lid and brushed my fingers across the keys.

The piano will be yours when I am gone.

The piano was mine now. *Would* be mine, I amended, once I gave Michael his letter. I glanced at the doorway again where he was carrying on a grim exchange with Sam in a voice too low to hear. Now wasn't the right time.

You're gonna have to confront the empty places.

Can't.

Gets harder the longer you wait.

Shut up! Shut up! Shut up!

Without thinking about it, my fingers picked out the familiar strains of *Moonlight Sonata,* and a sudden stab of pain went through me. I flubbed a chord and grunted out a breath that wanted to be a sob, and started again. I was no good at funerals or mourning or grief but music I could do. Every note hurt but I forced myself to play anyway, grinding out the melody, tone by tone, note by note, trying to pretend she was somewhere Out There, listening, like she always did.

When the movement ended, I gasped for air as if I'd been holding my breath. I heard a polite smattering of applause and I felt a slight brush of relief. Maybe I belonged here after all. Feeling calmer, I began another song. Something she would have liked. I closed my eyes and tried to pretend she was still standing behind me. The longer I played, the easier it got until I could breathe again. People drifted back into the room at the sound of the music. I let it rise through the wood and strings, feeling it through my fingers and feet. The applause was louder this time when the song ended. A few people were even smiling. I glanced around the room: maybe I could do something right after all.

Then I felt a hand on my shoulder and I flinched.

Michael.

Without a word, he reached over my shoulder and closed the lid of the keyboard gently but firmly. The spell broke and reality crashed back in around me. I was at a funeral— Dearie's funeral. She was gone and she was never coming back and all the music in the world wasn't going to change that. The last tenuous thread of my sanity snapped and rage overtook me.

"What the fuck is your problem, Michael?!" I snapped.

"Damen, please. This is a funeral. That's not appropriate—"

"Appropriate?!" I snarled. "Who fucking cares about appropriate at a time like this?"

"Language, please—"

"My language? You got a problem with fucking *language* right now? Dearie's dead, Michael, *goddamnmotherfucking* dead. She's a pile of fucking ashes. It's not like she can be disappointed."

Michael flinched as I hit a nerve but I didn't care. He wanted inappropriate? I'd give him inappropriate. I slammed the piano lid open and launched into a jangling showtune, *Get Happy*, singing the lyrics at the top of my lungs even though I couldn't remember all the words.

"Damen."

"Sing, motherfuckers!" I shouted to the people in the room, pounding out the chords with all the force I could muster. A real crowd had gathered now—if the music hadn't attracted them, then the commotion certainly had.

"Damen!" Michael barked over the music. "Stop! People are grieving."

"Yeah? So?" I screamed at him. "You wanna whisper around death like we're in a church? Everybody's just supposed to be quiet and desperate? Death's not fucking *nice*, Michael—"

"Michael—" I heard Mom catch his arm and guide him to the doorway.

"Gloria, this is—"

I slammed out the notes of the song, struggling to drown out the sound of his voice, but I could still hear it, no

matter how loudly I played. I was the only one still singing. I missed one note, then another. My flailing fingers
turned clumsy and stupid and the music began to unravel.
Still, I banged against the keys until it decayed into mean-
ingless noise. I slammed the lid shut and pressed my hands
over my ears trying to block out the sudden ringing silence.

This had been a mistake.

"Damen?"

I felt a hand on my shoulder: Father Jesse.

"I'm fine."

"I think we'd better go."

"I said, I'm *fine*." I shrugged off his hand with more force
than I intended and the back of my fingertips clipped him
across the face. I felt one of my rings hit one of his teeth
and saw blood bloom on his lip. Father Jesse staggered
back a step, not angry, just shocked. He pressed a hand
to his mouth and his eyes widened at the sight of the
blood. I froze.

"I'm sorry—I didn't mean to—" I stammered.

Someone reached out to him with a handkerchief and
Father Jesse's face closed down: angry and tight.

"Don't!" he snapped with force I'd never heard from him
before. The helpful Samaritan recoiled and Jesse softened.
"Sorry, 's okay, I got this. Excuse me." The crowds parted
as he withdrew toward the kitchen.

"Jesse, wait—I'm sorry—I didn't mean—" Fumbling my
words, I tried to stand up. My guts sloshed with wine and
the toe of one of my boots caught beneath the pedals of the
piano. I lost my balance, knocking over the bench with a
crash, scattering sheet music everywhere. I reached for

the piano, trying to catch myself but there was nothing to grip on the polished lid. My fingers brushed the padded cover and I grabbed for it but I was too late—I was already going down in horrifying slow-motion. I tumbled across the fallen bench, pulling the cover and everything on it down on top of me. I heard something fragile hit the floor and shatter in a cloud of dust and a thousand glittering shards.

For a minute, all I could do was lie still and wait for the room to stop spinning. Eddies of dust swirled in the air like smoke overhead, making me dizzy even lying flat on the floor. Everybody in the room stood frozen in a single nightmare moment. As the dust settled, I could see the faces of onlookers overhead, various expressions of shock and disgust, and anger. And then there was Michael, wearing a face of such piercing disappointment I couldn't breathe.

There was no salvaging this.

It was Edward who broke the curse. He emerged from the crowd without a word and hauled me to my feet. I tried to shrug him off. Couldn't. The grip on my arm might as well have been made out of railroad couplings. I realized I was covered completely in grayish powder. It tasted like bone in my mouth. I sneezed.

"Bless you."

Edward handed me a Kleenex and escorted me through the stunned crowd to the door. I could hear whispering all around me as guests took in the disaster I'd made of the living room.

"'M sorry," I mumbled again, slurring as the dust turned to mud in my mouth. I spat into the Kleenex and tried to enunciate. "Father Jesse, is he—?"

"I'll make sure he's okay."

I only realized I was at the front door when I saw Edward opening it. A sudden dread came over me: I hadn't wanted to be here, I'd hated every minute of it but the only thing worse than being here was not being here. *Edward was going to throw me out.* My mind circled the thought, unable to approach it directly.

"Listen, I'm sorry," I begged. "Please—I didn't mean it."

Edward's eyes were sympathetic and sad but he still stood beside the open door, waiting for me to go through it.

"I had too much to drink," I said, my voice turning into a pleading whine. "I lost my balance. It won't happen again—" but even as I said it, I could feel the floor tipping beneath my feet. A fresh wave of vertigo and nausea overtook me. The wine was coming back up. I fled out the door and made it as far as the cement railing on the front steps before my guts erupted. I hurled my guts out in a spray of red that cascaded over Grandma Dearie's rose bushes, cropped back to thorny brambles for the winter. Then I collapsed over the cold stonework and started to cry.

I was a disaster. I ruined everything.

Edward closed the door, cutting off the murmurs of the crowd inside. I felt his arm across my shoulders. He helped me to sit on the steps and handed me another Kleenex. I was too wrung out to take it. Edward cleaned my face and unbuttoned the collar and cuffs of the shirt.

"You want a mint?" he asked. From one of his pockets, he produced one of Grandma Dearie's peppermints. I took it but the thought of putting it in my mouth was more than I could take. "You got a coat?"

I shook my head. "At home, I think...maybe...I dunno."

Edward took off his suit jacket and put it over my shoulders. I didn't know why he bothered: I was just going to ruin it too. Before I could protest, the door opened again and Father Jesse came out. I groaned and leaned my face against the cold concrete, wishing I was dead. He wore a pair of latex gloves and was holding an ice cube to the cut on his lip. He gave my shoulder a slap and joined us on the steps.

"You okay?" Edward asked him.

"You should see the other guy," Father Jesse said. He gave me a sideways grin from the far side of Edward. "Just caught me wrong, is all. Already stopped bleedin'."

"You heading out?"

Father Jesse nodded. "I already called a ride. Tell your dad I'm sorry for his loss."

"Will do."

I felt Jesse's hand land on my shoulder. "C'mon, buddy. Let's get you home."

25

THAT OLD WRECK

ATHER JESSE drove me back to the comforting squalor of the Cursèd Place, and half walked, half carried
me up the front steps. Tombstone opened the door
with a look of surprise, took in the dark-colored suits, and
stepped back to let us inside. Father Jesse dragged me as far
as the living room and dumped me face down on the floor.

"Take care of him?" he said to Tombstone who nodded. The
two of them performed a complicated handshake I couldn't
follow and then Father Jesse walked to the door and let
himself out.

I heard the front door close. Tombstone's footsteps
padded past me into the kitchen where I heard a tinkling
of glass as he opened the refrigerator door. He came back
to the living room and flopped down on the couch beside
me. He opened a can of beer and held it out to me: hair of
the dog. I took it with an effort and held it in my lap.

"I don't wanna talk about it," I said, answering the question that he hadn't asked. We sat in silence staring at the
television as another turd in a jersey performed a victory
dance upon learning he was *not the father!* The show cut to

commercial and I saw myself appear on the screen: standing like a titan onstage at Lollapalooza while a thunderstorm closed in overhead.

Ain't it a shame when one more hit and you'll sell your soul/ always on the run and you're outta control! The mangled chorus of 'GoatRodeo' played beneath a slow-motion beauty shot of Firestone All-Weather Radials that showcased how engineered grooves wicked the water away from the tread, then cut back to me on the stage as the heavens opened up and lightning leaped into my hand to emphasize that this was a *Limited Time Offer! Act fast!*

I wondered if I'd ever be able to catch lightning again.

There was a jingle of a ringtone. Tombstone glanced at his phone, then sprang to his feet. Dragging my arm over his shoulder, he pried me up off the couch and deposited me in the corner nearby, propping me against a wall to keep me upright.

"The hell?" I protested but I stayed put, too exhausted to move.

Tombstone didn't answer. He smoothed his hair and straightened his shirt. Realizing there was a stain on the front, he peeled it off and turned it inside out but the stain showed through. Grimacing, he glanced around the room and his eyes settled on me, sizing me up. I stared back dully, unable to parse what was going through his mind. He knelt in front of me and began to unbutton Michael's dress shirt. Rolling me forward, he peeled the shirt off my back then set me upright again as he slung it over his shoulders.

Tombstone's laptop began to dingle with the familiar sound of an incoming Skype call and he hurried across the room to answer it buttoning furiously. He landed hard on the couch and accepted the call, smoothing the front of the shirt and doing his best to look casual. In his hurry, he'd buttoned the shirt crooked, leaving one side of the collar gapped open but it was too late to fix it now.

I heard a digital clatter on the far side of the call and then the voice of his older daughter, Lacey. "Dad? Can you hear us?"

Tombstone's face split into a grin and he waved.

"Hi, Dad!" His younger daughter, Piper, was there too.

"Hah-hah-hai!" he stammered.

"Why are you all dressed up for?" one of the girls asked—I couldn't tell which one.

Tombstone straightened an invisible tie for her benefit. "Y-you." He grinned again.

"Are you coming for Christmas?"

"Shh—you're not supposed to ask him about that—"

"Ow! Don't pinch me! Why not?"

There was a struggle of slaps and jabs on the far end of the line. Tombstone clapped his hands to get their attention again.

"I-I-I do-don-don nuh-know," he managed, his voice constricting as conflicting emotions tangled his brain's wiring.

"Just give Mom her check, *Gawd.*" Lacey's disdain was bitter with disappointment.

"Yeah."

"You got the money, right?"

Tombstone glanced at me where I lay, still slumped on the floor, watching him. His expression tightened. He didn't have the money. The show had been canceled. I'd gone AWOL.

"Muh-muh-mar—" he struggled. "Your muh-mom there?"

"Mawm!" I heard Piper yell.

"Piper, don't *yell.*" The voice of Tombstone's ex-wife, Marla, came into focus—the faulty connection chopping it into a stutter of her own. There was another clatter as the laptop on the far end was handed over to someone else, and the sounds of the girls faded into the background. "Where's my money, TJ?" she demanded.

The smile was gone from Tombstone's face now, leaving only grim pleading.

"Www-www-wor—" The 'w' got stuck behind his lips. He gave an annoyed whistle through his teeth and changed tactics. "T-tryin'," he managed.

"*Trying* doesn't pay the property taxes, TJ." Marla's voice dropped to a tone of genuine worry. "If we don't pay this tax bill, they're gonna take our house. The IRS don't mess around."

Tombstone had no response for this. He held up a hand helplessly, mouth open with no sound coming out except for an annoyed choke: *I don't know what to tell you.*

"Don't *keh* me," Marla imitated Tombstone's sound and probably his gesture too. "You promised you'd take care of this. Get me the fucking money or spend Christmas alone."

Before Tombstone could force out another sound, I could hear the bloop as Marla ended the session without saying goodbye.

"Fuck!" Tombstone slammed the computer closed and paced around the room, his fingers tangled in his hair and his face screwed up in disappointment. He picked up the beer I'd abandoned on the table and chugged it, crushing the empty can in his fingers before throwing it on the floor. It hit the ground near my head and bounced away with a clatter.

On the television, the show cut to a commercial for Victory Autowreckers.

That old car IS worth money!

The ad hadn't changed in thirty years. I could picture it in my head: a long-haired dude pulling the door off a seventies-era junker. The exchange of cash in bills so old they didn't exist anymore.

"Sell the RV," I said.

Tombstone stopped pacing and stared at me for a moment, then out the window at his now-abandoned RV parked in the backyard, then back to me. He gave me the finger.

"Yeah, yeah," I said. "Fuck me, I know." I gestured toward the back of the house. "Sell it to Jumbo—he'll give you the money. See your kids for Christmas. Buy it back after."

Tombstone's younger brother Jumbo owned a scrap yard on the west side of town near the train yards. He was only a couple of years older than me but already balding and paunchy with a tendency to flatten his As into a smear of grease coating everything he said. Like Tombstone, he had been born poor to poor parents from a long line of poverty-stricken ancestors but unlike Tombstone, who treated money like a foreign language, Jumbo had a good sense of numbers and a knack for turning junk into cash.

If anyone could come up with the money on short notice, it would be him.

"I can give you seventeen hunnert," was Jumbo's appraisal, when he arrived at the Cursèd Place somewhat later. He didn't need to look at the RV to know it was a piece of shit. "Any more an' it'll look like I'm cookin' my books."

Tombstone sighed and collapsed on the couch with his head in his hands. It wasn't enough.

"How much ya need, bro? I'll lendja da money. Whaddya payin'? Mortgage? Credit cards? Yer not in widdat loan shark again, are you?"

"Taxes," I supplied. Tombstone glared at me.

"Aw sheeeit." Jumbo pressed his fists into his kidneys as if the very mention of the taxman was enough to twinge his back. "On the house?"

Tombstone nodded.

"I ain't got that kinda cash, not this time of year—not many folks payin' to Pick-N-Pull." He stared out the front window for a moment, in thought, and then his gaze slid sideways until it found me, sizing me up. I didn't like the look of it.

"What?"

"You still drivin' that GTO?"

"I don't like where this is going."

"You're valued at, what? Twenty-five? Thirty? Knock off a few for the scratches and dents—" He turned back to Tombstone. "That be enough for you, brother?"

I made the mistake of glancing at Tombstone who was watching me with pleading eyes. He nodded. My car could pay off his tax bill.

"Hang on—you don't have enough cash for a loan but you got enough to shark my car?"

"*I* don't," Jumbo said, "but your brother Edward does."

"First of all, no. Hell no. Fuck you. Eat a bag of dicks."

"You know he's good for it—he's been sockin' away cash for months to buy it,"

Edward who finally had enough. Edward who'd given me the coat off his back.

"He'll jump on it in a second; you know he would," Jumbo persisted. "Gimme the pink slip an' I'll take care of all the paperwork. Get your cash for Christmas. You still got your van? I'll give you free pull for whatever parts you want to keep it runnin'."

Tombstone made a pleading gesture and got down on his knees. He was not above begging. He was looking at me like I was his personal lord and savior.

"Get up," I muttered.

Tombstone clasped his hands together and crawled forward on his elbows.

"Fuck you, stop it."

He grabbed my foot and held on when I tried to kick him away.

"Don't you dare, motherfucker."

Tombstone stuck out his tongue—ready to lick the sole of my filthy, salty boot if that's what it took. And if that didn't work, he'd find something else and keep coming.

"Fine! Fine. Goddamnit," I kicked him away. Tombstone relinquished my foot and wrapped me in a bear hug that lifted me off the ground. He might have been crying.

"Goose!" I shouted into the house at large, regretting it immediately as the sound of my voice echoed back to me and crashed into my headache. Goose poked his head into the room. "Pink slip. For the Goat. Give it to Jumbo."

Goose disappeared into the dining room on a mission. The title to the GTO was somewhere in the heap of paperwork along with our concert contracts and fan mail and overdue bills: a needle in a needle-stack but if anyone could find it, it would be Goose. Jumbo trailed along behind him to watch him work, leaving Tombstone and me alone in the living room.

Tombstone released me from his embrace, depositing me on the dirty carpet in the middle of the floor. The carpet stank of mildew and feet but still, I sank into it, boneless with exhaustion. I rolled onto my side and curled into a ball. With my ear pressed against the floor, I could hear the thud of Tombstone's footsteps as he took a lap around the room, still gesturing his thanks every few steps

"Yeah, yeah. Don't read too much into it." I mumbled, closing my eyes. "Now go away and lemme sleep."

26

THE MAYAN APOCALYPSE

sssssssssssssh.

A sound like the hiss of a snake found its way through my unconscious mind and pulled me back to the waking world. I cracked a swollen, scummy eye to find myself still lying in the middle of the floor. I was still shirtless, but someone had peeled off my shoes and covered me with a heap of blankets. It was late and the windows were dark. I raised my head with an effort and searched around for the sound.

I didn't have to look far. Gorey stood over me with a bag of rock salt under his arm which he was pouring out onto the carpet in a wide crystalline line as he walked a slow backward circle around the place where I lay. A spray of granules hit me in the face and I winced, feeling the brush of salt on my eyes.

"Ow, fuck!"

"Oh, hey—you're up!" he said. "Yo! Guys! He's up!"

"What the hell are you doing?" I asked.

Gorey paused for a moment in his salting of the earth and stared at me. "Is that a trick question?" he demanded.

"I'm trying to contain whatever *muló* you done dragged in. The place is already cursed, dude, you don't need to make it worse!"

I looked towards the couch where Tombstone reclined with his acoustic guitar, Tallulah, on his lap to see if this made any more sense to him than it did to me, but Tombstone shrugged and continued picking out an ongoing stream of thought in a minor key. Kilroy and Mungo emerged from the kitchen wearing matching expressions of concern. I pushed myself upright, and Gorey hissed at the sight of the Ouija board alphabet tattooed on my chest.

"*Fuck*, dude! Fuck, fuck, *fuck* no! Are you trying to invite spirits?" He spat on his fingers. "Nope, nope, *fuck no*, nope. I swear to Saint Sarah, tryin' to keep bad luck off you is like trying to disarm a Claymore mine while riding on a goddamn tilt-a-whirl! You're lying there in the middle of the floor with a goddamn Ouija board on your chest covered in...whatever the hell is in your hair..."

I reached up to run my fingers through my hair. They came away gritty and gray, and my throat got tight as I remembered the disaster I'd made of the funeral. Tombstone gave Gorey a Look but Gorey was not sympathetic.

"I'm—I can't even...I'm gonna need Granddad for this..." He stowed the bag of salt in the corner of the room and pulled out his phone.

"Where the hell have you been?!" There was a clatter as Jojo banged her way in through the front storm door trailing cold air and smoke off her winter jacket. She headed towards me across the carpet. Gorey held out his hands to stop her.

"No! Don't cross the circle!"

"Why the hell not?" Jojo stopped short and looked to me and then at Tombstone who shrugged: *it's Gorey*.

"Just don't, okay?"

"Fine, fuck—whatever." Jojo gave an exasperated sigh and stood over me with her toes on the line but didn't go any further. "Judge sent you this," she said holding out a bottle of scotch that looked like it was probably old enough to grouse about having *durn kids* on its lawn. She shook her head in disbelief. "You walk off the fucking stage in the middle of a goddamn sound check and disappear for four days and somehow you still come up smelling like fucking roses." She broke the tax label with a thumbnail and yanked the cork out with her teeth to sniff the contents, then shook her head again. "Fucking witchcraft," she muttered, holding the bottle to me but Kilroy took the bottle from her before I could grab it.

"He heard about your grandma. We all heard," he said, flopping down on the couch in a cataclysm of elbows and knees, folding his long joints into a tidy stack of bones. "Sorry, bro."

"This is ridiculous." I tried to get to my feet but my vision went black and I sat again, dizzy and lightheaded.

"No! Stop fucking flailing!" Gorey ordered from across the room with enough force to startle me into obedience. "You *sit*. Stay in your circle and think about what you've done." He waited until it was clear I was going to do as I was told, then finished his conversation on the phone. "Grandad's on his way. He'll sort this whole...*thing* out." He gestured toward me: the thing. He sank down to sit cross-legged on the floor outside my circle and lit a stub of a candle.

"C'mon, dude, cut him some slack." Kilroy gave him a meaningful look. Gorey's expression softened.

"Sorry to hear 'bout your grandma," he said. "It's just... spirits of the dead like to wander. If you get wrong with them, they can have trouble...you know, letting go."

"I'd deserve it," I croaked around the tangle of emotion in my throat. "I fucked up the funeral...Dearie must hate me. I hate me. I fuck everything up—"

Gorey poured out a generous portion of the whiskey into an empty mason jar and placed it furtively on the line of salt. Then he yanked his hand back as if afraid I might contaminate him. I reached for it, ashamed of how desperately I wanted it but Kilroy snatched it up first.

"Listen, dude..." Kilroy looked like he was bracing himself to say something that I didn't want to hear. He leaned in until his long pale face was inches from my ear and spoke in a hushed undertone that wouldn't carry to the other guys in the group, even though I was pretty sure they already knew what he was going to say. "I know things are...you know, fucked up right now but...you gotta get a handle on your, you know, drinking."

I glanced around the circle of worried faces penning me in on all sides.

"I'm fine," I mumbled. I wasn't but I also wasn't about to go to rehab over it.

"You're not fine, you're in fucking freefall." Jojo's hands were clenched into fists. It looked like it was taking all her willpower not to grab me and shake me. "You blackout for days at a time. You disappear completely till we see you on the fucking internet! Hell, you walked off stage and never came back!"

I looked around the circle of worried faces penning me in on all sides.

I nodded, too tired to fight, and pressed the tips of my fingers into the ridges of my eyebrows as if I could press away the headache settling in behind my eyes. "M' sorry. I really am. I just..." I didn't have words. She was right: it was one thing to go on a rockstar bender of booze and pills and it was another thing to wake up four days later with only the haziest notion of where I'd been and what—or whom—I'd done. Even thinking about the events of the past week felt like dragging my heart across a razor blade. "I overdid it. I'll walk it back for a while, but I can't..." I drew in a shuddering breath and did my best to sound clear-headed enough to warrant another drink. "I can't start tonight. Please...?" I looked to Kilroy again. "C'mon dude, you know me, right? I can party pretty hard but you know I can cool it whenever I need to. Just right now..."

Kilroy did not look convinced but Jojo took the mason jar out of his hand and handed it to me. "C'mon, give him this one," she said, "he just lost family."

Kilroy pressed his lips together in a grimace of reproach but didn't try to take the jar from me again. I sipped the whiskey and breathed a sigh of relief as the smoky warmth rolled through me.

"You're on a slippery fucking slope, dude," he said.

The front door opened and cold air puffed into the room again, this time carrying a tendril of cigar smoke heralding the arrival of Gorey's grandfather. He stopped for a moment in the doorway, leaning on his gold-headed cane as he sized up the six of us with his black, bird-eyes. He *tsked* at what he saw but he stepped inside anyway and turned his unblinking stare on me.

"*Marhrime,*" he growled phlegmatically.

"I know," Gorey looked pleading. "Can you do anything?"

Gorey's grandfather squatted beside the circle of salt, blowing smoke over me in a series of concentric rings. "Vwill rechquire sacrifice."

"Whatever you need."

The two of them exchanged a conversation of glances. Gorey nodded and got to his feet. He disappeared into the basement and came back carrying Mary May under his arm, petting the rooster's head to calm him. Rom Lazlo nodded once in approval.

"A zhing pure," he said. He held out a hand like a surgeon expecting a scalpel and waited expectantly for someone to fill it. Gorey hastily undid a gold chain he was wearing around his neck and dropped it in the old man's palm. The old man closed his fist around the chain.

With a deft flourish, the old man wrapped the chain around the rooster's legs and hoisted it into the air, wringing its neck in a single swift movement. There was a brief, choked squawk, and Mary May fluttered his wings, then went limp and still.

"Shit!"

"Whattheactualfuck?!"

Rom Laszlo dropped Mary May's carcass onto the carpet, arranging it so that it lay across the line of salt with wings spread wide and bound claws reaching skyward. Then he stood and stared down at his handiwork with a critical eye.

"Rhum," he said.

Nobody moved.

"What?"

"Rhum. I rechquire rhum."

"He wants rum," Gorey supplied.

"Like the drink?"

"Yeah, we got any?"

"Goose!" I shouted at the house. "Rum!"

There was a pause as we all listened for the distant sound of pattering feet as Goose searched the house for rum and then appeared in the doorway with a bottle of Kraken in his hand. He held it out to Gorey's grandfather. The old man pulled out the cork and took a swig. He swirled the liquid around in his mouth a few times, then spit it out through porcelain teeth.

"Is ekhceptable."

He upended the bottle over the bird carcass pouring it out until the black feathers were soaked in the spicy-sweet smell of the alcohol. Then he sucked on his cigar until the ember on the end glowed red and turned to snowy ash, and dropped the burning stub onto the carcass. It transformed instantly into a pillar of flame.

"Shit!" I leaped backward, feeling the singe of heat against the side of my face and arm. There was a stomach-knotting smell of burning feathers and rummy, roasting meat. Kilroy, the vegan among us, clapped a hand over his mouth and gagged. Escaping steam whistled out of the sizzling meat like the screech of an unclean spirit. The rooster's fat bubbled and hissed until the flames died down to a ghostly blue rising from the charred remains. Rom Laszlo watched the carcass burn without expression until the last lick of fire winked out leaving only the pinpoints of embers still glowing. The rest of the house was lost to profound darkness and foul smoke.

"Kheurse is lifted," Rom Laszlo said. "Is made clean. Go vwalk free." He kicked aside the line of salt, breaking the circle, and gestured me out into the world. He brushed his hands against one another like a dealer in a casino showing his hands to a pit boss, then he spat on the ground and walked out the door without a backward glance.

"What the *hell* just happened?" I asked, breaking the shocked silence. The living room was so thick with haze it was impossible to pick out anyone's face in the darkness. Gorey flicked a lighter and his grinning face floated into focus, his features all lit up from below.

"Rom banished the curse!" he enthused.

"Oh, is *that* all." Jojo's voice was thick with sarcasm and the smoke seemed to tickle her throat with every word until she coughed.

"It's complicated." Gorey touched the lighter to a stub of a candle and flicked it closed to shove it in his pocket. He lit a second candle off the first and handed it to Jojo, then lit another for Tombstone and another for Kilroy and another for Mungo until I was surrounded by a circle of flickering lights.

"What happens now?" I asked.

"Now we sit."

"Sit?"

"Yeah, sit. Drink. Remember the dead. Comfort the living."

"Like a wake?"

"Or sitting Shiva." Kilroy nodded, catching on.

You're gonna have to face the grief sooner or later but you don't gotta do it alone. A surge of emotion rose in me and I broke down and wept, letting the raw sorrow pour out of me until I couldn't breathe. I couldn't fight it anymore. I let it overtake me and pull me down, knowing I would never be able to haul myself back into the light again.

But I didn't need to. I wasn't alone.

Let me take you to your people. Father Jesse's words floated back to me and I realized at last that he had been right: I did have people. Gorey, Tombstone, Jojo, Kilroy, Mungo—*these* were my people. They had come together not because of money or fame or music but because I needed them to be there for me. To be there *with* me.

Jojo climbed into the circle with me and wrapped me in her arms, strong and tight against her whole body. Then Kilroy and Goose followed suit, the three of them anchoring me to the earth and burying my grief in their warm physicality. Tombstone struck up a tune, pulling the longing and loneliness out of the air and distilling it into music while Mungo offered up distillates of a more literal nature by pouring out shots of the scotch into Solo cups and passing them around the circle.

We huddled together in the reeking, candle-lit darkness long into the night, laughing and weeping and drinking and smoking until the bottle ran dry and the candles burned out. After a while it was only me and Gorey left, staring at one another across the guttering flame on the candle stub in front of him.

"It's the end of the world, you know," he said as we watched the last candle flame burn low and blue as it approached the pool of wax soaking into the carpet. "That whole Mayan calendar thing? Today was supposed to be the day. Winter solstice, 2012."

"So, did the world end?"

"You tell me."

The flame winked out, leaving only a pinpoint ember still glowing on the charred wick. A ghostly tendril of smoke rose into the air like a silvery thread visible only by the faint light seeping through the windows from a street-light outside. The rest of the house was lost to profound darkness.

"It sure as hell feels like the end of everything, everywhere."

"Yeah, it always does." Gorey flicked a lighter and put the flame to a fresh candle, preparing to continue his vigil over me until morning. "You know, they say that if you're going through hell, keep going."

"They also say if you find yourself in a hole, stop digging," I said. "How the hell do you know which one is right?"

"Just one way to find out," he said. "Pick one, and don't look back."

27

DON'T COME HOME

DESPITE THE Mayans, the world was still there when I woke up the next day. And it was still there the day after that. On the third day, Tombstone dragged me downtown to a clinic to get tested, and in a minor miracle, the results came back clean. I offered up a silent prayer of thanks and a heartfelt promise to never ever do it again.

For a while, at least.

I returned to the house to discover that Kilroy and his Yoga-Voiced girlfriend had taken it upon themselves to get rid of Mary May's earthly remains. They had vacuumed up the rock salt and done their best to clean the ash off the walls and furniture, but the old shag carpet was beyond recovery and now occupied the front yard in a stinking heap. The floor underneath turned out to be a span of scuffed parquet, serviceable but marred with a greasy black stain where the immolation had occurred. No amount of scrubbing was going to get rid of it. In spite of the cold, every single window in the house was thrown open as wide as it could go but nothing—*nothing*—was going to get rid of the bitter stench of burned meat that had saturated every porous surface in the house; including but not limited to, my own hair and skin.

It had taken three days of restless sleep and night sweats but I'd managed to dry out enough to pass as a functional adult, at least for short periods. The trip to the clinic had pretty much used up my energy reserves for the day. I shouldered my way in the front door, my mind was already back in bed upstairs but before I could drag the rest of my crude matter up the stairs to the bedroom, Jojo intercepted me.

"Hey, soooo your mom's here?" she said, nodding towards the kitchen. Her head was cocked with the question she wasn't quite ready to ask.

"Here?" I wasn't even aware that Mom knew where I lived much less cared enough to make a house call.

"Yeah, she showed up at the back door while you were downtown. Goose let her in."

I groaned. I was too tired to deal with Mom right now but it didn't look like I was going to get much choice in the matter. Jojo made a sympathetic face, offered me a Valium, then sent me on my way with a smack on the ass for good luck.

I found Mom in the kitchen, tearing the newspaper off the south-facing windows to flood the room with winter sunlight. Nearby, Goose struggled to pour her a cup of tea with shaking hands. Illumination did not improve the state of our habitat. Mom frowned as she took inventory of the filthy room: the unwashed dishes, the overflowing trash can full of empty liquor bottles, and the heaps of takeout cartons.

"Charming," she said.

Her frown deepened as she identified the oversized shirt Goose was wearing as the one she'd given me for the funeral. Goose cowered under her stare and proffered her the mug of tea.

"Go on, get lost," I told him as she took it. He fled gratefully out of the room, leaving Mom to turn the full force of her attention on me.

"You're looking better," she said, brushing the hair behind my ear by way of greeting. "Are you sober?"

"I'm dried out."

Mom settled herself against the cabinets across from me. "That was...quite some performance you put on at the funeral."

"I got carried away," I mumbled. "Overdid it. I'm sorry. I'll do better. I promise—"

Mom cut me off with a sharp gesture. "Don't—" she snapped but stopped herself before she could finish the thought. *Don't make promises you know you can't keep.* She inhaled the steam off her tea as if to calm herself and her expression softened. "Just...please tell me this is the exception, not the rule?"

I nodded dully, too tired to fight, and picked at a seam in the countertop with a fingernail without saying anything. Better to let her have her say and be done with it.

"Michael is very upset, of course," she continued. "Edward cleaned up your mess. I understand you sold him your car. That is an acceptable gesture of thanks. He is very happy."

Don't expect to buy it back.

I nodded that I understood but still said nothing.

Mom gauged my reaction carefully before continuing. "We will be gathering for the reading of the Will after the New Year," she said. "I understand Dearie already spoke to you. She left you her piano? Is this true?"

"Yeah but she had a condition," I said, remembering the envelope with Michael's name on it.

"Oh? And what was that?"

"Doesn't matter. I haven't done it." I wondered if it was too late.

"Well, in the meantime, we will keep the piano at the house," Mom said. I could tell she was angling toward something and I braced myself for what she was going to say next. "On which subject...The house will likely go to Michael. He is still rather fragile—I daresay we all are—in these uncertain times but...it would be best if you didn't come there anymore."

Thou shalt.

I waited for the stab of resentment and pain but it never came. It was just another place that didn't want me. Nothing new about that. Mom appraised my silence, waiting for me to respond.

"Okay," I said at last.

"Okay?"

"Okay, I'll stay away," I said. "It's not like I've ever been welcome there anyway. I only went to see Dearie, so..." *Why wasn't I feeling anything?* The eerie tranquility creeped me out: like the calm before a storm. Mom felt the same—I saw two lines furrow between her eyebrows as she measured my response.

"What about you?" I asked to change the subject.

"What about me?"

"If Michael gets the Big House, where will you go?"

Mom's eyes came into focus as the question made it to her brain and she started. I realized I'd taken her by surprise.

"Hmm. Yes. I hadn't thought of that," she said. "I expect he will ask me to leave. I should make arrangements. Thank you." She let her mind chase the thoughts for a while longer then shook herself as if trying to shake herself back into human form. Standing silhouetted against the window, I could see the light catch on the individual hairs standing out from her head like a luminous aura, both beautiful and terrible in her brightness.

There came a rap on the back door. Through the half-frosted storm door, I could see Quetzalez standing on the back stoop. He held up a wrist and pointed to his watch and Mom nodded in understanding.

"I regret that our time together has come to an end," she said, gathering her purse off the counter and hooking it over her shoulder. She pecked a kiss onto my cheek and pulled on a pair of gloves one by one. "Please, promise me you're being careful?" she said. "I do love you; you know." Only Mom could say 'I love you' with all the warmth of a surgical instrument but she meant it and I nodded.

Quetzalez opened the door to usher her out, then lingered a moment after she passed to size me up.

"You stayin' out of trouble?" he asked, leaning on the metal frame of the storm door until the sheen of frost melted, outlining the shape of his arm and shoulder against the glass.

"More or less."

"Well, keep it up," he said. He reached an arm into the kitchen to slap my palm and then knock his knuckles against mine. "I know where you live now." He winked before extracting himself from the door, and let it hiss closed behind him.

28

NOT ANGRY, DON'T HATE

I T WAS Christmas Eve and I had nowhere to go.

I was no longer welcome at the Big House, and, while I hadn't spoken to Melody since she'd maced me in the face, it felt safe to assume I wasn't welcome at her place either. The rest of the guys were scattered to the four winds: Tombstone and Gorey off with their families and Jojo gallivanting around some tropical resort with her biggest fan, Khaki Thackery. It was just me and Goose and Kilroy left in the house: Kilroy because he was Jewish, and me and Goose because we didn't have anywhere else to go.

I expected the house to be quiet with everyone gone but when I emerged from my bedroom sometime during the mid-afternoon, I found the living room crowded with hollow-eyed strangers bonding over cheap coffee and regret: Kilroy's recovery group. More than half of them looked like they'd already fallen off the wagon in a big way.

"All our normal meeting spots are taken," Kilroy explained when I cornered him in the kitchen. "I told everyone we could meet here over the holidays."

"You're welcome to join us," his yoga-voiced girlfriend added, handing me a cup of coffee with a candy cane hooked over the edge.

I took the coffee but I was not yet prepared to join the droning ranks of the wrecked and recovering. Instead, I took a bus downtown and wandered along the Magnificent Mile where luminous window displays sold make-believe holiday cheer to the empty sidewalks. The only other people around were vagrants like me: lump-shaped shadows drifting along the deserted street like restless ghosts.

At the corner of Michigan and Erie, I waited at the crosswalk behind a family with a couple of young kids dressed in their Sunday best who were headed to a Christmas service somewhere.

"You need to *sit still* do you understand? We're going to church," the dad was saying, trying to impress good behavior on the kids who were too young to care about church etiquette. I crossed the street behind them and followed them along the sidewalk, letting the patter of their conversation wash over me:

"Dad—Dad is Santa coming tonight?"

"Is baby Jesus coming tonight?"

"Does Santa bring baby Jesus?"

"Jethuzs!"

There was the smack as the youngest one, a toddler, tripped and hit the ground. The first hiccupping wail of pain was quickly absorbed by soft, warm, cozy parents in soft, warm, cozy coats. I looked up from the tableau and realized I was standing on the sidewalk in front of St James. The cathedral loomed overhead, pointing at the heavens like a mocking, holy finger.

An usher opened the door for the parishioners, who trundled inside in a cheerful, yuletide flock until I was the only one left on the sidewalk.

"Evening," the usher said, noticing me standing there. I felt an irrational surge of panic at having been seen and wished I could disappear into the sidewalk. I felt certain that he was going to tell me to go away but the usher bobbed his head politely, reached into a bucket beside the door, and scattered salt on the steps to melt the ice. "Here for the service? The next one starts at eight."

"No thanks."

I was pretty sure lightning would strike me down if I dared to cross the threshold.

"Okay, well...everybody's welcome," he said. "Merry Christmas."

"Yeah. Thanks," I mumbled and slunk away down the sidewalk pretending like I had someplace I needed to be. I wondered if I should have gone to Kilroy's meeting after all. I sure as hell didn't have the bandwidth to deal with children and families and Christmas and church. Hell, I didn't even have the bandwidth to deal with myself.

Why the fuck had I come here of all places?!

I struggled for breath around the fist in my chest and dodged around the next corner only to find myself waist-deep in a host of angels. I almost screamed. Then I realized it was just a choir of little girls, dressed up for a Christmas pageant. They were being herded along the sidewalk by a middle-aged woman in glasses and a Christmas sweater. I didn't think I could handle being seen again but there was nowhere to hide: the north side of the cathedral was fenced off and covered with construction scaffolding. A Metron Construction sign warned *Danger. Construction Site. Unauthorized Persons Keep Out.*

I ducked into the shadows and pressed myself against the fence, praying for the heavenly host to pass me by without noticing me. Like magic, the chain-link gave way to afford a human-sized gap. I wriggled through with an effort, feeling my coat catch and tear on the jagged edges. I found myself standing in front of a door that didn't look like it got a lot of use even when it wasn't under construction. The light overhead was burned out, and the concrete stoop was gray with old snow and waterlogged cardboard from some previous itinerant who had sought shelter there. I tested the handle and discovered it was unlocked. Easing it open, I slipped inside and pressed it closed behind me as quietly as my trembling hands could manage.

I was in a subterranean chapel that crouched beside the main sanctuary like a beggar. The room was dark, lit only by the thin, watery light of streetlights that managed to find its way through the windows but it was warm and quiet and, most importantly, *empty.*

I was safe now, safe and invisible and alone but my panic attack was still gaining momentum. I staggered towards the edge of the room where a jumble of pews stood shrouded in plastic like a haunted graveyard and curled up on the floor with my arms wrapped across my stomach as if I could keep myself from flying apart by physical force alone.

I wanted a drink.

Needed a drink.

Stop it.

My fingers slipped beneath my shirt to the place on my ribs where I'd scratched my skin bloody during the long sleepless nights of detox. I dug my nails deep into the raw skin until the physical agony burned away the smothering darkness of my emotions. It helped for a minute or two—long enough for me to catch my breath and pull myself together.

"The peace of the Lord be always with you," boomed a voice through the thick plaster wall as the service began.

The chorused response of the congregation was too dull to hear and was quickly drowned out by the thick, round tones of a pipe organ playing a Christmas carol. I felt myself relax, letting the music wrap around me in the wooly darkness to soothe my jagged nerves.

Feeling somewhat calmer, I took in my surroundings for the first time. The room was a wreck. It had been stripped of sacramental trappings to undergo renovation and was a shamble of sawhorses and power tools and a gentle snow-fall of dust. A large plaster angel lay on the ground nearby, her face turned to the floor as if prostrated with grief. The altar, stripped of artwork and linens, was little more than a dull slab of molded cement at the far end of the room. It stood in an alcove where there had once been a cross on the wall. It was gone now, leaving only a pale shadow where the flaking paint gave way to the bare plaster.

I dragged myself up out of the dust and brushed myself off as best as I could. Peeling back the plastic sheet-ing, I settled onto one of the pews and stared up at the stained-glass windows where sad-eyed saints and hopeless evangelists gazed down on me in pity. The city lights refracted through the colored glass in a thousand glowing fragments and I stared at them, transfixed, searching with my mind for peace, finding only emptiness instead. There was no God here—just a God-shaped hole.

I dozed for a while, listening to the drone of the service taking place on the other side of the wall, and awoke to a hubbub of voices as the congregation went in peace to love and serve the Lord. I crept to a door leading to the main sanctuary and pressed my ear against it, listening to the sound of families talking and laughing and wishing one another a Merry Christmas, all of them eager to get home to Santa Claus and Christmas Eve dinner. Alone in the chapel, I was glad for the safety and solitude of the darkness but I longed to be on the other side, in the light with everybody else.

"Michael, where are you going?" It was Mom's voice on the far side of the door, low and emphatic but unmistakable. I heard her precise footsteps approach and stop.

"I need a minute alone," Michael responded. I startled backward as if I'd been struck. His voice had been inches from my ear—so close that I'd felt the vibrations of it through the wood against my cheek. He was outside the door. His hand closed on the handle. I felt it move beneath my hand and realized it wasn't locked. It had no lock. I froze in place, terrified of what was going to happen when he found me there.

"*Michael,* please stop. It's Damen—" Mom said.

I bit back a scream. *How did she know I was there?!*

"—he's disappeared again. It's been three days—I'm

worried about him out there alone."

"I can make some calls," Michael said. "He'll be alright. He always is."

But I wasn't, couldn't he see that? I felt my face twisting under the crushing force of all the emotion I was trying to hold back. How could they be so close, talking about me and not know I was there?

All I had to do was let them in.

Even as I thought it, I cowered back into the darkest corner of the vestibule. My foot came down on something hard and angular. It skittered away with a raspy wooden rattle. I poked around for it with the toe of my boot until I felt it in the darkness. It was a wooden wedge used for propping the door open. Without thinking, I shoved it under the inside corner of the door and braced my boot behind it as tightly as I could.

Michael's hand closed on the door handle again. I felt him push against my foot, felt the door give way by a quarter of an inch. I pressed my body against it, shoving with my whole weight to keep it closed. Michael tried again with more force. I could feel my muscles trembling with a surge of adrenaline. How long could I keep him out? How hard would he try?

The lever released with a click but I didn't let go of the door. I heard him try the handle again, a gentle jiggle of the door against the frame.

"Door locked?" Mom asked.

"I guess so...I didn't think it had a lock."

The lever released for the final time and I heard them walk away, their voices blurring to low murmurs in the distance. I slid down the door and curled into a ball against the smooth wood. Tears flowed down my cheeks, soaking into the collar of my t-shirt. There didn't seem to be any point in holding them back anymore. I was alone now.

I waited until the sanctuary went silent then retreated back to the street. Fog had come in off the lake and wrapped the streetlights in hazy auras. The wind seemed to know its way through my coat. I shuffled along the street to the subway and tripped down the stairs to get out of the cold. Underground, the air smelled stale and wet but at least it was out of the wind. I hopped the turnstile. Nobody stopped me.

Down on the platform, a late-night busker was singing Christmas carols and accompanying herself with the caustic warble of a midi keyboard. A train was already there at the platform absorbing passengers. The doors closed with an electric chime and the train swept away on a fetid wind leaving only me and the busker behind.

I found her sitting against a pillar beneath a phone booth with no phone. She was plain and dark-skinned with crooked teeth—neither old nor young, wrapped in layers of scarves and shawls. Her voice was deep like a smoker's.

"Change, mister?" she asked when she sensed me staring—I realized belatedly that she was blind. Her head twitched to the side as if she heard someone call her name. "She say she see blue," she said as if that were supposed to mean something to me.

"Is that so," I didn't have the slightest clue what she was talking about but it didn't seem to matter.

"Not angry. Don't hate," the woman said.

I nudged the keyboard with my foot. "I heard you sing-ing," I said. "Can I?"

"You play?" the woman asked, handing it to me. I thumped down heavily beside her on the dirty cement of the plat-form. A cloud of dust from my coat puffed over her and she sneezed.

"Dust and bone!" she muttered in the tone of an invective.

"Sorry."

"Forgive. Forgive." She made a dismissive gesture and asked again: "You play?"

"A bit." I ran a quick scale to test the keys

"'O Holy Night'?" she hummed a few bars of a carol I most-ly recognized. I picked up the tune then branched into a harmony. The woman laughed and clapped her hands in delight then she threw her head back and began to sing: *O holy night, stars were brightly shining—*

Her voice was round and rich like a cello. She sang like a child, head thrown back, the sound coming from deep in her gut, bouncing off the curved tiles of the station and reverberating through the space until she was singing with a chorus of a thousand voices as if the whole city were singing with her. Every hair on my body stood on end and I stopped playing, mesmerized, wishing I'd thought to record it. When the last note died away, we sat in silence, side by side, watching a scrap of paper drift to the ground on an unseen wind.

"See in the middle," she whispered, at last, breaking the silence. "Blue sea."

"Sorry, what?"

"See in the middle."

"I don't know what that means," I said, still mystified.

The woman shrugged. "Don't know. She say."

"Okay."

Easier to agree.

I noodled around on the keyboard some more, letting my hands choose the tune. A note dropped out leaving an awkward gap in the tune like a smile with a missing tooth.

"See in the middle!" The woman cackled as if this somehow proved her point. She reached over and pressed the key—the middle C, and a weak, warbling note came out. I pressed it myself but it was silent. I felt a sudden knot in my throat, thinking about the old practice piano up in my old bedroom at Dearie's house. The one with the dead note right in the middle: right at middle C.

"Dearie?"

"Blue see."

"Can you—" My throat was so tight I couldn't breathe, much less speak. "Tell her I'm—" but before I could finish, a train howled into the station and drowned my voice in the metallic squeal of its brakes. A crowd of passengers began to disembark, filling the platform with joyful noise.

The woman labored to her feet and gathered her belongings into a shapeless bundle. She shuffled toward the nearest set of open doors without the need of any obvious assistance and felt her way inside.

"Wait! You can—can you see her?!" I jogged after her, desperate for answers to questions I didn't know how to ask.

The blind woman shrugged and smiled. "*She* see," she said. "Not angry. Don't hate. Forgive. Forgive." The doors chimed a warning that they were about to close and her hand darted out to catch my wrist urgently. "Believe?"

"I—"

The train doors chimed a second time and the woman let me go. "*Make* believe," she insisted stepping backward into the train car.

"I can't. I'm sorry—please!"

The woman shook her head and smiled again. "Nevertheless," she said, and the doors slid closed between us leaving me staring at my gaunt reflection in the dark window.

There was no arguing with a 'nevertheless.'

29

MAKE-BELIEVE

CLIMBED THE stairs to Melody's apartment feeling the weight of defeat sloshing around in my guts. I could hear the sound of laughter and voices on the other side of the doors that I passed—at least someone was having a good Christmas.

Melody answered the door with a glass of wine in her hand. I got the feeling it wasn't her first drink of the evening: her cheeks were flushed red and there was a smile playing around her eyes and mouth that I didn't get to see very often but even her evident holiday cheer wasn't enough to stop her from narrowing her eyes and blocking me out of the apartment with her arm on the door frame.

"Hey," I said.

"Hey, yourself."

We stared at one another in an awkward silence that thickened around us like glue. Inside, I could hear a television blaring and the sound of Girl Child laughing. The front room was lit with flickering blue light like the inside of an aquarium.

"Can I come in?" I asked at last.

"You been drinkin'?" she asked.

"No."

Melody gestured me towards her so she could sniff my breath and gave a curt nod, satisfied by what she didn't smell. But she still didn't step aside. "You scared me when you were drunk," she said.

"I'm sorry."

"You scared Vico."

"I was in a bad place but I'm...it's over now." It was a lame excuse—no excuse at all, really but it was the truth. "Is Girl Child okay?" I asked.

Melody huffed out a laugh. "Yeah, she's fine. She won't shut up 'bout you, you know. I kep' askin' her what she wanted asa Christmas present but she just kep' saying she wanted you to come back..."

She trailed off into silence and cast a shy glance at my face. *An opening.*

"Will you let me?" I asked, my heart in my throat. "Come back?"

The corner of her mouth twitched in a smile. "It's a free country," she said, stepping back from the door.

A Christmas miracle.

I didn't wait for her to think twice. I squeezed past her into the living room to discover that Christmas had come early. One whole wall was now occupied by an enormous flat-screen television playing *The Wizard of Oz* in four-dimensional resolution that made my teeth hurt. I stopped short, mesmerized as a sepia Dorothy wandered through the bleak landscape, running away from a home she thought didn't understand her.

"Damen!" The Girl Child charged across the room and wrapped her arms around my knees in a hug rocking me back a step at the force of it.

"You're back! Mama, Damen's back! I tol' you Santa would bring him!" she crowed in triumph. "I told him I wanted you to come back an' here you are!"

"Yup, here I am."

"Best Christmas EVER!" she squealed. "And look, this is my house!" She let go of my knees and pointed towards the empty cardboard box that the television had come in. A blanket had been draped over the ends to turn it into a fort, not-quite-covering a large, glossy, photograph emblazoned onto the cardboard that depicted a television family from the 1950s—Mother, Father, two kids, all gathered around a Sunday dinner. The American Dream: now available in liquid crystal high definition.

Home, sweet home.

The Girl Child pulled aside the blanket to welcome me inside. "We're having dinner," she said. "Are you gonna come?"

"That's up to your mom," I told her. Melody choked on her wine.

Shedding my coat, I dropped down to my hands and knees and crawled inside the box. The Girl Child had filled it with blankets and pillows from the bed and the couch like a plush nest. I managed to fold myself into a corner, feeling oversized and monstrous in the tight space.

"Nice place you got here," I told her.

"I like it."

Melody crawled in after her and took a seat beside me

with her legs tucked under her and a fresh glass of wine in her hand.

The Girl Child busied herself with scraps of cloth and paper napkins to create place settings on the blanket between us like a proper picnic. Her pumpkin bucket was once again serving as a lantern thanks to an overturned flashlight, and it filled the box with a warm glow. She handed me a paper plate printed with a Santa Claus and passed a second one to Melody.

"Dinner is served!" she announced grandly, whisking a piece of cloth off a carton of KFC chicken and tubs of potatoes and sides.

What's this I see? It's a house! With a picket fence...

It was a lot of food for two people. More than enough for three. I looked at Melody who studiously avoided my gaze.

"You sure you didn't plan this?" I asked once the Girl Child had helped herself to a drumstick and retreated to her side of the box to gnaw on it like a caveman.

"I figured you'd come 'round again sooner or later," she said, affecting a blasé tone as she scooped mashed potatoes onto my plate, using her thumb to push the sticky paste off the spoon. "I got your phone, by the way. You left it downstairs."

"Oh, yeah. Thanks." I mumbled. "Listen, about your neighbor—"

But Melody held up a hand. "I don't wanna talk about it. It's Christmas."

I nodded but caught her hand in mine and wrapped her thumb in my lips to suck it clean. "I'm sorry," I said, "for everything."

Melody smiled and stroked my cheek. "Yeah, me too."

Outside the box, I could hear the wind and wrack as a tornado tore through Uncle Henry's farm, uprooting trees and panicking the horses but here in the land of Make-Believe, the world was cozy and safe. Here, we were a real family: mother, father, and happy child gathered around Christmas dinner. The American Dream. Or so we could pretend. The chicken was lukewarm, and the potatoes tasted like paste but I didn't care and neither did anybody else. We huddled around the KFC bucket consuming our feast of salt and grease and wishful thinking.

At last, I pushed my plate away and curled up on my side, and put my head in Melody's lap. She ran her fingers through my hair, absently, stroking my head as I drifted towards sleep wondering what Technicolor world waited for me on the other side of my dreams.

APPROBATIONS & REPUDIATIONS

First of all, thank you to my best belovèd, Danellyn, for continuing to support my writerly aspirations even after finding out that self-publishing doesn't pay big bucks and he probably won't get to retire early.

I remain indebted to my Alpha Readers: Whitney Vendt, Logan Rose, Bryan Wilkerson, Royce Shockley, Kim Ellis, Danellyn, and Dad (thanks for saying you actually liked it!); to my Beta Readers; and to the members of my Writing Group past and present for being a constant bright spot in These Benighted Times. Thanks to Jeannette Spohn for copyediting services rendered. Thank you to my eagle-eyed proofreaders Madison, Logan, Sayre, and Caitlin for helping me catch every wayward typo and misspelling. Once again, thank you to Joey Peebles and Ben Stone for the insight into the workings of the live-performance world. And a very special thanks to Emily Bratton for the marvelous formatting and cover design.

Finally, to the Particular Individual I called out at the end of Book I: no, I haven't forgotten, and yes, I'm still mad.

ABOUT THE AUTHOR

GWYDHAR GEBIEN
(Pronounced Gwed-ra Gay-bin)

Gwydhar Gebien is a writer, an artist, and a filmmaker; originally from Chicago now transplanted in Los Angeles in pursuit of a career in film production.

With a background in theatre from Illinois Wesleyan University and a master's degree in film production from the University of Southern California, she is currently putting her training to good use at Skydance Animation as a Production Coordinator.

An eldritch creature of introverted disposition, Gwydhar, lives a quiet life in a pink house with her husband and a cat and a minivan, but can occasionally be coaxed out into the open with music, snacks, or a single-malt whisky.

CPSIA information can be obtained
at www.ICGtesting.com
Printed in the USA
JSHW031613210522
26212JS00002B/14